Clues
From The
Canines

CLUES FROM THE CANINES
© 2022 by Darlene Dziomba
ISBN: 13 979-8-9850655-0-3
e-Book ISBN: 979-8-9850655-1-0

Publisher: BCD Publishing

Printed in the United States of America

Cover Design by Chariz Abucejo

Book design by SeaGrove Press

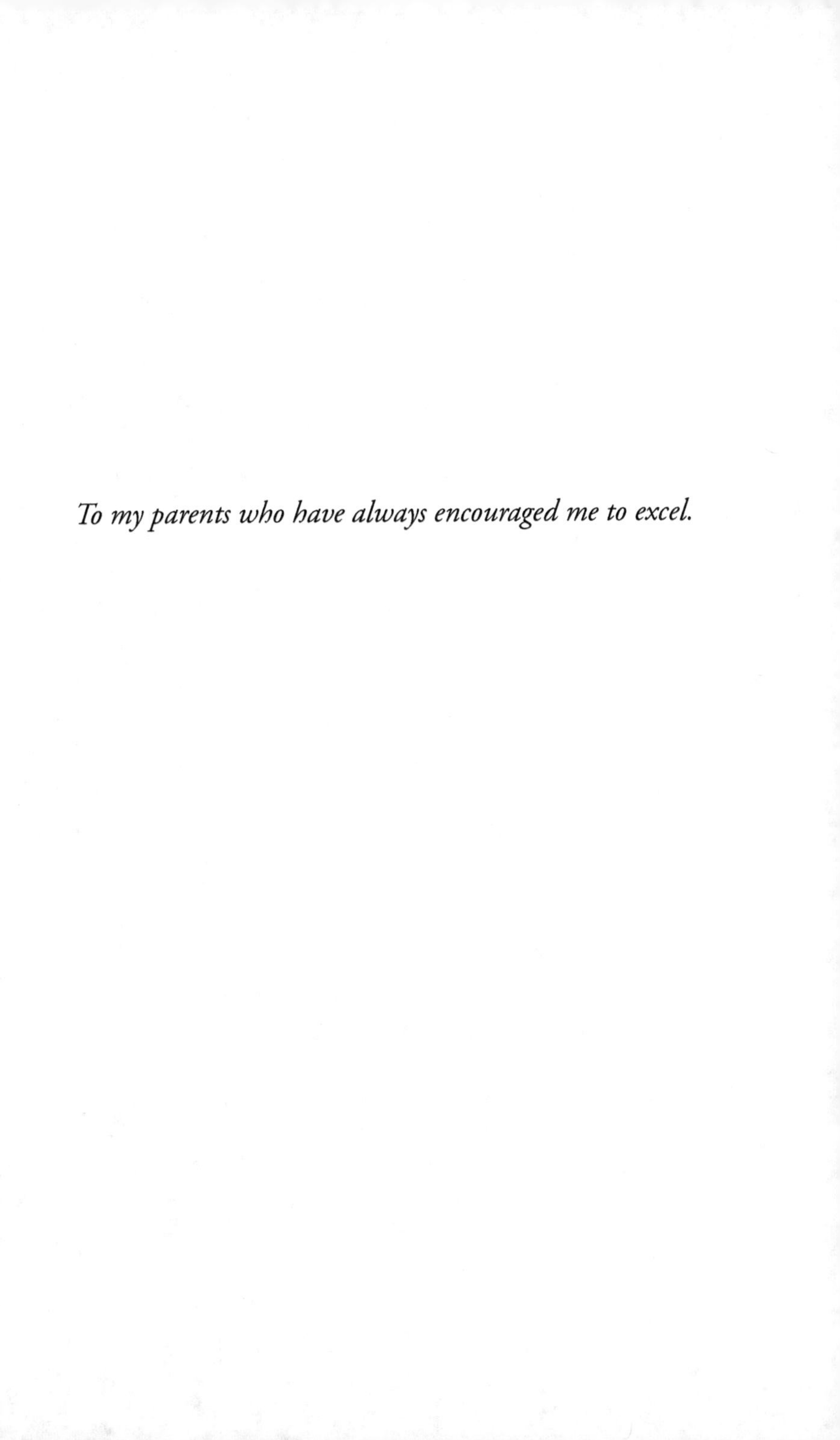

To my parents who have always encouraged me to excel.

Clues
From The
Canines

A Lily Dreyfus Mystery

Darlene Dziomba

CHAPTER 1

Pete rubs his temples in small circles using his first two fingers, attempting to massage the headache away. He had slight pain before his cousin arrived, now the rest of the day is probably a wash. He leans back onto the couch cushions, relieved he and Burrow did a five mile run this morning.

Burrow stares at him, his black eyes looking concerned.

"Dude, stop staring at me," he implores. "You're intensifying the headache."

The black and tan German shepherd saunters over to an extra-large dog bed that resembles a small couch and curls into a ball, facing Pete.

Sipping water from a mint green plastic tumbler, Pete thinks about yesterday's picnic date. A friend of Lily's had told her about the Mt. Cuba Gardens in Delaware, and Pete wandered the grounds there with Lily until they came to a secluded spot by a lake. He spread the faded blue and green plaid blanket from his childhood summer shore vacations on the grass, placing the picnic basket in the center, then listened as Lily relayed memories of trips to Parvin State Park with her family and the families of her parents' friends. One of the adults gave the children crazy nicknames. She was Smokestack, Lily said, and her sister Ivy was Monarch. He can't remember the others.

The corners of Pete's mouth turn up as he remembers Lily dropping potato salad in her lap. She got flustered, and the blush that spread across her face made her even more beautiful. He commented that her skin perfectly matched the pink in her shirt, which further deepened the blush. He leaned over to kiss her and set his hand on top of a potato salad-filled napkin, which left them both laughing. Being with Lily is softening his edges, he admits, helping him enjoy life again. He decides to call her after this headache passes.

He opens his eyes to glance at Burrow. "Dude, if it hadn't been for you, I would've never met Lily. You're a better wingman than Jim." Burrow's lips part and an enormous tongue drops out as he pants.

The cell phone rings. He sets the tumbler on the side table, checks the number, then swipes to answer. "Yo," he says, tapping the speaker phone icon.

"Hey, Pete. How ya doing?" Matt's cheerful voice comes across.

"Fighting a headache," Pete grumbles. He knows he should have let the call go to voice mail. Matt means well, but his youthful naiveté drains Pete's reserves.

"I'm sorry to hear it. Have you talked to the doctor about getting some medication for them? Mom was telling me about this thing she takes for migraines—"

"I'm sticking with Tylenol," Pete grouchily cuts Matt off. The VA doctor said they could prescribe something. They believe the headaches are caused by grief over tragically losing his parents in an auto accident coupled with the PTSD from his military deployments. Pete knows these are things he has to work through emotionally, not cover over with medication. He's a marine, and retired or not he'll tough it out.

"Okay, I was only trying to be helpful," Matt apologizes. "I found out I can get into Rowan summer classes, no SAT's required."

"That's great," Pete mumbles.

"The admissions guy I talked to had ideas about majors, too. He suggested public relations." Matt pauses.

"What does that mean, exactly," Pete asks, continuing to massage his forehead.

"You know, making impressions, um, being creative," Matt pauses.

"Matt, you've got a lot of thinking to do, about who you want to be and what you want to do." Pete hears the lecture in his tone, and feels guilty. Matt went straight from high school to the Marine Corps, and at twenty-six, he is trying to figure out the rest of his life. Pete knows he needs to be a better mentor.

"You know, Pete, all of us didn't have our dad map out a post-Corps life for us," Matt spits out.

Pete grits his teeth. He and his dad had a great plan to start a business. He blinks his eyes closed, pauses before opening them.

"I'm a little grouchy from the headache. I don't mean to lecture you," Pete apologizes.

"I'll let you go. I wanted you to know I'm working on making a plan. I'm not trying to ride your coattails. I hope you feel better." Matt disconnects.

Pete leans back onto his purple and gray geometric-patterned sofa and resumes massaging his temples. He thinks about yesterday, about Lily's stories of her childhood. As an only child, he never had to fight for his parents' attention the way she had to. He glances over at Burrow on his dog bed.

"I think this headache is going to need some Tylenol, my friend." He heads to the bathroom, swallows two caplets, then lies down in his bedroom and waits for them to work.

CHAPTER 2

"No peeing, no biting, no howling. Be good boys," Lily says as she leaves her Bassettville, New Jersey home.

Crockett gives her a forlorn stare, seemingly worried about Lily's distressed state. Boone continues to chew his Dentastix, altogether ignoring any behavioral suggestions.

Lily Dreyfus pauses on her driveway to take a deep cleansing breath, inhaling the heady scent of wisteria, which has replaced the syrupy smell of lilacs. She watches two young rabbits scamper across the lawn before climbing into her car for the short commute to work.

During the drive, she muses over her relationship with Pete. When they're together, her heart beats as fast as a hummingbird's wings, her palms get damp, and she's sure a sly smile of satisfaction shows on her face. What she can't figure out is if Pete shares her feelings.

On Saturday they drove down to the Mt. Cuba Gardens in Delaware. They toured the gardens, learning about the educational and plant propagation programs. A delightful day that culminated with a picnic lunch. The corners of Lily's mouth creep upward as she remembers them holding hands, then plummet at the memory of dropping potato salad in her lap.

She thinks of the text she sent Pete on Sunday, suggesting an activity for the weekend. Three days have passed with radio silence. She mentally weighs the pros and cons of following up—will she seem interested and assertive or just needy? She wonders for the thousandth time why relationships with humans are so tricky to navigate.

Lily pulls into the parking lot at work, parking in her usual space. As she leaves the car, her posture is straight and her shoulders are square. She may not be able to eat lunch sitting cross-legged on a blanket without dropping something in her lap, but this is a job that illuminates her talents. She even enjoys this job. It's a change of career that's become a passion.

As she enters, she greets each occupant she passes. Her hair, brown and loosely pulled up into a ponytail wags from side to side as she turns to call out their names. Lily moves on to the next wing, dropping her shoulders with an audible sigh. "Good morning, C–wing," she says.

"Don't you think you might hurt their feelings?" her coworker Chelsea teases. Jutting out one hip, she swings her ponytail of bouncy red curls across her ivory, unblemished cheek. If there is one person who knows how to use her sensuality, it is Chelsea. She is twenty-three, a perfect size two and looking so glamorous in the typical job attire of a T-shirt and jeans. On her, a T-shirt appears sculpted. Lily knows she does not have the same appearance or the same impact on male customers.

Tilting her head at Chelsea, Lily says, "Well, let's get cracking on adoptions and perhaps get them all to homes where their feelings are considered twenty-four hours a day, okay?" She smiles smugly, then adds, "Don't forget we have some new arrivals from the ASPCA coming in this morning. Please, enough with the TV character names."

"Hey, those weren't my choices," Chelsea answers shrugging her shoulders, scrunching her face as if she's just tasted something terrible.

The "C" stands for Cat. It is a large room with forty-five cages stacked three high. There are five stacks of cages along the leftmost wall and ten against the wall directly opposite the door. Along the right wall are cabinets containing towels, toys, and bags upon bags of kitty litter. Today, twenty of the cages contain cats.

Lily and Chelsea work at the Forever Friends Animal Shelter, part of the Camden County animal shelter system. It can be a bit of a postal place to work. Much like there is always junk mail to be placed in mailboxes, there are always dogs and cats to be placed with families.

Lily, the shelter's Adoption Coordinator, interacts with agencies nationwide to bring dogs and cats to Forever Friends. She then evaluates the animals and works to find them homes.

"Besides if we're lucky, Lucy and Ethel will be going home today." Chelsea smiles. "That was such a great family. They're supposed to come back tonight when the father gets off from work."

The proper procedure in animal adoptions is for all people who live in the home to interact with a prospective pet. While the staff realize that some people wanting to adopt a pet are willing to cut corners, Forever Friends does its best to follow best practices.

"Yes," Lily says. "Ingrid told me about them. She got a weird vibe from the woman when she told her the dogs had to meet all the family members. It was almost like they wanted to have the dogs already be at the house, and then tell the dad when he came home there wasn't a return policy. It worries me a bit, but I'll share your optimism the family will be back tonight. Lucy and Ethel are precious."

Lily knows she invests herself far too much into each adoption, but each adoption brings satisfaction. Witnessing the joy of people leaving the shelter with a new friend warms Lily, as if she were seated in front of a cozy fireplace.

She heads for the staff space as Chelsea begins the breakfast routine for the animals. The staff space is a ten foot square room. Three of the four corners have small, single-person desks, large enough to hold a computer monitor and the bare essentials of office supplies. She appreciates the window that lets in natural light.

Lily turns on her computer as she sits down at her desk. She brings up an email to check on the actual number of animals coming in the ASPCA transport. Their protocol is twenty kennels per transport. However, they consider four Chihuahuas as one kennel. Thankfully, this time there's only a single file for each kennel. Printing out the photos and stats, she starts on what feels like an endless stream of paperwork.

Jarred by the growling of a motor in need of a tune-up, Lily peers out the window to see the ASPCA transport van rolling to a stop.

"Chelsea, van's here," Lily calls.

"Okay, Lil" Chelsea calls over her shoulder.

Both Chelsea and Lily grab padded gloves, leashes, and towels as they head towards the van. They hear a cacophony of barks coming from the back of the van, then a very distinctive howl. Lily and Chelsea share a smile. They've heard that sound before; it's a coonhound. Coonhounds have a unique bay.

The ASPCA workers get out of the van. They greet Chelsea and Lily, then head inside to use the restroom and stretch their legs after a long ride. Chelsea and Lily get the new arrivals unloaded from the van and settled into temporary kennels. The women hang a clipboard with an "I've just arrived" sign on the enclosures, alerting volunteers not to attempt to walk these pups until they have had a little one-on-one time with seasoned staff.

Lily goes into the laundry area to thoroughly wash her hands before touching any shared surface or her computer terminal.

Chelsea pokes her head around the door frame, eyelashes aflutter. "Lily, Honeybuns is on the phone for you." Honeybuns is the younger workers' pet name for Officer Honeycutt, who works with the state police and seems to get the task of bringing in strays and runaways more often than any other officer. He's quite good looking, but Lily knows one day someone is going to slip and call him "Honeybuns" to his face, severely embarrassing the poor man.

"Howdy, Officer Honeycutt, what can we do for you today?" Lily says as she lifts the receiver to her ear.

"Lily, I've got a dog, and I'm pretty sure he was one of

your adoptions. Do you recall a German shepherd mix named Burrow?" Honeycutt asks.

She knows the dog, having seen him last Saturday. At a loss for words, she takes a deep breath, "Of course I know him. He belongs to a retired marine. Pete is one of our volunteers. He often brings Burrow to shelter events."

Officer Honeycutt cuts in, more cryptic than usual today. "There's no easy way to say this. We were called in for a wellness check. Neighbors heard the dog howling for over an hour, which the neighbors said is unlike this dog, and apparently not what the owner allows. We entered the residence and found Sergeant Russo dead. We need a place to house the dog until we can notify the family of the deceased. Can you take him?"

The phone falls from Lily's hand and hits the floor. She sits stunned, trying to imagine how a healthy, forty-year-old man could be dead.

Lily hears Officer Honeycutt's voice speaking from the dropped receiver. "Lily, are you there? Can you hear me?"

Lily grabs the phone from the floor. She pushes the door to the staff area closed. "I'm sorry. I was stunned by the news and I dropped the phone. What happened?" Her voice trembles as the palms of her hands moisten and tears well in her eyes. She takes a deep breath, and uses the back of her free hand to wipe her eyes.

"Now, Lily," Officer Honeycutt intones, "you know I'm not at liberty to discuss an ongoing investigation. I do need to secure a space for Burrow, though. Some of my fellow officers were trying to hide him under their desks." He chuckles. "One of the K-9 patrol officers suggested he'd take him home, but the major put the kibosh on that."

"We can take him, but I'm not certain we're the best placement," Lily says as she takes a deep breath to steady her nerves. Maybe if she focuses on the work aspect of this situation, she can keep the tears gathering in her eyes from bursting forth. "You know once an animal is surrendered to us, anyone who wants it has to go through adoption procedures. Is there a family member or neighbor who can take the dog?"

As the tears hover on her lower lashes, she recalls Pete attending shelter events, and how she congratulated herself on Burrow's perfect placement with him. Burrow brought Pete out of his shell. Lily even talked Pete into becoming a volunteer by channeling her inner-Chelsea and turning on the charm, emphasizing the positive impact Pete might have on people who need a furry companion in their lives.

Saturday, she had broached the idea to Pete that he and Burrow join her on a new outreach program She developed a plan to take dogs to schools to aid children with learning disabilities. She convinced Martin, her boss, to let this be a regular shelter outreach activity. She smiles to herself. Martin loved the idea. It could lead to future adoptions because animals and children worked so well together.

"I did check with the neighbors," Officer Honeycutt says with an audible sigh. "One neighbor said he thought there was a cousin who came to visit a few times. He didn't have any contact details. Another neighbor told us of a marine buddy who visits. They hadn't seen him recently. No contact information for him either. Darn these days of technology, all the sergeant's contacts must be on his cell phone, which is password protected. We couldn't find any paper with names and phone numbers anywhere in the house. We have a call into the Marines, but we haven't heard back yet. As I said, the staff thinks the best thing is to keep the dog. I don't think that's the most appropriate action."

Lily clears her throat before trying to speak. "Well, I can understand your dilemma. Let me check with some of our foster folks. Since there may be a family member who wants to take him, it's probably best not to put him on the site for adoption. Can I call you back in about an hour?"

They agree and disconnect. Lily puts her face in her hands, conceding defeat, and allows the tears to flow down her cheeks.

Chapter 3

"Soooooooooooo." Chelsea has opened the door and is staring at Lily, eyes wide, "is Honeybuns…," she begins, then notices the tears. "Is something wrong, Lily?"

"Chelsea, stop calling him that," Lily snaps. "Unfortunately, the owner of one of our adoptees was found dead in his house. Officer Honeycutt wants me to find a foster family until they can notify the next of kin. I've got phone calls to make. Is Ingrid in yet?"

"Oh my God, that's horrible. Yes, I'll send her in." Shocked, Chelsea wrestles with leaving Lily to compose herself or hugging her. Lily solves the dilemma by holding up one hand in a stop gesture.

"No, no, ask her to take over the assessments. And for goodness' sake, tell her no TV character names," Lily says dabbing at her wet cheeks with a tissue.

Chelsea backs out, closing the door behind her. She turns around to face the other employees at the front desk.

"Did Lily yell at you?" Ingrid asks, flipping her tightly braided black hair over her shoulder. Her hand rests on Martin, the shelter manager's, forearm. Ingrid is the guiding force of calm in the workplace. Like a lighthouse that ably guides ships to safety, she steers her coworkers from controversy and confrontation.

"She's had a bit of a shock," Chelsea says waving her hands as if trying to dry wet fingernails. "Officer Honeycutt is bringing us a dog to foster. His owner was found dead."

Ingrid's free hand covers her mouth as her mahogany eyes go wide.

"That's not an excuse to yell at Chelsea, though," Martin mutters. Ingrid's hand squeezes his forearm in a silent request for patience.

"Lily wants you to take over the evaluations," Chelsea continues. "Though how we're supposed to get back to normal after this piece of news I'm not certain."

"We'll find a way," Ingrid says stoically.

"You two go back and start the assessments. I've got things covered here," Martin reassures them. Martin's buzz cut accentuates his prominent cheekbones. He tries very hard to be assertive, but he's often stymied by Lily and Ingrid's determination.

Chelsea and Ingrid move off to D–wing, bending their heads together to whisper their perceptions of Lily's behavior.

Martin pauses to clear his mind. Whatever the cause, a raised voice is never acceptable around the animals. Concerned, he moves to the staff area and opens the door. "Everything okay in here?" he asks Lily's clenched back.

"Sure, Martin. I had a bit of a shock, but stiff upper lip, I'll carry on," Lily responds, but does not turn around to make eye contact.

"You'll be fine talking with foster families and making a placement for the animal," Martin adds in a flat, toneless voice.

There are five seconds of silence then Lily swivels in her chair. "I think I'll take him," she begins, conspicuously making no eye contact.

Martin blows out his breath then slowly inhales before speaking. "That's not the protocol."

"We can do an official meet with my dogs," Lily protests. She and Pete haven't taken the three dogs out together, but she could use the comfort of having Burrow with her. And Burrow could use the support of someone familiar.

"We could do a meet, but you're an employee of the shelter, not a recognized foster parent for us," Martin admonishes.

"Well, I'll just get one of those foster parent applications and evaluate myself. I think I'll find that Lily Dreyfus is a stellar candidate," she quips, raising her head to make eye contact. Her tear-stained eyes glare with indignation.

Martin holds up his hand to stop her talking. Lily opens her mouth, then reconsiders and closes it. She and Martin lock eyes, as if to see who will draw first in a western standoff. "You've had a shock, which is clearly impacting your judgment. You think about which foster family would be most suitable and get in touch with them. I'm going back to the front desk." Martin maintains eye contact for a few extra seconds to make sure she will follow his instructions, then turns and retreats, closing the door behind him.

"Darn it," Lily mutters, shaking her head. "I thought I'd finally found the lid to fit my frying pan. And when does a healthy, forty-something man just drop dead for no reason?" She stamps a foot on the linoleum floor, and slouches against the back of her chair with her arms folded across her chest.

After stewing in her misery for a minute, Lily swivels the chair around to face the computer. Grabbing the mouse in her right hand, she clicks to open the excel spreadsheet where the list of foster families is kept. "I'll find an appropriate foster family. And I'm going to find out how Pete died."

Scrolling through the spreadsheet, Lily begins to review the available foster families. Emitting a weary sigh, she stops searching. She'd like this dog to be fostered by Mickey and her giant Newfoundland Nero. She is one of Lily's closest friends, and the reason she applied for this job. Mickey knew Lily's previous job, working with sick children and victims of domestic violence, was taking a toll on her, and thought the physical labor of the Forever Friends job would suit her. Being cooped up inside and mostly bound to a desk in her old job left Lily lethargic.

Lily sends Mickey a text. "Need a foster home ASAP. You're perfect. Give me a call." Smiling to herself, she thinks "perfect" is the appropriate word. She thinks of sending a second message saying, "Remember the guy you encouraged me to talk to at events? He's dead, and his dog needs a home." The cynical side of Lily wonders if this latest development in her love life will get everyone off her back regarding her single status for a bit. Then her phone bings signaling a text message.

"Can do, but lots of clients today, can I come by with Nero at 6?" Mickey is retired from corporate life and has a dog walking and dog sitting business.

Lily texts back, "Perfect." She picks up the handset of the phone on the file cabinet and dials Officer Honeycutt at his state police station.

"Troop D Road Station, Major O'Shea"

"Um," Lily stammers. She is perplexed as to why the commanding officer is answering the phone. "Excuse me, Major. This is Lily Dreyfus from Friends Forever. May I speak to Officer Honeycutt?" She slaps her free hand to her forehead, as she realizes her focus is lost when she can't even say the name of the shelter correctly.

"Oh good, Lily, did you find a temporary home for Burrow?" the major asks. "Honeycutt's out on a call. My other officers seem to think getting the dog to catch a football is therapeutic. I think it's an excuse to be outside."

"I believe I have, sir," Lily answers. "Can someone bring him by? You know the drill, we'll have a meet with the foster family and their dog, but I think I have a perfect fit."

Major O'Shea assures her he'll have someone bring Burrow down as soon as he can order a halt to the football toss.

Lily wants to be involved in the handoff to Mickey tonight. Of course, staying until then will make for a very long day. She has two dogs of her own to feed and walk. She sends a text to her brother, Tyler. "Can you feed and walk the boys tonight?"

There is an instant reply. "Yep, wzup?"

Lily responds, "Dog surrender, I want to be here. Be home about 6:30."

"K" comes in reply. Tyler, ten years younger than Lily, often pokes fun of her full word text messages. Lily wipes her face one more time with a tissue before standing and opening the door to the front desk area.

Martin and Anna are behind the front desk. They both stare at her, their concern evident.

"Which foster family will be taking the dog, Lily?" Martin asks.

"Mickey Sterling's coming at six." Lily tries to act natural, but she is not fooling Martin.

"Okay, let Ingrid know since she'll be here tonight," Martin says.

"Well," Lily starts, "I thought I'd stay and see the handoff through." She starts walking towards the D-wing.

"Hold it," Martin says his face in a tight line. "I don't think you need to stay late. Ingrid's more than capable of handling this."

Lily thinks to herself, *why must he be difficult?* She smiles as best she can and says, "It's not a big deal. I can work on assessments and have more animals ready for the weekend adoptions."

"Lily, don't make me have to be a jerk, okay?" Martin stares at her. "I'm trying to be sensitive." Before she replies, Martin continues, "It's obvious this surrender is upsetting you. I don't know why. What I do know is you're not in a frame of mind to stay at work three extra hours."

A woman comes up behind Lily saying, "Hi, I want to adopt one of your cats."

"Of course, let me come with you," Lily says. She turns, walking back to the C Wing with the woman.

At the front desk, Martin shakes his head, perplexed. If he insisted a staff person work three extra hours, he's considered unreasonable and demanding. If he tells the staff person there is no reason to work extra hours, they argue with him. He looks at Anna and asks, "Will you be okay alone for a bit?"

"Sure thing," she says.

"I'm going to talk to Ingrid," he says and walks to the D-wing.

CHAPTER 4

Finding neither Ingrid nor Chelsea around the dog kennels, Martin heads outside to the outdoor pens. He sees the two of them with a large black dog. He walks over to the pen, observing from the perimeter. Unbeknownst to all, Lily watches the interaction from one of the walking trails used to exercise the dogs, having stepped outside for some fresh air to clear her mind. Anna willingly took over the application processing for the cat adoption.

Chelsea loosely holds the dog's leash. Ingrid tries to grab one of the dog's front paws. The dog jumps from its seated position to standing and wags his tail. Ingrid tries to grab the leg again, and the dog does a puppy bow.

"He doesn't seem aggressive." Ingrid smiles at Chelsea, and notices Martin outside of the kennel.

"Boss, step in here and let's see how he is with men," she says.

Martin opens the gate and steps inside. The dog turns, and his tail droops. Martin slowly approaches and holds out his fist for the dog to smell. The dog backs up two steps, then tentatively walks forward and stops. He leans forward to smell Martin's fist then drops to a puppy bow again.

"I think he likes you," Chelsea says.

"It seems he does," Martin says, as the dog begins to bat his paws at Martin's calves.

"Do you want to take him for a bit of a walk, and we'll get the next one?" Ingrid, their Animal Behaviorist, asks. This is her second career, having moved on from being a systems analyst after her job got outsourced.

"Not right now. Chelsea, why don't you take him? I want to talk to Ingrid," Martin says.

"You bet. C'mon boy," Chelsea calls to the dog.

"Well that sounds ominous. What'd I do?" Ingrid asks playfully.

Martin waits until Chelsea leaves the pen, then says, "Something's up with Lily. She looks like she's about to burst into tears, but she's insisting on staying until the foster shows up tonight for the surrender."

"Ugh, you know Lily. Her canine handling skills far outweigh her interpersonal skills," Ingrid says.

"Yeah, and she's a master at avoidance," Martin scoffs. "A woman came up and said she wanted to adopt a cat while we were talking, and Lily hightailed it to the cat wing."

Ingrid starts laughing.

"It's not funny," Martin shouts, although he smiles. "Whatever has her so upset, working three extra hours isn't going to solve it." He tilts his head to one side, grimacing.

Ingrid puts a hand on Martin's shoulder. "I'll talk to her. I'm not making any promises, but I'll try to get her to see reason."

"Thanks, Ingrid," Martin says.

Chapter 5

"We didn't finish what we were talkin' about this morning." Quinn is wearing a black Skillet T-shirt that's two sizes too big, over jeans with frayed hems. He and Eva are walking their bikes away from the Haddon Township High School.

Eva halts. She holds the pink-banded handlebars of her bike with one hand and uses the other to flip her lank, blonde hair over her shoulder. "There's nothing more to discuss," she spits out like an irritated llama.

Quinn flinches, as if she had spit on him, then musters his courage. "I don't agree. I don't think you've thought this through. You have options."

"I don't, though. I don't have options." Eva's throat tightens as her voice rises. Her free hand slices the air like a knife. "People say shit like that because they don't know what it means not to have options." She begins to step off a curb when a dented Hyundai from the '90s screeches around the corner on nearly bald tires.

Quinn's bike clatters to the sidewalk as he grabs Eva's shoulders, yanking her backward. Eva holds on to the handlebar, and the front wheel of her bike jerks into the air, whirring as it spins on its axle. There's a hiss, and a mini-tornado of stones spins down to the ground. "Geez, Eva, that crazy bitch almost ran you over."

Eva sets the wheel back onto the pavement. She rubs a fist into her left eye, then the right, clearing the dust from them. "Now that would've solved my problems. I forgot death is an option," Eva mumbles. A tear drips down the line of her cheek.

"You say stuff like that, and it makes me want to run to the police," Quinn grunts, as he picks up his bike.

Eva's pupils shrink to pinpricks as she glares at Quinn. "You'd better swear you won't talk to the police," she growls through gritted teeth. "They'll kill me for sure."

Quinn puts his free hand on her shoulder. "I think that's a baseless threat. They know they've got you scared. They're saying shit to keep you scared."

Eva turns her gaze away. She turns her head to the left to make sure no other cars are coming around the corner and starts pushing her bike across the street. Quinn's hand falls from her shoulder. Hitching up his jeans, he follows her. They continue in silence.

At the next corner, Quinn says, "Any idea who almost ran you over?"

"That creepy, cafeteria lady," Eva says and checks for turning traffic before continuing across and down the street.

"Can you narrow that down?" He smirks, hoping to get a laugh from her.

"The jittery one, who looks like she drank a case of Red Bull," Eva mumbles.

"Shit, the other day she was working the tray collection station, dumping shit all over the floor. Then steppin' in it and makin' it worse. I swear someone's gonna post it on America's Funniest Videos." Quinn's now wholeheartedly laughing. Eva makes no response. "Seriously, didn't you see it?"

"No," Eva mumbles.

"Oh my God, how'd you miss it? Seriously funny shit. You think she's retarded or something?" Quinn asks.

"No," Eva says, more adamantly than she intended. Her shoulders have started slumping as if a ghost has been putting rocks into her backpack, making it heavier. "She's a junkie," Eva mutters.

"F…" Quinn's cheeks redden. "Sorry, Eva, I guess you'd know the signs, huh?"

"Right, the signs," Eva responds, keeping her eyes on the ground. She stops at the next corner. "Listen, this is where we part ways."

Quinn turns serious. "I don't like it, Eva."

Eva holds up one hand, palm out. "Enough." She turns left to cross the street. She looks over her shoulder. "And don't think of following me." She pushes the bike across the street. At the next corner, she gets on the bike and pedals off, hair billowing like a curtain in a spring breeze.

He watches her head off towards the park, berating himself for making fun of the cafeteria lady. He didn't know the woman has a drug problem like Eva's mother. When Eva is no longer in sight, he throws one leg over his bike and rides home vowing to bring the subject up again with her tomorrow.

Chapter 6

Lily leaves the shelter at quarter after four and walks over to her parked car, feeling like she's been voted off "Survivor." She gets into her car and turns the key in the ignition. The latest ballad by Taylor Swift comes on the radio. Lily quickly punches the button to WMGK, knowing love songs are rare on the classic rock station. She pulls out of the lot for the short drive home.

As she pulls the car into her driveway at home, she sees Boone lift his head from the couch through the large bay window of the living room. He peers out the window. Suddenly, it's like someone pulled the cord on a lamp; his ears lift and his eyes shine with glee. He sees Lily is home.

Boone gives himself a good shake and jumps off the couch. Then, with a mighty baying, Crockett streaks into the room. The glee in Boone's face turns to a scowl. Lily laughs out loud. She wonders for the thousandth time if Boone will ever forgive her for bringing home Crockett. Crockett came into the shelter shortly after she started her job. He is a beagle mix, and he gave her the pathetic stare for which the breed is known. She thought having another dog in the house would be good for Boone. Instead, Boone tolerates Crockett, but barely.

Lily gets out of the car and heads up the three steps to the front door. She looks into the entry, and sees the door to the upstairs residence is closed. She shuts the entry door and opens the door to her house, squatting to let Boone lick her face. He may not have minty fresh breath, but dog kisses wash away any feeling of inadequacy.

"It's been a rough day, Boone," she says tasseling his ears. "Mommy's latest romance was found dead. Can you believe that?"

Tears start to fall down her face again, and Boone licks her cheeks. Crockett smells up one leg and down the other. "Okay, Crockett buddy, I know I smell like dogs and cats, but you're getting a little too personal there with your snout."

"Yo, you said you'd be late." Tyler comes in the door. The building they occupy is a brick duplex. Lily lives on the bottom floor and Tyler the top. Tyler bought the place several years ago when the couple who lived upstairs were selling to move to North Carolina for retirement.

Lily surveys what Tyler is wearing, jeans so faded they are barely blue, and a T-shirt she believes was once emblazoned with the Green Wave of Audubon High School. She shakes her head, wiping a hand across her cheek. "Let's say Martin insisted I come home."

"Good deal," Tyler responds. He moves through the room to give Crockett a scratch on the ears. "I won't have to put on shoes."

Lily scoffs. Before she can comment further, Tyler smirks and adds, "Um, not like YOU are a 'fashionista' when you go to work."

"I didn't say anything," Lily protests. She thinks her younger brother is the epitome of millennial.

"You don't have to. You have that same look mom gets." Tyler gives her an exaggerated scowl.

"Okay, I'm going to walk the boys. I think there's lasagna in the freezer. Would you put it in the oven? Crockett is climbing my leg. He must need a walk."

"He's a faker. I took them on a walk around two."

"Oh, but no one walks him like his mommy." She giggles. Lily grabs two leashes from the hand-painted rack by the front door. She attaches them both, checks her pockets for plastic bags, and heads out again. Lily smiles at the boys. They have such personalities. Boone, a canine garbage disposal, has his nose to the ground, sniffing away. Someone might think it is for rabbits, but truth be told he's happy to find an errant roll or pizza crust. Crockett, on the other hand, has his head up and is surveying the landscape. He thinks it would be fabulous to catch a squirrel. He is scrappy, but the squirrel would put up a fight Crockett is not prepared to have.

The long, pleasant walk helps Lily clear her head while giving Boone and Crockett a chance to stretch their legs and gather in the neighborhood smells. They walk until the grumble in Lily's stomach reminds her she hasn't eaten since breakfast. She steers the boys towards home. As they reach the steps, Lily looks down at the poor pink and red flowers Kelly gave her. Oh boy, those flowers sure need some help, she thinks. Kelly's said they're virtually unkillable, but they may have met their match with her.

She climbs the three steps to the front door. Tyler has left the door to the front entry open, a habit that tends to annoy her, but tonight she's grateful to only have to unlock one door. The hearty smell of garlic and cheese fills her nose. Boone sticks his nose in the air as well, his whiskers twitching with anticipation. Lily unhooks the leashes, and Boone and Crockett charge into the kitchen. She hangs up their leashes, and locks her front door.

Lily follows the boys through the living and dining room. As she glances down at the maple Pergo flooring, she mentally puts sweeping the floors on the list of things to do. In the kitchen, Tyler is sitting at the round, pub-height table, perched on a stool. He has his laptop open. Boone and Crockett are rooted in front of the cabinet where Lily keeps the bin of dog kibble.

Lily picks up the dog bowls from the floor and sets them on the countertop. Boone leaps to his feet and starts shuffling from one front paw to the other. Lily gives each dog a bowl of kibble and a fresh bowl of water. As they gulp down their food, she grabs an open bottle of red wine and pours a big glass.

"Crap, Lil, why not stick a straw in the bottle?" Tyler teases her.

"You know, I considered it," she counters. She faces him, leaning one hand on the counter, the other holding the glass of wine aloft.

"Seriously, you're not yourself, what's up?" Tyler asks.

Lily turns back to the cabinet to get both Boone and Crockett a Milk Bone. She puts down her glass so she can hold a treat in each hand. Crockett sits perfectly still. Boone has his haunches a whisper above the floor ready to pounce. She hands the treats to the dogs, and picking up the wine glass to face Tyler, spits it out.

"Well, we had the state police call asking us to take a dog. They got it from a house where they found the owner dead," she starts.

Tyler opens his mouth to speak. Lily puts up her empty hand as if to stop something from crashing into her.

"Hold that thought. The dead person happens to be Pete, the guy I had a date with last week." Tears start to flow down her cheeks again.

"No way. You finally go on a date, and the guy ends up dead? What are the chances?" Tyler asks. He has swiveled the chair to face her fully.

"The chances are pretty good. It happened." Lily turns from him and buries her face in her hands. "I'm sorry, Tyler. I don't mean to be snippy with you. Seriously, what *are* the chances?"

"Oh, geez, Lil, please stop crying. You know I'm not the emotional one in the family. I don't even know what to say to you," Tyler sputters.

"I know," she gulps air. "You chose a career with the most minimal human contact. I need to talk with one of my girlfriends." Lily pulls a wad of Kleenex from her pocket, and blows her nose. She reaches under the sink to put the wadded tissue into the trash can.

"Yeah, but you know I'm going to tell the guys, right?" Tyler tries to cheer her. "Guy kills himself rather than date my sister."

Lily takes another sip of wine and then forces a smile. "You do, and it's the last meal I cook for you, brat."

"Um, technically I cooked tonight."

"Putting lasagna I made and froze into the oven is not cooking." She turns from him and goes to the bathroom off the kitchen for another Kleenex. Tyler is silent as she returns to the kitchen.

"Let's see if the lasagna is cooked." She puts a potholder glove on her hand. She opens the oven door and pulls the oven rack out a bit. She grabs a knife and cuts into the lasagna. Steam pours out.

"It looks like our walk was long enough for it to cook through," she says. "Get some silverware and napkins out for the dining room table. I'll dish this up and refill my wine glass."

"You got it, sis," Tyler closes his laptop, gets silverware and napkins, pours a glass of wine for himself, and heads into the dining room. Lily has the wooden table collapsed to its smallest size, with only three of the six ladder-back chairs around it. Tyler puts down his wine and positions two place settings, the second perpendicular to his.

Boone has been following every movement. Tyler goes back into the kitchen with Boone at his heels. Tyler takes one of the plates on which Lily has put a chunk of lasagna. He looks down at the dog. "Boone, the chances of me dropping this are pretty slim, buddy."

The dog sits and looks over to Lily. "I'm not giving you lasagna either, my friend. You had your dinner." She refills her wineglass and takes the other plate into the dining room.

Lily is grateful for the comfort food and wine. She feigns interest in what Tyler is telling her about the security patches he pushed out to his clients that day, and her mind keeps flashing back to Pete. She remembers the day he adopted Burrow. She and Ingrid were working on assessments. As they were bringing an assessed dog back to its kennel, they saw Pete sitting cross-legged in front of Burrow's kennel. A baseball hat was shielding his face, both hands were interlaced in the fencing that separated him from Burrow, and he was leaning forward.

Burrow was sitting tall on the other side of the fencing, with his head forward so he and Pete were nose to nose. It was as if the two of them were sharing some vital secret. Lily remembers wishing she had her phone to snap a picture of the poignant scene. She was transfixed until Ingrid opened the kennel for the dog they were returning. The noise jarred everyone from their reverie.

Pete stood up, but his eyes never left Burrow. Ingrid breezily approached asking, "Would you like to have a meet with Burrow, here?"

Without turning his head, Pete responded. "We've met. We're ready to go home."

"Earth to Lily," Tyler says.

Lily shakes the thoughts from her head. "I'm sorry, Tyler. I'm probably not much company tonight."

"You weren't even in the room with me, sis," Tyler teases.

Lily uses her napkin to wipe the tears forming at the corners of her eyes. "I was remembering the day Pete adopted Burrow."

"It must be a pretty intoxicating memory," Tyler smirks. "Or you've had too much to drink."

"A bit of both," Lily says. "So, you were saying something about security patches?"

Tyler lets out a laugh. "About five minutes ago. Geez, I know my work can make people's eyes glaze over, but crap." He forks a chunk of lasagna into his mouth and chews.

Lily looks down at her plate. She realizes she's no longer hungry, but takes another bite anyway. "Tyler, I'm ready for a shower." She lowers her fork and pushes her chair back from the table.

"Yeah, and bed, too, I think. Go on. I'll finish what I'm eating and clean up."

"Thanks," she mumbles and heads off towards the bathroom.

Once in the shower, she lets the tears fall freely from her eyes. She sobs until there are no tears left. Then she washes her body and hair, quickly rinsing off. She turns off the water, dries off, and towel dries her hair. As she's combing out her wet hair, she catches sight of her face.

Crying left deep crevices under her eyes. She grabs Oil of Olay from the medicine cabinet and spreads some liberally under her eyes. Hopefully, it will work its magic overnight.

Feeling clean, Lily gets into her pajamas and heads for the kitchen. She finds Tyler has taken his laptop and gone home. She goes to the living room to find Boone on the recliner and Crockett on the couch. Boone is snoring loudly. Lily sits down on the couch. Crockett comes over and lays his head in her lap.

"Gosh, buddy," she says to him, "I know you drive Boone crazy, but you're so cute and snuggly." She pets his back.

He sighs contentedly as if to say, "Yes, I know how cute I am."

Lily continues to stroke Crockett's fur and thinks to herself, *Pete, what happened to you?*

CHAPTER 7

While Tyler and Lily are enjoying comfort food, Mickey and Nero are on their way to Forever Friends to pick up Burrow in Mickey's new red GMC.

Oh boy, oh boy, we're getting a new buddy to stay at our house. I'm thumping my tail with glee in the back of the car. I can't help myself. I love it when we get new buddies to hang out with. We're pulling into the shelter and it's time for a giant WOOF to let everyone know we're here. I see Ingrid and Martin coming out of the shelter. I better Woof Mom to hurry up and let me out of the car. She's got the hatch open and she's leashing me up.

I'm gonna jump on Ingrid and give her a slurpy kiss. Oh my God she smells like cat. I can smell it all over her. Mom is yelling at me to be polite but holy cow, cat, cat, cat. Martin's taking me to the play area to meet my new buddy. I know the drill, I've been through it lots of times, we each sniff, then we usually get some play time. I won't be too exuberant but it's hard. I'm a big guy; I have lots of enthusiasm.

Oh, there's Ingrid with a German shepherd. I think I know this guy. I'll get a good whiff when they get closer. Yep, we've met.

"Hey, Buddy, remember me? Nero, Nero Woof. Buddy, come on now, if we get along, you get to come home with us. We've got a huge comfy couch and lots of fluffy blankets." I am enthusiastically wagging my tail and smiling my biggest smile. Friendly, I must be friendly. Boy oh boy, this guy is one sad looking fellow. How low can a tail hang down? He stops walking, standing away from the side of the pen. I'll encourage him. "Buddy give me a sniff, okay?"

"Hey, I'm Burrow, not Buddy, and I'm having one lousy day."

"Dude, I get it but give me a sniff and they're gonna let you in the play area. Believe me, you want to come home with us. It's much better than the shelter."

He's coming over and now he's giving me a sniff through the fence. Mom is telling me to sit and stop the barking. I always try to give the new guys the lowdown. It can be scary, whatever reason that someone is coming to stay with us, but I work hard to let them know it will be okay. I'm taking a seat, but my tail is still wagging on its own, sending up a nice cloud of dust.

Ingrid's got the play area gate open and is waving Burrow in. Geez, does he have one drooping tail? Burrow's walking around following all of Ingrid's instructions, but he doesn't seem interested. Man, I can't help myself.

"Dude, seriously, come over here and give me a sniff, would you?"

"Listen, I'm not Buddy or Dude, and my best friend is dead. So back off."

Whoops, this guy has quite the bark on him. And how did he get every hair to go straight up like that? The most I can ever manage is one strip down the back. Ingrid's backing him up and talking to him. Good idea. She's good, that Ingrid. Okay, they're coming over again, I'll zip it and sit still.

"Hey Nero, sorry, it's been a completely bad day."

Oh, that was a playful bump Burrow just gave me. I see Mom and Ingrid are smiling at each other like they did something grand. I'm so hard to resist. No one stays mad at me for long.

"No problem let's get you to our house and I'll give you all of the space you need."

Ingrid's taking Burrow's leash off. That's good, he can roam a bit. But he's sitting down next to me and gives me another bump. I guess he wants company. Now he's lying down on the ground. I'll lie down too to show we're buddies. Look at those big wild grins on Mom and Ingrid. They must think they're the ones making Burrow comfy. It's all me. I am so charming.

Mom's putting my leash back on and Ingrid's doing Burrow's. I guess it's time to leave the play area and walk back to the shelter. Ah, it's a little cooler here by the front desk. I guess they're doing the papers that'll let Burrow stay with us. Oh, a biscuit and a pat on the head. That's nice. I think I'll check out the cat smell on this worker. Yep, she's been working with the cats. But she likes me better. I'm the one she's giving the biscuits to. Oh yes, they do think I am entirely charming. I am lovable. I know how to work it to have them eating out of my paw. Mom's back and it's time to get me and Burrow loaded in the car for home.

Chapter 8

"How much money do I have on me?" Clarissa asks while washing her hands in a cracked porcelain sink. The soap stings as it touches the exposed cuticles of her ragged, bitten nails. She frowns at her hands. Red Bull has kept her steady through this shift at Wawa, but she'll need a more potent stimulant to get through the next job, not wanting a recurrence of last week's events. She sighs, remembering the laughing, cell phone-toting teenagers filming her as she was putting dirty cafeteria trays on a conveyor belt.

She pulls the ID holder from her back pocket and unzips the money section. She steadies her hand and pulls out the wad of bills stuffed in there: a ten, two fives, six ones. Deciding to check the ATM before leaving Wawa, she appraises herself in a warped, foggy mirror. Her sunken eyes seem to be stained a permanent red. She glances at her hands again as she stuffs the money back inside the ID holder.

She exits the bathroom and goes over to the ATM. She inserts her card and waits for the account balance slip. A chime sounds, and she glances over to the front door where two police officers are entering. Cringing, she says a silent prayer that they did not notice her car's expired plate and bald tires. There is no money for either.

A slip of paper kachunks from the ATM, and Clarissa grabs at it. She grimaces. Her pay from the school has not been deposited. She will have to see what $26 can purchase.

The two officers are pouring large cups of coffee and

chattering. The day shift has come in, and people are silently preparing for the morning commuters. Clarissa slips out the front door and gets into her car, wondering how long she can continue making sandwiches midnight to six, four days a week, plus 10 to 2 cafeteria duty five days a week. If only her cousin Pete cared as much about her welfare as he does about his stupid dog.

She resents his judgmental attitude that working two minimum wage jobs is her first choice. The law firm's refusal to extend her medical leave beyond twelve weeks for her unhealed broken leg rankle. And the boyfriend who took her on the ski trip leaving her for a bimbo he met in the emergency room while she was waiting to be seen, that was a bummer.

The officers have left the Wawa, so Clarissa puts the car in gear and pulls from the parking lot. The sun is coming up, so she grabs her sunglasses to keep the glare out of her eyes. The car swerves slightly, causing blasts of horns. She admonishes herself to concentrate rather than add to her woes with a car accident. She exits Route 70 and takes the back roads through Cherry Hill into Westmont, then back around until she comes to the street that borders Cooper River. She parks the car at a curb and gets out without bothering to lock the car door. She removes the ID holder from her back pocket and pulls out the ten and two fives. Folding them in half and half again, she slips them into her front pocket. She puts the ID holder into her back pocket. She looks around and sees no one walking dogs or jogging, then heads towards the woods that border the river, believing all she needs is something to help her stay awake during her cafeteria shift.

Chapter 9

It is Thursday morning, and Lily arrives back at the shelter. Her nerves are steadier. Unfortunately, her mouth is as dry as a wad of cotton. Her head reverberates as if someone is trying to pound a nail into it. She is more than a bit hungover. She picks up the plastic bag from Wawa with two bottles of water, one liter each, and exits her car. Hydration will bring her around.

"Lily, you had a good cry last night. You will not burst into tears at work. Stiff upper lip, let's go," she tells herself. She crosses the parking lot and heads to the back door of the shelter.

Opening the door to the D-wing, the morning cacophony greets her. "Ethel, you're alone. Well, don't worry, sweetie. I know we'll find you a permanent home soon. Morning, Dylan. You've got an enthusiastic tail wag going there. Well, good morning to all of you new recruits who we still need to name. Don't worry. Everyone will get breakfast and a walk around the grounds very soon." She greets the dogs, embracing the comfort of a well-practiced routine.

Lily moves on to the C-wing to check out the cats. "Good morning, my cute, furry, companions. Kibble and aluminum foil ball chasing will commence shortly."

"You're a riot," Chelsea laughs as she comes down the corridor. She does a double-take at Lily's red rimmed eyes, but does not comment. "I'm going to start assembling doggie breakfast."

Lily nods in acknowledgment, and turns her gaze through the window to the cat playroom. Despite feeling raw inside, she laughs out loud. The feral kittens arrived, and Ingrid gave each a colored collar and a name. The list reads Puma, Cheetah, Snow Leopard, Tiger, Sierra, and El Capitan. After Ingrid's systems analyst job got outsourced, she went back to school and got a degree in animal behavior, garnering animal training certifications along the way, and then found herself at Forever Friends. She jokes that the cats have better personalities than the IT people with whom she worked.

"Well, you said no names of TV characters, so Ingrid named the kittens after MAC operating systems," Chelsea says, dimples showing as she smiles. "You have to admit they're good names for cats."

"You're right, there," Lily retorts. "Let me check through the paperwork from last night and see if there are any special instructions for our recruits before we get to cage cleaning and walking." Lily moves down the corridor, enters the staff area, and sits down at her desk. The first item she picks up is the adoption paperwork for Lucy. It appears Ingrid's odd feeling was correct about the family that came to look at Lucy and Ethel. They didn't return.

Another family did adopt Lucy last night; Brandon became Bandit and went home; Luke, also adopted, became Duke; and two more cats found forever families. Doc is going to do some further assessment on the coonhound that arrived yesterday. The note says short walks only.

Lily goes to the tiny staff kitchen located behind the waiting area. She opens one of the bottles of water and downs half, then puts it and the unopened bottle in the refrigerator. She rolls the plastic bag into a ball and puts it in her pocket to use during the morning dog walks. She drops her tote onto her desk and heads back to the D-wing.

Lily and Chelsea get moving with the cage cleaning, feeding, and walking. The shelter has a distinct morning routine. Every morning there are crates and kennels to clean, then clean blankets for the dogs and clean towels for the cats, breakfast to hand out and exercise for them all. Lily's friends sometimes criticize her for pulling her hair into a barrette and not wearing makeup at work. She often wonders how fabulous eyeliner and mascara would look after her morning work routine. She directs her focus to the movements and personalities of the new dogs.

When all the dogs have had a walk, she returns to the staff area. Ingrid has arrived and is at her desk.

"Lily, how are you?" Ingrid asks.

"I'm okay, thanks." Lily wipes sweat from her brow with her sleeve. She sits in her chair. "How did the meet go with Mickey and Nero?"

"It started a little tense. You know Nero comes on a bit strong. I think he freaked Burrow out a bit," Ingrid begins. "Once Mickey got Nero to rein in his personality things went smoothly. She's probably treating Burrow like a king this morning," Ingrid answers.

"That's good. I'll call her later," Lily sighs.

"I know you wanted to stay last night," Ingrid begins in a judicious tone.

"No, you were right to tell me to go home." Lily shyly smiles. "Don't tell Martin I said that, okay?"

Ingrid winks at her. "Your secret is safe with me. Listen, it was probably quite a shock to hear someone you know was found dead. It's not what we expect to have to cope with coming to work in this job." Ingrid puts a hand on Lily's shoulder.

Lily's previous job was as a social worker at the Children's Hospital of Philadelphia. While CHOP is prestigious, finding hospice services for sick children, dealing with state and county protective services bureaucracy, and being around the sick every day took a mental toll on her.

"Sure," Lily concedes. "Let's go through what we need to do today."

Ingrid understands Lily's need to shift her focus to work. Lily's eyes look like the "before" shot of a Visine commercial. "Let's get cracking," Ingrid says.

Ingrid and Lily head to the D-wing and continue assessing

the dogs that arrived yesterday. It is difficult to know an animal from the first meeting. It's sort of like a blind date. You want it to go well, so you avoid anything negative. Finding ways to showcase a dog's positive characteristics helps to get them into a permanent home.

The women take the dogs one at a time into a pen and let them run off a little energy. Then they try some basic commands: sit, stay, leave it. If the dog is responding to the commands, they introduce it to another of the dogs to see how the new one reacts. They pick a dog that has been at the shelter for a few days and that has shown itself to be comfortable around other dogs.

Then, with each on a leash, they bring both dogs inside the pen. They walk them around each other to get them more acquainted. If the dogs are tolerant of each other, they'll release them one at a time from the leash. Sometimes it is obvious one dog is not going to tolerate another. One can feel the dog's muscles tighten up from the pressure on the leash. Of course, there are other telltales: a dog's hair going straight up, a low rumbling growl, and worst, one dog lunging for the other.

Lily and Ingrid go through this process with each of the new dogs. Tomorrow they will move to the next process, a similar assessment between the dog and a cat, in an indoor enclosed space. Depending on how the dogs are responding, the process will move on to working with different people. They will introduce one of the male coworkers into the mix to see how the dog reacts to men.

There is also a process to try to see if a dog is receptive to children. It involves a doll about the size of a four-year-old child. It's hard to assess whether an animal will be good with kids. Sometimes the staff will bring in a family member to play around the animals to see how a dog reacts, but they can't hire a five-year-old to run into the pen and see what happens. Besides the child's safety, there are labor laws and insurance liability to consider.

After a few hours, interspersed with water breaks for Lily, she and Ingrid return to the staff area. Martin is singing, badly and off-key, some Bruno Mars.

"Phew, Martin, I don't mind watching you but the listening gets a little tough," Lily chuckles.

"You should hear me on Karaoke night. I get rounds and rounds of applause." He stands up, hands on hips, and tries a few dance moves.

Ingrid asks, "Does the applause happen when you're leaving the stage?"

"You know, I sure hope the new employee who starts next week will give me some respect." Martin hangs his head down as if defeated.

"Oh, bossman, don't cry." Ingrid gives a mocking pout.

"Yes, bossman you have so many traits that we do love and appreciate," Lily adds. "For instance, there's your incredible sense of humor."

"Here I say I hope I get more respect from the new staff, and you two mock me further. This is wrong, wrong." Martin throws his hands in the air.

"We're saving up all of our respect for the new guy. We don't want to scare him away," Ingrid chuckles.

Shelter work isn't for everyone, and it has a high turnover. The thought of a job where one doesn't smell like an animal kennel is sometimes appealing. Still, Ingrid and Lily joke about being respected more by the cats in the shelter than the executives they met in their other careers. They will take smelling like a kennel over thinly veiled sexual innuendo.

"I accept your disrespect for my singing since it's made Lily laugh again." Martin smiles his million-dollar smile. "I was worried about you yesterday."

Lily's cheeks flush. She stammers, "Um, well, that was hard news to take."

"Oh, Lily, that's right. I forgot to tell you." Ingrid leans across the desk and lowers her voice. "It was Officer Jarvis who brought Burrow in."

"Not Honeycutt?" Lily asks.

"Nope," Ingrid answers.

Officer Jarvis is one of few female state troopers.

"Was Chelsea terribly disappointed?" Lily asks mischievously.

"I do believe so, but she took it on the chin," Ingrid giggles.

Martin reaches over and closes the door to the staff area. He walks over and leans between Lily and Ingrid to whisper, "You two are terrible. You do tease Chelsea a lot."

"Well, Martin, so you see we spread our disrespect around." Lily spreads her arm in a circular motion as if she were spreading mulch over a garden.

"You have to admit, Chelsea is an incredible flirt," Ingrid says.

"I'm leaving this discussion. There is no male supervisor answer that will be considered appropriate." Martin opens the door and walks out to the front desk.

Ingrid turns to her computer.

Lily reaches into her desk and removes her cell phone from her bag. She has quite a few text messages.

"Out 2nite," from Tyler.

Lily is happy to hear it. First, she worries Tyler spends too much time with "virtual people." Second, she could use a "no people" evening herself. She realizes the irony of the situation, worrying about Tyler being lonely while wanting to be alone herself.

"Burrow settling in." A message from Mickey.

"He and Nero are demolishing the grass in my yard." Another from Mickey.

"BBQ Sat," comes from Lucinda.

Lily smiles at this. A girls' night will cheer her as long as no one asks about her dating status. None of her friends met Pete, though some knew she was in a new relationship. She sends Lucinda a response.

"Be there with sangria."

Lily puts her cell phone away. She looks through the recent adoption files and makes some phone calls to see how adoptees are settling in. It's regular working hours for most people, but she finds one or two at home. The two calico cats adopted by twin girls are settling in nicely.

Ingrid leaves the staff space to interact with the cats.

Lily updates the computer records on the completed assessments. She knows the more information she can provide to future owners, the better the chance for adoption. She prints out updated sheets, goes to the D-wing to hang them on the clipboards and remove "I've just arrived" signs, to let volunteers know which dogs they can handle.

Looking up at the clock, she realizes it is already 4:30. She goes back to her desk to get her bag, gives Martin and Ingrid a wave goodbye, and heads out to her car.

As she walks through the lot, Lily notices Chelsea has just sashayed away from a young man in mirrored sunglasses. "Another admirer?" Lily asks her.

Chelsea bats her eyelashes at Lily. "He's looking into Rowan summer classes. I ran into him last week after he talked with an admissions officer. I've taken some of the classes he's thinking about, so I offered him the books to look through."

"Good thing you hadn't resold them," Lily says, as her gaze strays to the young man who's casually leaning his muscular, jean-clad legs against the bumper of a dusty Toyota Rav 4. A pile of books rests on the hood.

"Resale on textbooks stinks. I try to choose classes where I can get the books on Kindle. If I can save someone else the cost, I'll do it." Chelsea casually wraps a bouncy curl around her forefinger. "Sometimes I get dinner or a few drinks in exchange…" She looks over to the young man and gives him a coquettish wave.

"I've heard enough. I'll see you tomorrow." Lily gives Chelsea a playful pat on the back then walks over to her green Chevy. The man in the mirrored shades is making a call on his cell. He's talking loud enough for Lily to hear and he's put the cell on speaker.

"Jim, I recognize you've only been an official civilian for a few months, but you need to stop thinking everyone is waiting to jump at your command. How about if we start this conversation over? Good afternoon, Jim. How are you?"

There's an extended inhale and then a loud exhalation from the phone. "I'm not in the mood for your games, Matt. I'm concerned. I've left voicemails and I've texted. And nothing from Pete." The voice pauses.

"I wasn't playing games with you, Jim. I've been a bit caught up in things. We've each had some items that needed some personal attention. I wanted to talk when there was a solid case to present to him." Matt pauses.

Not wanting to be caught eavesdropping, Lily opens her car door and slides into the driver's seat, carelessly tossing her bag onto the passenger's seat.

CHAPTER 10

When Lily arrives home, two eager dogs greet her. She leashes them up and heads for a nearby lake with a walking trail. En route, she sees people mowing their lawns, reminding Lily this chore is on her to-do list as well. Both Boone and Crockett are enjoying the walk around the lake. Wildlife is abundant; squirrels scurry in the underbrush, while ducks and geese swim on the lake's surface. Some evenings at dusk, possums can be spotted. There have even been deer occasionally tiptoeing through the trees.

Crockett tries to run after a flock of baby geese. Six adult Canada geese loudly hiss at them. Boone picks up the pace, forcing them to walk faster. When the geese can no longer be heard, he stops and lets loose an incredible stream.

"Boone, they're only geese," Lily laughs.

He looks at Lily with a scowl. Lily imagines if he could talk, he'd say, "Easy for you to say, you're bigger than they are."

Lily steers the dogs towards home. Once there, she gives each a bowl of kibble and a fresh bowl of water. When the dogs finish drinking, they walk over and plop at her feet. She gives them each a Milk Bone.

When Lily leaves for the bathroom to take a shower, Boone jumps up on the couch and spreads himself out. Taking the non-subtle hint, Crockett hops on the recliner, curls himself into a ball, and falls asleep.

Lily emerges from the bathroom wearing a pair of denim shorts, a green tank top, and sandals. She goes into the kitchen, puts the leftover lasagna from the night before on a plate, and sticks it in the microwave. Boone scampers off the couch and walks into the kitchen. He gives Lily a look like he has not eaten in days.

"You sure do have a short memory, Mister Boone," she says to him. "You ate dinner thirty minutes ago."

He continues to stare.

"Oh, you want a lasagna snack? Because you had such a long walk tonight?" The microwave clicks off. Lily removes the plate and sits down at the kitchen table to eat. When she finishes, she puts the dishes in the dishwasher. She fills a glass with water and walks into the living room followed by Boone.

Crockett has seized an opportunity to move to the couch. Boone glares at him, then settles on the recliner. He gives a mighty sigh as if the burden of the world rests on his shoulders.

Lily sits on the couch cross-legged, tapping the remote to turn on the TV. She turns to the NBC Nightly News with Lester Holt. Coverage of the approaching Freddie Gray police misconduct trial continues.

The cell phone rings and Lily checks caller ID. It's Mickey.

"Hello, Mickey."

"How're you doing?"

"Probably be better if I wasn't listening to the details of Freddie Gray's injuries."

"That situation is dreadful. But you know that's not what I meant. How're you coping with the news about Pete?"

Lily squints back a tear. "Honestly, I'm still incredibly shocked. I also feel guilty."

"Guilty?" Mickey exclaims. "Why do you feel guilty?"

"I was getting all angry with him because I sent him a text on Sunday and he never answered it. Now I know he didn't answer because he was dead. How can I not feel guilty?"

"You can't beat yourself up. It's not like Pete called and asked you to take him to the hospital, and you refused," Mickey says, attempting to rationalize the situation.

"Maybe I should've called him instead of texting. Maybe he was in distress, and no one knew."

"You have to stop this, Lily. You'll make yourself crazy with what-ifs. Can you find out how he died?"

"Well, I'm not sure how." Lily pauses. "I guess I could ask Kim for the emergency contact on his volunteer application. Of course, she'll want to know why I want it…" Lily trails off and drops her forehead to her free hand.

"Crap, I suddenly realized. Officer Honeycutt said they needed Pete's next of kin information. We probably have the name of a contact person at the shelter. I didn't even think to mention it," Lily groans.

"That could solve your problem. You could tell Kim you need the contact information for the police," Mickey states. "Ingrid was worried about you yesterday. She said you were rattled."

"It was such a shock. And…" Lily breaks to stifle a sob. With a deep inhalation, she continues, "I don't know how to say this. Do you know how everyone talks about their soul mate? I think Pete may have been mine."

"Lily, you two weren't together long enough—" Mickey starts.

"I didn't realize there was a timeframe associated with knowing whether or not somebody was the person you would spend the rest of your life with," Lily snaps. "Perhaps there is. Fate was showing me Pete wasn't mine by killing him."

Mickey makes no sound on the other end of the phone. Lily listens to her inhale and exhale several times, then continues. "I would have preferred a more subtle clue."

"I didn't mean to make light of your situation, Lily. I've never heard you refer to anyone as a soul mate. I was quite caught off guard." Mickey draws out each word with precise enunciation.

"I'm sorry, Mickey. I don't mean to be ungrateful for your support." Lily draws in an elongated breath and slowly exhales it out. "I guess this is better than being told I'm too 'whatever'…," Lily says.

"That's the spirit," Mickey says. Lily pictures her raising a fist, and chuckles.

"I'll think about your suggestion about the contact information. It could work. How are Burrow and Nero doing?" Lily changes the subject.

"Funny you ask. The weirdest thing happened. I overdid it a bit today and decided to take a few Tylenol. The boys were in the living room. I got the bottle of Tylenol out of the cabinet. When I opened it, Burrow flew in here and knocked it out of my hands. Caplets spilled everywhere. Honestly, that dog moved faster than if I had pulled out a bag of Beggin Strips."

"That's odd. Hey, was it expired? Dogs have an enhanced sense of smell. Maybe he could smell the difference between usable and expired medications?" Lily furrows her brow. Crockett rolls over onto his back, and kicks her with one leg. She starts to rub his belly. He rocks from side to side, and pants.

"Golly, I don't know, but I had to get him out of the kitchen to clean up the spilled tablets. Do you remember his history? Did he fail out of drug sniffing school for the police academy?" Mickey chuckles.

"Very funny, but I don't think his history was anything glamorous. Burrow was one of the dogs that came to us from the ASPCA. They removed him from a kill shelter somewhere down south," Lily recalls.

"While I was cleaning up, he and Nero made quite a ruckus. A true barking duet, those two were. Whatever the problem was, I wasn't about to see if they like Tylenol."

"True that, I wouldn't want to have to induce vomiting on either of them. Those are some big dogs. Those would be some big vomit puddles." Lily begins wholeheartedly laughing. "Are you coming to Lucinda's for the barbeque?"

"I don't think so. I'm not sure how Burrow would take to Tigger. Pooh is easygoing, but Tigger can be a bit much. I'm not too sure of Mr. Crockett either," Mickey adds, with a judgmental tone.

"Yes, well, it isn't as if Pete and I reached a point in our relationship where we had our dogs meet," Lily snaps.

"I'm sorry, Lily. I wasn't thinking." Mickey sounds chastened.

"I'm the one who should apologize. This is walloping my emotional state," Lily mutters. "I need to accept that dogs will be my only life companions."

"Now don't go feeling all sorry for yourself. Why don't we meet at Cooper River and try walking the four of them together?" Mickey suggests.

"That's a good idea. Since it's lighter later, can you meet tomorrow at 7?" Lily asks.

"That'll work," Mickey says. "If I need more Tylenol, I'll hide in the bathroom to take them."

"All right, I'll see you tomorrow," Lily says, and disconnects. She continues to rub Crockett's belly. "Crockett, you're going to meet someone new tomorrow. I want you on your best behavior."

Lily glances across the living room to the sleeping Boone. She doesn't have to worry about Boone. He takes meeting other dogs in stride. Crockett, though, gets too enthusiastic, barking up a storm and jumping around. He's a good companion for Lucinda's Tigger. Tigger literally bounces. He can jump from a standing position to lick someone in the face. Lily has never seen another dog do this. Tigger has short legs, too. His face is like an Italian greyhound and his body like a Basenji's.

Thinking about Tigger and Crockett brings Lily a smile. She pats Crockett. "Enough belly rub for tonight, my friend. Let's wake up Boone and take a walk around the block before bed."

Lily leashes the dogs up and pats her pants pocket to make sure she has a couple of plastic bags. She and the dogs head out as twilight is coming on. The thought of Cooper River makes Lily smile. Cooper River is where she and Pete had that interaction that led to their first date. Lily had gone to a fair at the Camden County Parks Environmental Center that her friend Kelly told her about. Kelly was there to promote and recruit for her garden club.

Neither Lily nor Tyler give much attention to the landscaping of the house. Lily was hoping for some simple solutions to add curb appeal. She picked up several free plants to put in the beds flanking the front door of the house. As she was putting them in the car, a dog's barking caught her attention. Looking up, she spotted Pete and Burrow.

Pete waved at her. She walked over to say hello. He invited her to take a walk with them, and she did. After the hike, they went into Haddonfield for water ice at Gracie's.

Lily is jerked from her reverie as Crockett leaps at a tree. A squirrel scurries up the trunk into the expanding branches. She shakes the cobwebs from her head; was it only a month ago she and Pete had water ice at Gracie's? Then, on the way back to the cars, his invitation to dinner at a restaurant with outdoor seating so they could people-watch.

She pays closer attention to the dogs as they make the last turn on the block to head home. "Well, tomorrow you two will meet Pete's dog. Sans Pete." She contemplates the irony of the situation.

Chapter 11

"UGH, New Jersey humidity." Lily gives an exasperated groan as she leaves the house with Boone and Crockett for their morning walk. The air that brushes past her feels like cobwebs hanging in a haunted house. She wants to recoil, but no matter in what direction she turns, the heavy weight of the air touches her skin. When they return home, she gives the dogs their breakfast. Then she goes into the bathroom and twists her hair into a scrunchy on top of her head. She gives a long, spiritless sigh. On humid days it is tough having to wear heavy pants to work. She weighs the alternative, wearing pantyhose, and decides jeans are less onerous.

Lily pulls a half gallon plastic water bottle from the refrigerator, then grabs two Dentastix from the cabinet. As they head to the front door, she gives the dogs a Dentastix each and asks for good behavior. She leaves the car windows closed today, and turns the air conditioner on.

Before heading into the shelter, Lily stops at the admin building. She's flooded with relief when she finds the building empty. Kim is one of the few coworkers who thrive on confrontation. Lily wonders if it's easier to be combative than competent. Her neck muscles pull tight at the thought of interacting with Kim.

Lily sets her tote bag down and makes a beeline for the file cabinets. She pulls Pete Russo's forms from the volunteer files and flips to the emergency contact information. Seeing what's there she drops the pages and covers her eyes with the palms of her hands. She inhales, ruefully shaking her head from side to side.

"Is there something I can help you find, Lily?" an irritated voice rasps.

With an involuntary jump, Lily drops her hands, looking towards the voice. Kim is standing in the doorway, squinting her eyes like a cheetah about to pounce.

"Geez, Kim, I didn't hear you come in," Lily stammers.

"That's obvious. What're you doing?" Kim's tone implies misconduct.

"Don't get all accusatory on me. I thought we might have information to help the state police. They need next of kin for the guy whose dog got surrendered the other night," Lily pushes out in a rush.

"And you couldn't wait until I came in to ask for the file, because...?"

Lily inhales slowly attempting to modulate her tone of voice. "Because I didn't realize these files contained state secrets." Realizing the slow inhale did not have the desired effect, Lily plunges on. "How well do you read these applications, anyway?"

"I look for a criminal record, as well as health conditions that might be an issue—the important things," Kim huffs indignantly. Her cheeks have begun to turn pink, mirroring the frustration in her voice.

"Well, this guy's emergency contact is John Doe, 856-111-1111. I'd say that's a fake number." Lily replaces the form into the file and slams the cabinet drawer. She walks towards Kim, who is blocking the exit.

"I guess I don't live up to your exacting standards," Kim harrumphs. "That's probably why you feel the need to push your way into my job all the time." She crosses her arms in front of her chest.

"Kim, for the hundredth time, the 'Read To A Dog' program was an idea. I discussed it with Martin. He told me to check things out and see what I could make work. I did the research on the benefits of children interacting with animals. I talked to several school administrators. I found a school willing to do a trial." Lily pauses, inhaling a long breath to steady her nerves. "If I had brought the idea to you, would you have done that leg work?"

"You could have talked to me before approaching our volunteers," Kim snaps.

"Again, I didn't approach a volunteer. I approached someone who is fostering a dog, that I thought would be a good candidate for the trial. I understand you question my competence, but believe it or not, I do know a bit about animal behavior." One corner of Lily's mouth turns up in a cynical half grin.

"I don't snoop around your space. I expect the same courtesy in return, Lily." Kim says.

"Sure, Kim, whatever." Lily waves a hand in a dismissive gesture. "If you move away from the door, I'll leave you to your privacy." Lily's voice is low and feral.

Lily retrieves her tote bag, and Kim moves aside with a rush of breath. Lily exits, her head high and shoulders square.

When Lily opens the door to the D–wing, she notices there are names for all the recent arrivals. Ethel and Dylan are still there. Joining them are newbies Rufus, Barkley, Skittle, Jethro, Rosey, Sage, Dillie, Peanut, Crackle, and Hooch. Some of these seem like odd dog names, but no names of TV characters. Or if they are, not from any shows she's seen recently. Hooch? It could be worse. A couple of them could have been named Jack and Daniel.

Lily stops in front of Barkley's kennel. He's lying on his dog bed, awake but not enthusiastic. For a coonhound, he should be baying with gusto. Lily makes a mental note to chat with Doc today and see what the vet's impression is. She moves to the next kennel. Skittle's case of the runs seems to have cleared up, but the poor little guy is still jittery. She wonders if the cacophony of barking might be too much for him. She considers ways to get him into a foster home. He is small, and the little guys tend to get placed quickly, even the barkers. People always seem to associate small with easy to control. Lily associates small with quicker to get into mischief, but to each his own.

Lily heads for the front desk and takes a peek at the schedule and remembers Chelsea will not be in today. Chelsea worked Sunday to Thursday; Anna will be working. Lily goes to her space and turns on the computer. Her email includes one from the ASPCA, which wants to send a transport of kittens next week. The feral population seems to be booming this spring. Lily decides to have a chat with Martin. She knows Doc and Mitchell have been busy with this latest transport of dogs. She doesn't want to overwhelm them.

It is time to serve up some breakfast. Lily goes back to the C-Wing. She opens the cabinet, pulling out a new bag of Friskies and several cans of Fancy Feast. She measures out portions onto small paper plates, while the residents begin to shuffle in their cages and purr. Lily reflects on how all cats purr at you when you serve them a meal.

The door opens, and Anna enters. "Good morning, Lily."

"Morning, Anna, TGIF," Lily beams, happy to receive a nicer greeting than the one from Kim.

"For you, maybe. I'm here tomorrow," Anna says with a shrug.

The "meow" chorus is going in earnest. Anna begins to clean litter pans while Lily hands out breakfast. They work in companionable silence until Anna lets out a squeal.

"Ugh." She pulls back from a kennel.

"What's up?" Lily asks.

"I think someone either can't digest their food or has a problem. This kennel is full of diarrhea." She grimaces and waves her hands in front of her face. "That's a nasty surprise for first thing in the morning." Her face scrunches like she's bit into a lemon.

"Crap. Sorry, no pun intended," Lily says walking over to the cage to peer inside. "Phew, let me take him to Medical for Doc to have a look at." Lily grabs a towel and carefully wraps it around the cat, Caesar, as he emits a pitiful meow. The towel prevents a sick animal from scratching the next person who's touching it. Lily carries him to the medical area, which is an extensive section in the shelter. It holds large kennels for dogs as well as a set of cages for cats. A scale, a large sink, and an exam table sit in front of the kennels. There are two tiny exam rooms to provide a private area for more complicated or potentially contagious cases.

Doc is standing by the exam table and gives her a quizzical look, "What do you have there?" he asks, grinning just enough to show his dimples.

"Someone had quite a bout of diarrhea last night." She places the towel containing Caesar on the exam table. "I'll get his clipboard for you. Do you want me to scoop you a sample?"

"Yes, that'd be good. I can run a few tests on it and see if we can figure out what's upsetting his tummy." Doc hands Lily a plastic vial then unwraps the towel as Caesar gives another pitiful meow.

Lily walks back to the C-wing. Anna is still replacing litter and handing out breakfast.

"What'd Doc have to say?" she asks.

"He's going to run some tests." Lily holds up the vial. She goes to the cabinet to get a pair of disposable plastic gloves.

"That looks like a joy," Anna responds.

"It's all part of the glamour of our jobs." Lily laughs as she carefully scoops some sample into the plastic vial. She places a lid on the vial, removes the gloves, and takes the clipboard from the front of the cage.

When Lily returns to Medical she finds Doc has put Caesar in a pen with a cozy cat bed.

"Thanks." Doc smiles down at her. His height always makes Lily feel petite. "We'll get him feeling better. At least it happened before we got him adopted out. Imagine if someone took him tomorrow and it happened there?" Doc's nodding towards Caesar and referring to Saturday, which is a high adoption day.

"I hear you. By the way, Doc, did you do an assessment on Barkley this morning? He seems a bit sluggish."

"We're going to have to get an X-Ray on his hind leg. He's

trying hard not to show it, but it's painful when he walks. He barely let me touch it." Doc crosses his arms in front of him and frowns in concentration. "I gave him an injection of painkillers last night before I left. He may have been in a fight with another dog before he got transferred up here. There isn't anything in the ASPCA records since he was picked up by animal control. And he doesn't have a chip, so we don't know his history." He shakes his head from side to side.

"If anyone can solve that mystery, it's you," Lily says, with a hint of flirtation. "We'll keep him off the adoption site for now. Maybe we should move him into one of the kennels here in Medical. Maybe get him away from the commotion and let him get some rest?" Lily inclines her head.

The medical area is Doc's domain. He decides who does and who doesn't stay in there.

"Good idea," Doc agrees nodding his unruly head of hair. "I'll bring him back here."

"I'm also going to take that little guy Skittle into the staff area. He seems quite overwhelmed by the other dogs," Lily says.

Lily leaves the medical area and heads for D–wing. Anna is getting the dogs ready for their morning walk.

"Do you need my help walking the dogs?" Lily asks.

"I think we're good. We have two volunteers to walk the dogs. And another two doing laundry. When the laundry gets running, they can help clean kennels."

"That's great. I'm going to let Skittle be with me today. He can keep me company while I tackle administrative stuff," Lily smiles.

"Ooohhhh administrative stuff. You have fun." Anna laughs.

"Well given the humidity today, I don't mind letting someone else walk the dogs." Lily gets a leash and opens Skittle's kennel. "Hi, Skittle, you're getting to watch me type." She loops a leash over his head, lets him out of the kennel, and closes the door. They walk back to the staff area, and she settles Skittle in the pen. Then she places a baby gate across the entrance to the staff area. The staff has to be very careful not to let animals get loose in the shelter.

Lily starts reviewing files and making updates to the electronic records as well as the shelter website. She removes Caesar from the site.

Around 11:30, the phone on her desk rings.

"Forever Friends, Lily Dreyfus speaking."

"Hi, Lily. It's Kathy Klapper from Haddon Township," says the voice on the other end. "I'm calling to find out if we're on for a read to the dogs afternoon next week."

"We sure are," Lily says enthusiastically. "One of my foster parents, Connie, is bringing the boxer mix that she and her family are fostering for us."

"Great, you'll be here as well, correct?" Mrs. Klapper asks.

"Absolutely, I want to be on hand to see how things run. You want us to meet you at the Thomas Edison school, correct?"

"Yes, I sent the directions to you. There will be four children," Mrs. Klapper adds. "We want to start small. We also had to ensure none of the children have allergies."

"I understand. Connie checked the dog treats she's bringing. There are no peanut products in them. We're hoping the trial is successful. This would be a terrific way to get exposure for the work we do at the shelter," Lily says.

"We think so, too. I'll see you next week," Mrs. Klapper says.

"Have a good weekend," Lily says, and disconnects.

Lily has high hopes for this program. She's learned so much from Eileen about learning disabilities, and how making corrections early in life significantly increases the chances for success. She and Pete had a conversation about K through 12 education. Neither of them has direct experience, since they don't have children. However, Pete met many individuals unable to pass the ASVAB test for service in the Marine Corps, due to poor skills from a lackluster education. Lily knows how hard her nieces and nephews study. Many times she's wanted to ask her sisters when do the children get to have some fun, but she knows it's a sensitive subject to avoid.

The thought of teenagers having fun brings another memory to mind. Last weekend on their walk with Burrow, Pete told her that he'd come across a group of teens smoking pot at Cooper River. He was stunned by Lily's naiveté when she thought he was joking and trying to shock her.

Lily wonders how far out of touch she is with today's teenagers and the issues they face. Insistent barking brings her from her reverie. She stands and stretches, then heads to the front desk to check out the barking.

Chapter 12

Friday night in Haddonfield, New Jersey Mickey is gathering Burrow and Nero to go and meet Lily.

Oh boy, Oh boy, I hear we're going to Cooper River for a walk. I'm running around Mom's legs to let her know I'm ready to go. Mom is yelling something about me breaking her legs and not being able to walk at all. Hey, I'm a big, strong Newfie. I can pull her along on a wheelie chair. Burrow can help. Oh man, she is finally getting the leashes. "Hey, Burrow c'mon."

He's hopping off of the couch and coming over. "Man, Burrow you are going to love this, there is a lake, geese, and lots and lots of smells. But we're not allowed to pull Mom into the woods. We just usually go up a trail and get some good squirrel sightings. But remember no growling at anyone, or else we have to come home."

"Listen, Nero, I don't growl at anyone unless they're suspicious. I'm a guard dog, and I'm trained to sniff out suspicious characters."

Burrow's starting to come out of his shell a bit. I give myself all the credit. It is tough to be around me and not be happy. My tail is wagging I am so ready for this walk.

Up into the back of the car and we're off. Mom has been leaving me at home a lot to keep an eye on Burrow. I usually go with her when she is visiting other dogs. Sometimes I even get to romp around other yards with friends. A lot of the time I stay in the car, but that is okay with me. We almost always stop at an off-leash park on the way home. I can rustle and tumble with whoever's there or run a few laps around, stretch my legs a bit.

We're already pulling into the parking lot. Oh Man, I see Lily and Boone. What a character that Boone is. Oh crap, there's Crock O'Shit, that's what Boone calls him. His real name is Crockett. Little guy is a nuisance sometimes but he loves a good game of chase. For having small legs, he runs pretty fast. Hey, Mom, it's time to let me out and say hi to my friends. I can see Burrow's eyebrows twitching. He's watching Boone and Crockett from out of the back window of our car. He's lifting his nose and sniffing at their musky hound scents.

Finally, the door's opening and I burst out of the car. "Boone, Crockett, how are you guys doing?"

I'm running right over to them wagging my tail. "Wait'll you guys meet my new buddy Burrow. He's the strong silent type, but I'm working on him."

I see Lily's got Boone wrapped up tight on a leash and Crockett's still in the car. We have to make sure Burrow can be civil to them. She always starts the introductions with Boone. My buddy Burrow 's ready to go over with Mom. She's muttering some crap about me jumping out of the car without my leash. I guess I'll walk over and let her put my leash on too.

I'm explaining I had to say hi to my pals but she's not listening. Where's Boone? There he is. Gosh his eyes are growing to the size of my water bowl and Crockett's going berserk with questions.

"Holy mackerel, that's a big guy. How fast does he run? Is he friendly? Does he like Beagles?" Crockett's got lots of questions. Lily's telling him to simmer down.

Now she's bringing Boone over on his leash. Hey, Boone's stopping a dog's length away, planting his feet like he's not coming any closer. He's just being cautious as usual. Now Boone's leaning forward as far as he can and taking a sniff. "Yo."

Good going, Boone. Now Burrow's moving a bit forward to take a sniff.

"Yo, yourself. What's with that yappy one in the car?"

Well the tension's broken and Boone's loosening up too, moving closer to Burrow. All right, Boone and Burrow are doing the circle dance, sniffing and nudging each other.

Boone's giving Burrow the lowdown on Crockett, to ignore him or give him a good growl and he'll go away.

Lily's walking Boone back over to their car. He's looking pretty smug. Now Lily's getting Crockett leashed. Crockett's straining at the leash. Lily's coming back holding tight to both leashes while Crockett barks away, "Howdy I'm Crockett I'm friendly and I'm great to play with ask anyone."

Oh oh Burrow's starting to growl, the one that's from deep in his chest where he lowers his head and flattens his ears. Boone is just grinning like he found a pile of rabbit turds and ate it in one gulp. Crockett's noticed the growl and is standing stock still. Boone's showing up Crockett now by giving Burrow a tail wag that Burrow returns. Looks like most everything's sorted out.

Finally everybody's ready to walk. Mom's taking Burrow and Boone and Lily's got Crockett and me. There's a flash of brown, did you see it? We're all stopped dead to look and now Crockett starts that infernal barking and the critter is gone. Well, one squirrel wasn't enough for all four of us to play with anyway. Besides where there's one, there's more.

I stop and give some of the tall grass a good dousing. "Hey, Crockett, if you had to hunt for own your food, you'd die of starvation."

"Au contraire, my good friend, I would flush out the prey for the rest of you to chase down for me with your long legs."

As if Crockett thinks there's something to prove, he lifts one of his little legs to give another patch of grass a dousing. Now Boone's stopping too. Look at him go, geez, he must have had a bucketful in there. "Hey, Boone, you been holding that all day?" But Boone doesn't like to be kidded much, I better do an apology tail wag.

Well, Crockett is right about one thing; his legs are short. Hey look, Burrow and Boone are stopped with their noses in the air. Let me try and get a whiff of whatever they're on to. Umm, that's something I've never smelled before. It sort of smells like that chicken Mom took out of the freezer and forgot to put in the refrigerator before we went to the shore for the weekend. Phew when we got back even I wasn't interested in eating that chicken. I hear Burrow making his deep growl again, he sure seems to know what it is. Hey, what's the weird smell?

Burrow's bark is low and menacing. "Pete smelled like that and that's what made me cry out for human help. Maybe there's a human in trouble around here, too. Boone, let's make a run for the woods." Boone gives him a look to say okay and they pull poor Mom off her feet. I can feel Lily tightening her grip on my leash. I'd try to follow, but I know Crockett isn't as fast as I am. They make it about ten feet and then Mom's got control again. She's got her feet dug in and she's using her weight to hold them back.

Mom's weight, she says I weigh more than she does. She is a tiny human, but that doesn't mean she's weak. She has a tight grip on those leashes. What's the human phrase, "small but powerful".

"Mickey, what do you think they're after? Do you see another dog?" Lily is slowly letting us get closer to them. I'm catching a whiff of tuna fish cans that have sat in the sun too long.

Boone's whiskers are twitching. "Whatever it is, I don't think I need to get any closer."

"I'm telling you, there's a human in trouble," Burrow growls. He lowers his head and digs his paws into the ground to charge into the woods if he can.

"I don't see anything," Mom says with a hint of confusion.

"We're close to the path anyway, let's head that way and see if we flush out what's exciting all of them."

"It had better not be a skunk. I'm not in the mood for two doggie baths tonight." Lily laughs.

Hey, that isn't funny, I know a guy who got sprayed by a skunk once. Phew, there was more than one bath needed. We all like to have our doggie scent on us, but Capital P, Capital U on that skunk smell. We're heading towards the path, I can see Mom's biceps tighten as Burrow pulls hard on the leash.

"Easy big guy" I give him a bit of encouragement. There's some thrashing nearby, but no time to be distracted by a rabbit until we find out what that smell is. We trundle along, and then Mom stops.

"That can't be." She says and leans her head past a tall tree. "How'd that get there?" She says with a strange frown on her face. Pulling her head back in front of the tree, they start up the path again.

Burrow's growling, and Boone's howling. What a racket. Mom shushes them and stops again. She wiggles her head forward like a turtle.

"Lily, hold up with the dogs." Mom says.

Lily does her best to get me to stop, but darn it, I want to know what that smell is. Burrow's ears are pointed forward, and his body is coiled tight. He looks like a pitcher ready to throw the winning strike.

Chapter 13

"What is it, Mickey? Is there a dead animal in there?"

"No, Lil, I think someone fell. I thought I saw a backpack a few steps back. Now I see a person's back." Mom is leaning farther forward. "Hello, hello, are you okay? Lily, I don't want to climb into the woods holding these two. Besides, I think Burrow has grown roots. He is planted."

Lily brings us closer. Boone is shuffling from one foot to another.

"Whatever it is, I don't need to find out," Boone barks.

"Shush, Boone," Lily says. "Mickey, you're right. There's someone laying there. What the heck were they doing off the trail?"

"I have no clue," Mom says, and shakes her head. "Here, you take Burrow's and Boone's leashes. Hold them tight."

"I'll do my best. You do realize I'm outweighed more than twice right now." Lily's voice is surly.

"If I took all four leashes I'd be outweighed three times," Mom shouts back. She turns sideways and wiggles around a tall tree. "I hope I'm not stepping on poison ivy," she says as she climbs over fallen branches.

Clustered around Lily, we watch Mom as she winds in between the tree trunks.

"Hello," Mom calls again. "Are you all right?"

Mom's voice is a little breathless like when we've been jogging. You know, for having longer legs than I do, she gulps air when we take a run the same way I gulp water on a hot day.

"Mick, is it a person?" Lily asks.

"It isn't a crash test dummy, Lily. It's a girl and she doesn't appear to be breathing."

"See if she has a pulse," Lily instructs.

"You want me to touch her?" Mom shrieks.

I don't get this. Why wouldn't one human touch another one? We dogs don't have boundaries. See another dog, sniff it. That's the way it is.

"Hello, hello," Mom calls, as she walks around the girl. There is a pause, and then an ear-piercing scream.

We all start barking in unison.

"Oh, my God, she's definitely dead." Mom covers her eyes with her hands and backs up a step or two. Her back bumps a tree trunk, and she slumps against it. "Oh my God, oh my God," she continues to mutter into her hands.

"Mick?" Lily's voice trembles.

"Oh," Mom groans. "Her eyes are open, and staring vacantly." Mom heaves another breath. "She's dead. Oh my God, she's definitely dead."

"Mickey, you'd better come out of there. We need to call the police," Lily says.

"All right." Mom takes her hands from her eyes, but holds her right hand against her face as she tentatively steps around the girl. "My phone's in the car," Mom says as she starts to rewind her way back through the trees.

"Have phone will travel. I've got mine," Lily says.

Mom comes back on the path and takes Burrow's and Boone's leashes from Lily.

"Let's get out in the open," Mom says. Her breathing is still as if she's been jogging.

"Keep taking deep breaths," Lily says. She pats Mom on the shoulder with the hand holding my leash. I can't stand it. I jump up and lick Mom's face a few times.

"Down, Woofy, down," Mom says, and takes a step

backward. "I can go a long time before I see something like that again."

"I bet," Lily says.

Mom and Lily turn around and lead us dogs back down the path until we're back at the trail entrance. Lily tells us to sit.

Of course, I plant my butt down right away, "Sit" is usually followed by a biscuit. Crockett, on the other hand, needs more encouragement.

"Crock-ett." Lily is more emphatic. He finally sits. "Good boys," she tells us. Now she has the infernal thing humans are always looking at and talking at, but oh yeah let a dog try to play with it once.

"Yes hi. I'm calling from the Cooper River trail, near Hopkins House. There's a dead girl in the woods." There's a pause. "My friend went over and looked at her. She's dead." Another silence. "Well, no, my friend did not touch the person or try to do CPR. She went over to the girl, and the girl's eyes are staring vacantly." She is tightening her grip on the leashes.

"Yes, right, no response, eyes staring vacantly." Lily is starting to clench her jaw, and she's stomping her foot as if keeping time to a drumbeat. I swear if a human could growl, Lily probably would.

"Lady, what part of DEAD isn't clear? I cannot tell you age, sex, distinguishing marks, I CAN tell you there's a DEAD person in the trees next to the trail." There is a much longer pause. "Yes, okay, I'll meet the first responders at the entrance to the trail. Tell them to look for a woman in jeans and a blue T-shirt with a black Newfoundland and a brown and white hound dog."

I perk my ears and put on my "I am so handsome expression". Newfoundland, that's me.

"No, a Newfoundland is a dog. A big black dog. Okay, okay." Lily sighs with an exasperated groan, and turns to Mom. "Do you think they give dispatchers IQ tests? Nutcase was asking me all kinds of crap. How old? Hair color? Maybe I should order Nero to fetch whoever it is out?"

Now there's a brilliant idea if I ever heard one. I could get whoever it is. Of course, the other boys would surely be jealous, me getting the first sniff and grab at it. Oh yeah, Nero the Hero.

"It's okay, Lil." Mom is starting to sound more like herself, less edgy. "Who are such good boys?" Mom opens the little purse she wears around her waist and starts handing out some biscuits.

Oh yeah, who are good boys? We're good boys. We all gather around sniffing and bumping each other. "They should let us get the person," I suggest.

"No way, I heard something about poison ivy. I don't need anything that's going to make me scratch," Boone says.

Burrow squints down at Boone, his brows fuse together as he squeezes his face tighter. "You don't want anything to make you scratch? Is that all you can think about, when there's an injured human?"

Boone backs away a few steps, "Honestly, I was thinking I could use a snack. That was a tense walk."

Burrow lets out a derisive snort.

Finally, we hear sirens approaching. Do you humans have any idea how much that sound hurts our delicate ears? We all shift a bit on our feet, trying to figure out how to make the noise less painful.

A blue and white car with Police on it stops on the road. Two people in blue uniforms get out and head our way. Blue is always good, especially blue with a shiny badge. There is always a friendly pat on the head from people in blue with a shiny badge. I let out a big friendly welcome to help them find us. Burrow, Boone, and Crockett join in. Mom and Lily shush us.

"Hi, I'm Lily, I made the call."

"Yes, ma'am, tell us what you saw." This one in blue is a

girl like Mom and Lily, but she doesn't look soft and cuddly like Mom. Sheesh, she looks like I could jump on her with a running start and not budge her.

"Honestly, I didn't see much," Lily starts to tell her. "Our boys here started barking madly and pulling us up the trail. My friend thought she saw a person lying in the brush. I took hold of all four leashes, and Mickey went through the trees. She called out. Then she went around to the front of the body." Lily shivers and takes a deep breath. "She said the eyes were open staring vacantly. We decided the best thing to do was call 911."

"Okay, we're going to go talk with your friend. Can I give these two a pet? Hey, who's this big handsome guy?" I get a gentle pat on the head. I wag my tail to show I know I am a big handsome guy.

"Hi, there. I'm Michelle," Mom is a little breathless. "We were about twenty to thirty feet up that trail there." She uses her head to point since both hands are still tightly holding leashes. "Honestly, I thought my eyes were playing tricks on me when I saw the backpack. Then I looked closer, and I could see sneakers." She takes a long breath, shakes her head, and continues. "With all the noise we were making, I knew whoever it was if they were conscious, they would have moved or reacted somehow. So I just moved back. I deal with lots of sick dogs and cats, but I don't have any human emergency training."

"It's okay. I'm Officer Jenkins, this is Officer Stewart. We'll go have a look, please stay back with your dogs." She looks down at Boone and Burrow. "What a handsome pair these guys are." Boone and Burrow both get their ears scratched.

Boone gives the grin that seems to please humans so much. Burrow, on the other hand, is all business. His eyes are focused; his ears are straight up. He wants to get this policewoman moving. There's more earsplitting noise as another car gets closer.

"These officers pulling up now will take your statements, and you can be on your way." She tips her hat and starts up the trail.

Mom purses her lips, and her cheeks redden. She glares over at Lily. She has that look from when I chew on one of her leather shoes. "Be on our way. Really? We find a body in the woods, and we should be on our way?" She shrugs and shakes her head. "Oh, hey, here are some sneakers nobody needs. I'll just drop them at a homeless shelter and be on my way." Her voice is getting louder, and I can see Boone is getting agitated. Mom's hand is waving Boone's leash making him dance side to side.

"Mick," Lily says in her best placating tone, "the officers are just doing their jobs. I mean, it's not like they patted you on the head and said, "Thanks little lady, now go home and rustle me up some grub." She uses her best John Wayne imitation.

Despite herself, Mom smiles, "True. However, you know now my curiosity is on fire. I want to know what happened to that person."

Oh, yeah, she's curious. We were curious, too, but we were told to stop barking and stop pulling, which is what we do.

Now there's more people in blue. And more talking.

We don't want to, but now we're headed back to the cars. In all this excitement I forgot to lay down a bit of Eau d' Nero. I make Lily stop so I can spray a good bit by the lake. Ha ha like magic now everybody's remembering to sprinkle some. And I do think Boone just tried to hit Crockett with his. That boy.

Well, back in the car and off towards home. I don't know about Burrow, but I bet I sleep good tonight. Maybe I'll even catch that squirrel in my dreams.

CHAPTER 14

It is Saturday morning and Lily awakes from a night of tossing and turning. She loosens the sleep in her dry eyes like a dump truck emptying a load of gravel. When she was able to fall asleep, she had a dream about Pete. She sits up with an involuntary shiver. In her dream, Pete was walking with a blonde girl. She called out to him, but he didn't turn around. She ran to catch him, but no matter how fast she ran, she never could.

Lily, your subconscious is having a field day, she says to herself. At the side of her bed, Boone is staring fixedly at her.

"Okay, Boone, I'm getting up for our walk." Lily gets out of bed and pulls on shorts and a T-shirt. She gets a clean pair of socks from the dresser and puts them on, slides her feet into her sneakers, and ties them with double knots.

She grabs a few plastic bags as she passes by the kitchen. Boone and Crockett are both waiting by the front door. She snaps on their leashes, pulls her Phillies cap over her head, and heads outside for the morning walk. Both the boys are raring to go, straining the leashes taut.

Lily is pleased it feels cooler today from the lower humidity. She hopes it stays low since they will be outdoors at Lucinda's tonight. Boone is moving intently, at a faster pace than Crockett and steering them towards something on the ground. Lily spots the object of his desire, an ice cream cone sitting in a puddle. She reins in the leash to steer him past it.

"Ice cream cones aren't breakfast, my friend," she tells him. Boone slows his pace. They head for the lake. Crockett's ears are riding high on his head. He is on full alert for anything that he might be able to outrun. Lily keeps her eyes peeled for baby geese. She does not want a repeat of angry adult geese hissing at her. They leave the path so that the two boys can sniff some shrubs for rabbits.

Lily reflects on yesterday's walk, aghast that they stumbled on a dead body. As she ruminates about the woman, who she was and what happened to her, Lily starts to guide the boys home. Even with all the death she has faced this week, she's hungry for breakfast. Boone is picking up the pace now that they're headed home. They arrive home and Lily gives each boy a bowl of kibble and a fresh bowl of water. She retrieves a dish from a kitchen cabinet and pours in some granola and milk. As she puts the milk back into the refrigerator, both dogs plop down in front of her.

"Okay, one Milk Bone each," she says, and gives them each a treat.

Picking up her bowl and spoon, Lily heads for the living room. She sits cross-legged on the couch, and turns the TV on to check out the news while she eats. David Murphy predicts low humidity and sunny skies for the entire weekend. Bryan Taft follows with the latest local news.

"Yesterday, the body of a teenage girl was found along the trails in Cooper River Park." A view of the park with yellow crime scene tape comes on. "Police have identified the girl as Eva Livingston of Haddon Township. They've not reported the cause of death. The county coroner will be investigating. The body was discovered by some casual walkers. We'll follow this story as more information becomes available."

Lily drops her spoon, which bounces off her lap and to the floor. Boone is instantly there to lick the pieces of granola from the spoon.

"Oh, good golly, Boone, I would've gotten a clean spoon anyway. Now I have to," she groans as she picks up the spoon from the floor. Boone's glare follows Lily as she stomps to the kitchen for a clean spoon. Returning, she flips to Animal Planet hoping to find a cute puppy show.

After slowly munching through the now mushy granola, Lily puts the bowl on a coaster on the end table. She shivers and rubs the goose bumps on her arms. Slouching back against the couch cushions to ponder the news, Lily reaches up with her right hand and scratches Boone's ears.

"What a week, buddy. First, I find out my latest dating interest is found dead in his home, then we find a dead body at Cooper River. I don't want to leave the house again."

Boone tilts his head to the left.

"Don't worry, silly boy. I know I have to take you and Crockett for walks." She lets her hand fall back into her lap and lets out a heavy sigh. Matching her exhalation, Boone curls into a ball on the cushion next to her. Lily stares idly at the TV, not paying attention to the show. Despite her best efforts, visions of her dream about Pete keep appearing in her mind.

Crockett runs into the living room with a tennis ball in his mouth. He stands in front of Lily, wagging his tail frantically.

"You know what? Throwing a ball for a while might help. Let's go outside," she says, expecting to relieve some of her tension.

She picks up the bowl from the end table and places it in the kitchen sink, then heads out the back door. Crockett is hot on her heels.

Lily and Crockett play fetch for about a half hour until Lily collapses in the grass. Crockett runs over and starts licking her face.

"Okay, okay, Crockett, enough. I'm alive." She sits up and stretches her legs out in front of her. Crockett hops into her lap, putting his paws on her chest, licking her face some more. She wraps her arms around him in a hug.

"Oh, Crockett, I'm so glad I have you boys. No one loves you quite like your dogs do." She nuzzles his neck with her nose.

Crockett jumps out of her arms and picks up the tennis ball in his mouth.

"I'd love to play all day. But if I do, I won't have any clothes to wear to work on Monday." Lily stands and brushes loose grass and dirt from her shorts and legs. She and Crockett go into the kitchen and get another Milk Bone. Lily gives the cookie to Crockett. Boone saunters into the kitchen and plops in front of her.

"And you think you deserve a treat because you slept so well while we played?"

Boone gives her a scowl and then turns his face into his irresistible "I'm so cute" look.

She reaches into the box and pulls out another Milk Bone. "You know I can't resist that face," she says.

Boone grabs the cookie with his mouth and eats it in short order.

Lily fills a glass with water from the sink and carries it through the house and out the front door. She pours half of the water on each of the flowers. She returns inside, closing the outside door behind her, and goes back to the kitchen to put the glass in the sink.

Going to the basement, Lily puts a massive load of jeans and Forever Friends T-shirts in the washer. After sorting the rest of the dirty clothes into piles, then heads back upstairs to the living room to check her phone for messages. Lucinda has sent a text asking if Lily can bring some type of side dish tonight.

Lily returns to the kitchen and opens the refrigerator. Finding carrots, celery, and mayonnaise, she decides to make a macaroni salad. She gathers the items, closes the refrigerator door, and almost steps on Boone.

"Boone, I swear you could hear that door open if you were miles away. Alas, you wasted your energy, my friend, no more food until dinner."

The boys saunter to the living room for naps. Lily completes the Saturday chores. When the salad is made and the laundry complete, she gets into the shower to clean up before going to Lucinda's. She keeps the water cool since the weather is so hot. There is no reason to steam up the bathroom.

Chapter 15

Casually dressed in shorts, a tank top, and sandals, Lily goes back to the kitchen and lifts the dog bowls from the floor. Eight paws hit the floor of the living room as she dishes up kibble.

While Boone and Crockett crunch away on dinner, she packs the macaroni salad, sangria, Solo cups, and dog treats, and loads everything into the car. Boone and Crockett are sitting by the front door when she returns inside.

"I'm almost ready. Let me grab my purse and phone, and we'll head off for our night out," she says. She leashes up the boys, and they go out to the car. Lucinda lives a short drive away in Robinberg.

Lucinda has a cute cottage with a glass-fronted porch framed by garden patches on either side of concrete steps. Her miniature rose bushes are starting to bud within a carpet of silver Artemnesia that surrounds them. Lily pulls into the driveway behind Lucinda's compact. Boone and Crockett are leashed and escorted to the back gate. Tigger is inside the house announcing their arrival with short, high-pitched barks.

Lily opens the fence's six-foot cedar gate and lets the boys into the backyard. As is his nature, Boone starts a sentry around the perimeter. He stops at each shrub and sniffs around the bottom. Crockett has shot straight through the gate barking. He runs on the flagstone pathway down the center of the yard. Lily secures the gate and then unpacks the goodies from the car.

Lily climbs three porch steps then shifts the box of food to her hip to open the porch door. As usual, the front door is unlocked. She reflects someday Lucinda will regret never locking her doors. Pooh is sitting calmly ensconced amid throw pillows on the settee. He lifts his face to look at Lily. Lily can see through the house to the back door. Tigger has his nose glued to the screen door, watching Boone and Crockett.

"How are you, Pooh?" Lily stoops and pets Pooh and is rewarded with a customary lick on the face. She hollers up the steps, "Lucinda, I came in your unlocked front door. I think someone stole your TV and DVR. They're no longer in the living room."

"Oh, good, now I have an excuse to buy a new smart TV. I'll be down in a minute, would you let Tigger out?" Lucinda answers.

Lily crosses the knotty pine floors of the living room and dining area to the kitchen. Tigger pogo stick jumps at her arrival, straight up in the air from a standing position. She marvels for the millionth time at how Lucinda's pine floors look so clean. Pooh and Tigger's dog hair must perfectly blend into the pattern of the wood.

She sets the package down on the celery-and-emerald-speckled, synthetic stone countertop. Tigger continues his pogo stick jumps. "Crazy guy, if you stand still for more than two seconds I'll pet you and let you out."

Tigger is *so* correctly named. Lily begins singing to him, "The wonderful thing about Tiggers is Tiggers are wonderful things." He continues to bounce around her.

Lily opens the back door, and Tigger bounces out to start a game of chase with Crockett. She lets out a laugh as she watches Tigger leap from side to side as Crockett chases after him turning one way then the other. Boone settles himself on the deck and gives an exaggerated sigh.

Lucinda glides into the room, her loose-fitting pants and striped swing shirt flow around her like foam following a wave as it reaches the beach. Pooh follows on the heels of her nubuck sandals. Lily notices the color of her layered bob hair looks like spring honey.

"Trying another new one, eh?" Lily asks pointing to indicate her hair. She unpacks the items from her packages, opening the Solo cups and pulling out one for herself.

"Yes, the last color looked too mousy." Lucinda smiles and glances at the packages, "Oh good, sangria. I have some burgers, and Kelly is coming over with hot dogs. I expect with the racket she knows you've arrived." Kelly and Lucinda are longtime neighbors. Ironically, they each bought their homes after divorcing their husbands. Kelly moved in first, Lucinda two years later.

Kelly also has a dog, but her friendly companion isn't good with other dogs, so she stays at home on girl's night. It's ironic as Kelly's dog, being female, would be a most appropriate companion for girl's night. But Kelly's dog doesn't miss out entirely. When Kelly hosts her dog gets all of the attention.

"And is Eileen coming?" Lily asks.

"You bet, with dessert. The poor dear-- did you hear about the student they found at Cooper River?" Lucinda grimaces and shakes her head.

"Um, hear about it? Oh, yes." Lily pours a large Solo cup of sangria and adds some ice from Lucinda's freezer. "Mickey and I discovered her."

Lucinda almost drops the platter of burger toppings that she's pulled out of the refrigerator, "What? Are you serious?" she gasps.

"Unfortunately, yes," Lily answers. "But if it's okay, I'll tell the full tale when everyone is here. Suffice to say it was a shorter than usual dog walk." Lily takes a sip of sangria and leans back against the counter.

"Helloooooo." Kelly comes through the back door, and Pooh wanders out to greet her. "I saw you pull up, so got my things and came on over. It's such a beautiful night. I'm so glad that you got us together, Lucinda. It's a great chance to catch up with everyone. Huh, your hair is a new color."

Kelly tilts her head from one side to the next as if to find the right perspective to inspect this color. "Yes, yes, I like it. I think that's the color you had when we first met so many years ago, right?" Kelly speaks faster than anyone else and manages to fit a lot of information into one breath of air. It is amazing. Like Lily she's wearing casual shorts and a tank top. Every thread in Kelly's outfit is pristinely smooth and seamless. Lily studies her shirt and shorts wondering if she owns an iron.

At the resounding thump of a car door closing, Kelly turns.

"Good, look, Eileen's here; I wonder what she brought for dessert? Here, I'll go help her with whatever she brought. Pooh, I almost fell over you; yes, you are sweet but don't sneak under someone's feet like that." Kelly scurries from the kitchen.

Lucinda and Lily share a glance and almost laugh. Kelly, while quite petite, sure seems to beat everyone in the energy and conversation departments.

Lily and Lucinda walk onto the back deck. Lucinda pours charcoal into the grill and lights it with a long-necked lighter. It will be ready for cooking after everyone is settled with drinks. Lily throws a flowered plastic tablecloth over the table and gets the Adirondack chairs placed around it. Experience has taught them to set the food inside, fill their plates, and eat outside. Otherwise, some of their four-legged friends do their best to steal food.

Kelly and Eileen come out on the deck, Eileen carrying a large glass of red wine.

"Yo, Ei," Lily chuckles. "You're getting to it as fast as I did when I got here."

"I need it. Yesterday was awful, so awful." Eileen shakes her head and sinks onto a chair. She is dressed in running pants with one of those T-shirts that have a built-in bra. Lily wonders how many miles Eileen ran today. She tells herself she gets the same amount of exercise walking dogs and cleaning kennels.

"I think I might have you beat, but you go first," Lily says.

"Wait," Kelly holds up one hand. "Lily, I hope you're watering those impatiens I gave you." She stares straight at Lily.

"Impatiens, yes. I was trying to remember the name of those

flowers. I watered them this morning as a matter of fact," Lily blithely responds.

"We won't ask when you watered them *before* this morning," Lucinda chuckles as she sits down in the empty chair. "Eileen, tell us your story."

Eileen sighs. "There's this student..." She stops and takes a sip of her wine. "I shouldn't be telling you, but I won't use names. She's in a single parent household, and that parent, her mother, is in drug rehab at Recovery Centers of America. "

"How's she still in the school system? Is she living with relatives? Who's taking care of her?" Kelly rattles off.

Eileen drinks more wine. "I'll get there. Her grandmother agreed to come and live in the house so she could stay in the Haddon Township school system, which is great. Yesterday rolls along, a typical day for me. The girl apparently never came to school." She shrugs; teenagers sometimes cut school.

"Anyway, as I said, a normal day. I go home and go for a long run. When I get back, there's a call from one of the teachers I'm friendly with. She's this girl's homeroom teacher. The girl's grandmother came home from work, and the girl wasn't home. She figured the girl went to visit her mother. The grandmother tried calling the girl's cell phone but didn't get an answer. Then, the grandmother called Recovery Centers of America and was told the girl hadn't been there that day. The grandmother was starting to get worried, so she tried calling the school, but it's Friday night, no one's answering phones at the school." Eileen pauses.

The women have inched forward on their chairs and are hanging on every word.

"Finally, the grandmother called the police." Eileen stops and takes another gulp of wine. Her face is starting to flush. "Okay, the point is, the girl was found dead in the woods at Cooper River Park."

Lucinda gasps and grabs the cup Lily is about to dump all over the table. Lily's hands are shaking. Eileen continues. "It's so awful. The girl had so many problems, and somehow she's killed in the park. Oh, and you'll find this ironic," she points at Lily. "I heard she was found by someone walking their dog." Eileen shivers.

"Um, not SOMEONE walking their dog," Lily whispers. "It was Mickey and me walking our dogs together."

Kelly slams her hands on the table, and everyone jumps. "You're telling us it was *you* that found the girl from Eileen's school? Oh my God, you saw her? What happened?" Her curls are bouncing like balloons in a breeze from one side of her head to the other. She's looking from Lily, to Eileen, and back to Lily.

Lucinda steps into the kitchen. When she returns, she has a plate with four hamburgers and four hot dogs on it. She places the items on the grill and takes the empty plate back to the kitchen. She stands to the side of the grill so she can watch the food and listen to the conversation.

Now Lily takes a large gulp of sangria, "Well, I wasn't the one who saw her first, Mickey was." She relates the tale of yesterday's grim discovery. She ends with, "Don't worry about confidentiality. Her name was announced on the news this morning. Eva Livingston."

Around the table, pale faces stare at Lily. Kelly asks, "Is that why Mickey isn't here tonight? Is she too traumatized to go out? Have you talked to her?"

The delicious smell of beef patties rendering fat onto charcoal begins to fill the air. All four dogs are on the patio, seated behind Lucinda. Small drips of saliva hit the patio at their feet.

Lily takes a deep breath. She lets it out, takes another one. "No, no, she isn't here because of the foster dog. We weren't sure how he would be affected and didn't want to worry about any bad puppy interactions. Although I'm sure she could've used this night, too. Unfortunately, we weren't told much. Once we gave our statements, the police made it clear that we were to leave. I was horrified to find out the dead person was a teenage girl. What are the theories?" she asks as she looks at Eileen.

Eileen takes another sip of wine. "This coincidence is incredible."

"What's incredible is that smell." Lily tilts her nose into the air. "I feel like Boone. My mouth is watering."

"I'll go inside and open up the rolls," Kelly says, going into the kitchen. The sounds of bags being rummaged through, and silverware being collected drift out the door.

Lucinda joins Kelly in the kitchen. "Any more alcohol for either of them, and I'll have four overnight guests," she whispers to Kelly.

"Well, I can take the humans, but you'll have to take the dogs," Kelly smirks. "I'm surprised the pitcher of sangria made it here tonight. If I were Lily, I might've stayed home and drunk it all." Kelly also whispers.

"Good thing we scheduled this get-together," Lucinda says. She picks up two of the plates on which Kelly has placed salad and empty buns and returns to the deck. She uses a spatula to put a burger in a burger bun on one of the plates. Then she delicately picks up a hot dog from the grill with thumb and forefinger to put in the other bun on the plate. She does the same for a second plate.

Lucinda hands the full plates to Eileen and Lily. "No more wine for either of you until you get some food into you," she says, stabbing a finger first at Lily and then Eileen.

"Thanks, Mom." Eileen grins at her. She continues her tale. "The school counselors and some of the teachers were called in today to talk about plans for dealing with the students impacted. We're going to have different options available for the students, mostly them talking to us one-on-one, and a session for parents as well."

Kelly comes from the kitchen with forks and two large glasses of water. She puts forks and glasses on the table, then slips back into the kitchen.

Eileen finishes chewing the bite of hamburger she has taken. "Anyway, there's a suspicion that Eva was selling drugs. We're not certain, but you know you hear students talking, and even with the code words they use, you get the drift." She shakes her head. Her mouth turns down in a considerable upside-down "U".

Kelly returns from the kitchen with two more plates with salad and empty buns. Lucinda places a burger and a hot dog on the remaining plates. They return to their places at the table.

"It's regrettable. We know the mother had an addiction issue, and so this girl may not've had the best supervision. You always want things to work out for the students in your school. It's very hard." Eileen shakes her head again.

"Do you think the police will let the school board know when they've got everything sorted out? I mean, if she was selling drugs the school should be informed, shouldn't they?" Lily thinks how grateful she is to work with dogs and cats.

"I'm sure we'll find out," Eileen continues. She wipes her mouth with a napkin. "But holy crap, Lily, seriously, you've had a year's worth of police interactions in one week. You get brought a dog because the owner is found dead, and then you stumble on a dead girl with said dog. How bizarre is that?" She takes a bite of macaroni salad.

"Too bizarre for me," Lily says, and takes another bite of her burger. A wet nose touches her toe. She looks down, and Boone is looking like he hasn't seen a meal in days. She wonders how he makes his face look so sad. "No begging, mister. You know I don't feed you from the table."

All the dogs are gathered around the table now, hoping for a scrap or a crumb to fall. Even Tigger is sitting still, a very unusual sight.

"For once I'm glad my life is uneventful," says Kelly.

"Me, too," agrees Lucinda. "No dead people amongst the books I audit."

They continue to chat, grill, and catch up, until they decide it's time to head home. Taking over cleanup and pack-up, Kelly assembles a take-home plate for everyone. All that energy does come in handy.

Lily leashes up Boone and Crockett and gets them in the car. Eileen's promised to let her know any details she finds out about Eva's demise.

Chapter 16

Skimming through the explosion of texts on his phone, Quinn slumps at the desk in his bedroom. "You two-faced A-holes. You didn't give Eva the time of day. Now you're all acting like she was your best friend. She was my friend, and I let her down," he mutters to himself.

His iPad is open to his English assignment in case one of his parents should walk by. Their mumbling has carried down the hall, alerting him to an imminent interrogation.

Then realizing he can no longer hear the mumbling, Quinn stops scrolling and listens carefully. The creak of a floorboard announces someone in the hallway. Thrusting the phone under a pile of papers, he picks up his iPad, pretending to concentrate. There is a cursory tap on the door, but he doesn't look up.

"Mom and I would like to talk to you," his dad says, casually leaning his six-foot-five bulk on the doorframe.

There is a fake hint of nonchalance in the tone. Quinn knows this will be anything but a casual conversation. He pretends to be engrossed in his reading assignment. There's another tap on the door. Quinn swivels his head on his neck and opens his eyes wide. He shifts in his seat, sitting straighter.

"Hey, Dad, what's up?"

"Quinn, Mom and I want to talk to you," George repeats. He's smiling, but the lines around his deep brown eyes are tight, and the greying eyebrows above them twitch.

"Uh, doing homework, Dad." Quinn shrugs his shoulders and looks back down at the iPad.

"This won't take long. C'mon downstairs." George makes no move to retreat from the doorway.

Quinn scrolls right to change the page, pauses ten seconds and then sighs. He flips the cover over the iPad's screen and tosses it on his desk. Without making eye contact with his father, he stands up and shuffles out his bedroom door.

George wrinkles his nose as his son passes in front of him. His eyes scan his son's back, from the top of his head to the frayed hem of his jeans. Quinn is in his typical attire of black T-shirt and jeans. From the smell, the T-shirt is long overdue to get into the wash. He bites back a comment on showering. When he was Quinn's age, he would not take a shower at his parents' suggestion. Besides, he has a more important topic to discuss.

He follows his son down the stairs and through to the kitchen. Mary is pouring lemonade into an octagonal glass half-filled with ice cubes. She forces a smile which turns her usual placid face a bit maniacal.

"There're my men. Either of you want some lemonade?" she asks, holding up a glass.

"No," Quinn mumbles, flopping onto one of the kitchen chairs, causing it to skid on the earth-tone laminate flooring.

Wincing, Mary locks her doe-brown eyes with her husband. George nods and gives her an encouraging smile. "I think I'm good, Sweetie, thanks," he says.

Mary and George move to the kitchen table and sit on either side of their son.

"We had a call from your school counselor yesterday, Quinn," George starts.

Quinn sighs deeply and folds himself a little more forward causing his unwashed shoulder length hair to cover his face.

"It wasn't a bad call, Quinn," Mary attempts to soften the message using a serene voice.

George interjects some anxiety as he clarifies the matter. "He wanted us to know the police want to talk to Eva's friends. They're investigating her death. They want to find out what happened."

Quinn's jaw locks as his teeth skid on top of each other from the pressure he's using to not speak. He doesn't want to have this conversation.

"You want that too, doncha, Quinn?" Mary queries, placing a hand on her son's arm.

The silence stretches like an eternity. No one at the table speaks for over a minute. Mary is the first to lose patience with the waiting game.

"Quinn, we've always encouraged you and your brother to talk to us if anything was…" She breaks off, searching for a word that won't cause her son to curl up even more inside himself.

Quinn shifts his forearm so his mother's hand falls off.

"You're mom doesn't go into work until late tomorrow. She's gonna go to school with you," George says.

Jerking his head up, Quinn's mouth falls open as he looks from one parent to the other. "I don't need to be taken to school. I'm not a baby," he shouts a bit too loudly. His hands ball into fists. He hits the left fist on top of the right.

George takes a deep breath, "No one's treating you like a baby. You can't talk to the police without a parent present. Mom doesn't start work until eleven, so she's goin' to school with you. Once the police have talked to you, she's goin' to work."

"I don't have anything to tell them," Quinn shouts again. He drops his head down, his gaze is back on the opalescent tabletop.

Mary tentatively sips from her glass of lemonade, and focuses out into the backyard. She lingers in that position. Suddenly, she slaps a palm on the table and starts to rise. George and Quinn both jolt with surprise gazing at her.

"Doggone squirrels, tryin' to chase the birds from the feeder." She retakes her seat.

Despite his attempt to say nothing, Quinn smiles and laughs.

Mary gives George a chastened glance. "Well, at least I made you laugh," she says, nodding at Quinn.

"Do you know what Eva might've been doing at Cooper

River Friday morning?" George asks. "It's not like it was on her way to school."

Quinn shrugs.

"Okay, Quinn, everyone knows her mother…" George starts.

"Eva wasn't doing drugs like her mother." Quinn glares at his father, his tone implying he does not want to have a debate about this fact.

Putting his hands up, palms towards his son, George says, "I didn't say Eva was doing…"

"Only 'cause I stopped you," Quinn says, dropping his head again.

"So why was she at the park?" George asks, looking to Mary, his eyes pleading for assistance. Mary shrugs, shaking her head unsure of how to approach this conversation.

"She wasn't like her mother," Quinn says, choking on the words. "She wasn't." He pauses. "She could be pretty stubborn, but she was determined to be better than a junkie."

"Dad didn't call Eva's mother a junkie." Mary soothingly pats her son's arm again.

"But it's what everybody thinks," Quinn says and looks his mother in the eyes. His face is a hardened mask of defiance. "We all know it. We know our parents are sayin' that they believe us, they trust us. But behind our backs, it's wink, nod, we sure don't want our kid hangin' out with that junkie's kid."

"Listen, Quinn, we admire Mrs. Livingston for admitting she needed help. We do," Mary says. She looks at George, who nods at her, encouraging her to continue. "It takes courage to get counseling. We admire Eva for keeping it together and staying in school. We know she's had to deal with other kids texting and instagramming about her. We're glad she has a friend like you." She pauses. "Um, had a friend…." Her cheeks redden slightly.

George leans forward and clasps his hands on the table. "It's why we want you to tell the police anything you might know. You were Eva's friend, a real friend. We know that. So, help make this right."

"All we're askin' is you don't keep information from the police that could stop what happened to Eva from happening to someone else," Mary says. She's leaning forward, and her flaxen shoulder-length hair is brushing her son's jet-black tresses. "Okay?" she queries.

Quinn looks up, making eye contact with his mother. Then he turns his head and makes eye contact with his father. "Yeah, okay," he agrees sullenly.

"Good, now go upstairs and put a clean shirt on. I think the one you're wearing is ready to walk itself down to the washing machine," Mary says, waving a hand in front of her face as if to clear away a pungent odor.

George shrugs, and with a glint of humor in his eye says, "I don't know what your mother's talkin' about. I don't smell a thing." He gets up from the table and walks off towards the living room.

CHAPTER 17

Monday morning finds Lily back at the shelter. There were numerous adoptions over the weekend. Lily is elated knowing dogs and cats found forever homes, even though she now has a mountain of paperwork to sort through. Lily and Chelsea are chatting away about their weekends as they finish up serving kitty breakfast. The door to the C-wing opens and a boisterous, "What is all of this chattering? I want to see work being done, work." Martin stands as tall as his five-foot-six-inches will allow, wearing his Cheshire Cat grin.

He loves to play the role of tyrant, which is ironic, as he's like a kitten with a rottweiler's voice. There is a lot of noise, but no menace behind it. Chelsea and Lily share a look, and Lily gives him a mock salute.

"Aye, aye, skipper, less talking, more litter shoveling," she says.

Despite herself Chelsea giggles. Then she turns her sweet face, all doe-eyed and lashes spread like peacock feathers to Martin. "How silly of me to think chatting while we worked would make the work less onerous." She bats those amazing lashes several times.

Lily coughs into her hand to stifle a laugh.

"Boy, it's a sarcastic crowd this morning. Did you two have good weekends?" Martin asks.

"The usual," Chelsea says quickly. Now Martin and Lily share a smile.

"Nothing too exciting, unless you count finding a dead teenager at Cooper River exciting," Lily adds.

"Je—" Martin begins. Lily cuts him off with a stern face. Chelsea's mouth opens, closes, opens again.

"I saw that on the news. Pray tell, how did you get involved?" Martin asks.

"Mickey and I went for a walk with the dogs. The dogs smelled something and pulled us up a trail." Lily shrugs as if finding a body is an everyday occurrence.

"Holy mackerel," Chelsea exclaims.

"I actually didn't see anything. Mickey noticed a backpack and then thought she saw someone. She scurried into the woods. When she walked around the body, she said the eyes were open and staring vacantly," Lily explains.

"Ewww…" Chelsea grimaces.

"Are you making this up? Seriously, you and Mickey found her?" Martin asks again.

"Bossman, I wish I were making it up. The police sent us packing after taking our statements." Lily waves her hand in a "move along" motion.

Martin lets out a whistle, which causes a brief chorus of meows from the C-wing. "I guess my wife deciding it was time for Pull-Ups instead of diapers for Christian pales in comparison?"

The three share a laugh as they return to their respective tasks.

Lily goes into the medical area. Doc's shadow shows through the frosted glass of one of the exam room windows. Walking over to the kennels, she peers in at Barkley. He gives her a lethargic glance. Skittle is sitting at the door of his kennel.

"Hi there, little guy," she says. "How about coming to watch me work today?" She grabs a leash from the wall rack and leashes Skittle up. They exit the medical area and walk into the staff area. Martin is at his desk and looks up as they enter.

"I was wondering why there's a pen in here with a dog bed in it," he states.

"This little guy can't deal with the noise of the shelter kennels. We had him in Medical over the weekend, but I thought I'd give him a chance to stretch out a bit. I'm looking for a foster home for him, because I think it's his best chance at adoption." Lily uses her most matter-of-fact, professional demeanor.

"I'll accept that for now because I need to talk to you about something else," Martin says.

When Martin's voice is in the lower octaves, Lily knows it will be an unpleasant conversation. Her arms are tense as she settles Skittles into the pen. Sitting in her desk chair, she swivels to face Martin.

"Kim cornered me…" he begins.

"Kim should concern herself with doing her own job correctly." Lily bolts from her seated position.

"Hold it, hold it." Martin raises his hands as if trying to stuff ten pounds of trash into a five pound bag. Lily reluctantly takes her chair. "You two can't get along with each other, for whatever reason," he begins.

"I wanted to see if we could help the state police with their next of kin notification," Lily huffs, her cheeks flushing pink.

"You could've asked Kim for the information," Martin counters.

"She would've taken two or three days." Lily folds her arms in front of her chest, squinting her eyes in anger.

"Then you come to me and tell me what you're trying to accomplish," Martin placates. "Lil, you're great with the animals. Our adoption stats have increased since you've taken this job. You need to show the same patience with people as you do with animals." He pauses and looks down at his desk, before returning his gaze to Lily. "You yelled at Chelsea last week," he states in a matter-of-fact tone.

"I'd been told someone I knew was found dead. Pardon me for not having patience with Chelsea and her relentless flirting," Lily snaps.

"Lil, if a member of your family died, or a close friend, you'd have had a reason for snapping at Chelsea. Your reaction was a bit extreme for a shelter volunteer being found dead." Martin pauses again. "Take a breath and count to five before starting a conversation. That's what I do with my wife."

Lily puffs air from between clenched lips.

"Give Kim space. You two need to work together. I know you have different ways of working. Try to understand her way works for her. And I told her to be understanding of yours. Okay?" Martin tilts his head to one side.

"Yes, okay," Lily sighs out.

"Awesome, now go find Skittle a good home. That's why we pay you the big bucks around here." His smile threatens to split his cheeks.

"Yes, sir. You know I'm in this job purely for the money," she says sarcastically. The joke eases the tension, and they laugh. No one works at a shelter for the money.

Lily maneuvers the conversation to emphasize her valuable animal skills. "I was thinking about bringing in one of the cats to assess Skittle's tolerance. I might be able to foster him in a home with older cats. It won't be as noisy, and we know older cats tend to ignore new things for a bit unless it's a catnip toy."

"Good idea," Martin agrees. "I'll let the troops know we're closing the door to avoid escapees. I think I know which cat would be just right, too." He wanders out and returns with Twinkle.

"You're right, she's perfect." Lily says, with a nod of agreement.

Twinkle is a tiny calico that has shown a tolerance for dogs. Her main interest is curling up on a blanket, so Skittle won't feel threatened. Martin puts a blanket down on the floor and lets Twinkle wander around. Skittle is up and on guard. Eventually, Twinkle lies down on her blanket, and he mirrors her by lying down on his bed.

The day is uneventful, allowing Lily and Martin to get caught up on paperwork. Lily is able to check the list of foster families to see if she can find a match for Skittle. After a while, Martin opens Skittle's pen so the two animals can interact. Neither turns aggressive.

Glancing at them as she works, Lily realizes she has found a way to foster both of them. Twinkle's chances of adoption are much higher than Skittle's. Cats are less rambunctious than dogs, and cat owners tend to be more patient in letting the personality develop.

CHAPTER 18

Around midafternoon the sounds of someone crying at the front desk are heard. Lily and Martin look at each other, and Martin says, "Let me check it out." As he reaches for the door, it opens a crack and Angelo peeks in.

"Can I come in?" he sheepishly asks.

"Sure," they answer in unison.

"Um," he stammers. "There's a woman here asking about a dog, Burrow. I see him in the system, but he's not up for adoption. I'm not sure what to tell her."

"It's okay, Angelo. I've got this." Martin pats him on the back. They head out front.

Lily's radar ears are turned to high alert. She hadn't received any messages from the state police about Pete's family being notified, and she hadn't been able to help as he hadn't listed an emergency contact on his volunteer application. She wonders if the person asking about Burrow is a family member, and if so whether she knows how Pete died.

About fifteen minutes later Martin returns. Walking over to Lily's desk, he picks up the box of Kleenex. "There's a woman who says she's related to Burrow's deceased owner. I've explained that since the dog was surrendered, she has to go through all adoption protocols. I'll get her started on the adoption forms. Would you call the foster parent and see when they can bring him over?" he asks.

"Sure, but what's with the Kleenex?" Lily asks.

"Darn, she's crying the Mississippi out there," Martin says.

Lily's nerves tingle at the prospect of meeting Pete's relative. She admonishes herself to be sympathetic.

Martin slips back out the door. Lily calls Mickey, but reaches only voice mail. She leaves a message to call back, then follows it with a text. "Person here related to Pete. Can you do a meet tonight?"

Next Lily places a call to the trooper unit that surrendered Burrow to make sure this person is legitimate.

"Troop D, Road Station, Officer Jarvis."

"Hi, Officer Jarvis, it's Lily from Forever Friends. There's a person here who says she's related to the owner of the dog you surrendered to us last week."

"Yes." Officer Jarvis pauses. "She was here this morning. She was at the house and one of the neighbors directed her to us," she states blandly.

"Well," Lily continues, "she wants to adopt the dog. We want to make sure it's procedurally okay. We were asked not to put him up for adoption."

"Hold on, I'll check." Officer Jarvis puts Lily on hold. Relishing the soothing feeling that comes over her when touching a dog, Lily reaches down and pets Skittle.

"Lily, the case has been turned over to Burlington Township because that's where Sgt. Russo lived. We asked you not to put the dog up for adoption because we hadn't been able to reach family members. I'd say it's fine to go through with an adoption." Officer Jarvis' words are succinct, and her voice shows no emotion.

"Thanks, Officer Jarvis. I appreciate it." Lily disconnects. She pulls out the file for Burrow to note the conversation, including the date and time. With the turnaround on shelter animals so high, it's hard to remember the specifics on all the animals, so the staff rely heavily on notes.

Lily's phone bings. She sees a text message alert.

"Can the person come tonight after six. Or tomorrow?" It's from Mickey.

Lily closes Skittles' pen with Twinkle in with him, leaves the staff area, and heads to the reception area. This space is just inside the front door of the shelter. It holds six small, white, rectangular tables. Each table is surrounded by four black folding chairs. The reception area is used by potential adoptive families to fill out their applications, and it's where they meet with adoption consultants. And where people wait if they're surrendering a pet.

Lily smiles when she sees Martin schmoozing the woman. He has taken two chairs from one of the tables so the two of them can sit side by side. The woman is almost purring at him. She looks about Lily's age with dull brown hair rolled in a padded rubber band at the nape of her neck. She wears what appear to be scrubs, and Lily wonders if perhaps the woman is a nurse. She chastises herself for her earlier doubts about the woman's worthiness. Lily approaches them.

"Hi, I'm Lily, the Adoption Coordinator. Our foster family could meet you tonight at six. We'll have them bring Burrow here."

"Oh, thank goodness." The woman blows her nose and lets out a heavy sigh. "I hadn't talked to Pete in a while, and I thought I'd stop by on my way home from work. The neighbor—oh, what's his name?" She waggles her hand that's holding the Kleenex back and forth. Then puts it to her forehead, "Darn, I'm blanking on his name." She scratches at her forehead.

"We understand," Martin says.

Tears seep from the woman's red-streaked eyes. She closes her eyes and uses the Kleenex to dry them. "The day I've had," she whispers.

"I can imagine," Lily says, remembering her own reaction when she found out about Pete's death. "So, we just need to make sure you and Burrow are compatible."

The woman opens her eyes, fixing them on Lily. "Wha… what do you mean?" she stammers.

Before Lily can answer Martin cuts in.

"Clarissa, as I was explaining to you, sometimes people don't fit well with a particular animal. Burrow's a German shepherd, a powerful dog. It wouldn't be acceptable for us to let you take him without being sure you can control him." Martin is making hand gestures of holding a leash. "We don't want him pulling you down or making you fall because he's too strong for you to control."

"No, no, you can't give Pete's dog to someone else." She turns and grabs hold of Martin's arm. "Don't you understand that's all I have left of Pete." She grabs another Kleenex and buries her face in it.

"I'm not saying you can't handle him. I've seen the smallest people handle a Doberman mix. We have to make sure. It's the normal procedure," Martin says.

"We can also give you some advice on walking and handling. Do you have any other animals at home?" Lily asks.

"No, no," she waves her hands. "It's only me."

"Okay," Lily says.

"I used to joke with Pete that I got my animal fix when I visited him." She tries to force her mouth into a smile as another tear runs down her cheek.

"That's what my brother says about my two pups," Lily adds. "So I'll go let the foster parent know tonight at six is good?"

"Yes, definitely, yes. I'll be here," the woman says, rising from the chair. Her shoulders are slumped forward. "I'm so glad I found him." Her mouth twitches, attempting a smile.

Lily slips back to her desk and sends a text to Mickey. "A go for 6."

Martin wanders back into the staff area, putting the box of Kleenex back on Lily's desk. "Well, there's our good deed for the week. We've reunited human and dog."

Lily turns towards him. "Not bad for a Monday. Does this mean we can breeze through the rest of the week?" she asks.

Twinkle begins rubbing her head on Martin's pants. "Good deed number two will be finding these two friends homes."

Lily looks at her watch and realizes it is almost 3:30. She

marvels at how fast the day flew by. "Not today. Where'd the time go?"

"Time flies when you love what you do," Martin says. He picks up Twinkle. "I'll take this princess back to her lodgings." He carries her back to the C-wing.

"Little guy, I'm sorry. I promise, tomorrow finding you a foster home will be priority number one," she tells Skittle, leashing him for a walk before returning him to his kennel.

They walk the trails that surround the shelter. Breathing the fresh air while listening to birds chirping gives Lily renewed energy. Following the walk, Lily returns Skittle to the kennel in the medical area. She does another check on Barkley. He is contentedly sleeping. She needs to remember to talk to Doc about him tomorrow.

Lily returns to her desk to grab her purse and phone. Martin is in the staff area.

"Oh, I remembered Ingrid's off today because she worked the event Saturday. Do you want me to stay for the meet?" she asks him.

"Nope, you get all of the paperwork ready so all she has to do is sign. I'm giving Chelsea a few hours of overtime to stay tonight," Martin says.

"I've got it right here on this clipboard," Lily says, handing it to Martin. "Leave it on my desk, and I'll update the records tomorrow."

"Thanks a bunch. Have a good night," Martin says smiling at her.

CHAPTER 19

Arriving home, Lily leashes Boone and Crockett, and they go for a lengthy walk. Taking to the streets of Bassettville, they pass by houses with flags that resemble graduation caps hanging from porches. These same houses have a significant amount of trash out for pickup. Lily muses about her own college graduation, astonished it was more than two decades ago.

Groups of children play on lawns. Some of them run over to pet Boone and Crockett. While petting Boone, one little girl throws her arms around his neck, giving him a hug. He looks up at Lily with the huge grin that always makes her smile. Little girls are drawn to Boone. Lily is never certain if it is his charm, or because he is low to the ground being part Bassett Hound. On the other hand, Crockett's nose follows balls being thrown in games of catch. Crockett would love to be set free to chase the boys around.

They gradually meander back home, to find Tyler at Lily's dining room table with his laptop.

"I think there were some serious graduation parties in town over the weekend," Lily says breezing past him into the kitchen.

"Oh yeah, I think Rutgers and Villanova had graduations last week," Tyler states.

Lily dishes up bowls of kibble and gets fresh bowls of water for the dogs. "Gosh, it would be great to see those stories on the news."

"Maybe if you and Mickey would stop finding bodies on your walks we could have more happy news stories," Tyler teases her. "Personally, I'd be happier with a Phillies win."

Lily opens the refrigerator and takes stock of its contents. "Hey, Tyler, you want some chicken stir-fry?"

"If you're cooking it, I'm eating it," he quips.

"Can you tear yourself away from the computer for a few games of fetch with Crockett?" she asks as she gives each dog a Milk Bone. "That way I'll only have one dog under my feet while I cook."

"Sure thing," he says, logging off from his laptop. He and Crockett head out into the yard with a tennis ball.

Lily chops carrots, celery, and an onion. She heats two pans with olive oil, tosses the vegetables into one and the chicken into the other. As she stirs and cooks, Boone is rooted by the stove on the off chance something would drop to the floor. Lily adds some prepared sauce to the chicken. The pungent smells of garlic and ginger fill the kitchen. She mixes the contents of the two pans together. Deciding to cook some rice, she navigates around Boone to get the rice from the pantry. "About five minutes to go," she calls out the back door.

Tyler and Crockett come inside, each with a tremendous thirst. Crockett heads for his bowl and laps up every drop. After washing his hands and refilling Crockett's bowl, Tyler opens the refrigerator and grabs the water pitcher. He pours two glasses and sets them on the table. He drinks from his and refills it.

"I got a new client today," he tells Lily, as he grabs two forks from the drawer and sits down.

"Awesome, tell me about it," Lily says, as she puts food on the two plates. Then she turns off the burners on the stovetop and moves the pans to the cool burners at the back.

"This woman is opening a used bookstore in Collingswood. She's a talker. Phew, I think I know the name of every member of her family. I also may know her entire life history. The important thing is, she needs a good website." Tyler tucks into the food Lily has put in front of him. "She also needs to make sure her credit card processing is secure and unhackable."

"Great, how'd she find you?" Lily asks.

"Like I said, she's a TALK-er. She's renting the store from my realty client. One of the many things she told them was she needed to get a website up and running, and they gave her my card."

"That's cool. You know I love bookstores," Lily says. They continue to chat about their days. When they finish eating, Tyler takes care of the dirty dishes, and then heads back to his house.

Lily heads to the bathroom to take a refreshing shower and wash off the musty reek of kennels. Putting on an oversized T-shirt, she goes back out to the living room to find Boone settled on the recliner, probably dreaming of eating an entire pizza.

She curls onto the couch with Crockett and "Dayshift," a book Ingrid lent her. The phone rings and before Lily can even say hello, Mickey is talking.

"Lily, I needed quite the glass of wine after that meet," she says breathlessly.

"Why?" Lily asks.

"Don't tell Martin I told you. It was awful. Chelsea met me outside, and we took Burrow back to the large play area. We were having a good time. Chelsea had him playing tug-of-war with one of those rope toys. Suddenly, he dropped the rope, his ears stood straight up, and his tail flared out."

"What happened?" Lily asks.

"Martin and Clarissa were coming up to the play area. I think Burrow heard them talking. He went over to the fence of the pen and got into a crouch. Then he started fiercely growling. Martin stopped walking, but Clarissa didn't. She kept coming, and I swear every hair on Burrow's coat went up. He started barking like a prison guard dog. I've never seen him behave that way. You remember when he first met Nero? He was a little gruff, but Nero comes on a little strong sometimes. This wasn't anything like that." Mickey pauses. Lily can hear her swallowing.

"He knew her?" Lily asks. "You know Pete didn't list anybody as emergency contact on his volunteer application. That made me suspicious about a family member suddenly appearing. I chalked it up to my overwrought emotional state. Clearly Burrow recognized her. What happened next?"

"Well, Martin asked Clarissa to stand back out of sight. Then he came over and talked to Burrow through the fence. Burrow was still tense, but he calmed somewhat. Martin entered the pen and gave Burrow his fist to sniff, petted him and put his leash back on. Chelsea left the pen to get Clarissa. As they approached, Burrow went ballistic. Chelsea took her back to the shelter, and we calmed Burrow down. I brought him home, leaving Clarissa for Martin to handle." Mickey pauses.

"How's Burrow now?" Lily asks.

"I had him and Nero out in the yard, and they chased each other. They're relaxing in the living room. Martin, the charmer, he called me to make sure everything was okay at my house. Then he apologized like somehow he might have done something wrong. He'd done everything we usually do. Honestly, Burrow was fine with him in the enclosure. He was fine with Chelsea and me. Like I said, she had him playing tug-of-war. Everything was going great."

"Mickey, this is weird. I'm sure we'll get to the bottom of this," Lily says to comfort her friend. "Clarissa was a piteous mess when she came into the shelter. But she'd had quite a shock. She'd found out from a neighbor that Pete was dead."

"Holy smoke, imagine that," Mickey exclaims.

"I know. I can relate. I know how shocked I was. I dropped the phone on the floor," Lily says.

"Did Pete ever mention Clarissa to you?" Mickey asks.

"No. I knew Pete didn't have siblings, but he didn't talk about his family." Lily lets out a rueful laugh. "He wasn't much of a talker. More a listener."

"You two must've been a pair. You're not the chattiest person either, Lil."

"We talked a lot about our dogs." Lily pauses, thinking back over her conversations with Pete. "Pete was immensely interested in my career change, being mid-forties and having devoted his life to the Marines. He was trying to figure out what to do next in life. I think the transition from the rigid structure of the military was difficult for him." Lily pauses.

"Well, whatever it was about her, there's one dog that doesn't like her," Mickey says. Lily hears her swallow again.

"It's a good thing Martin didn't have me stay tonight. I volunteered, but he gave Chelsea the overtime," Lily says. She frowns. "Thanks for the heads up. I'm sure I'll hear all about it tomorrow." She disconnects. Boone hops up on the couch between her and Crockett.

"Boone, buddy, are you actually going to snuggle up here with me?" Lily asks. He licks her face several times and then lays his head on her chest. Boone can be a standoffish dog. At times he's affectionate, but at others he just gives his "is food involved in this?" look, and if not just goes about his own business. "Boone, I wonder what tomorrow will bring for me?" Lily strokes his head, and he sighs, satisfied with his life.

CHAPTER 20

Pondering how to proceed with her life, Clarissa sits in Wawa's parking lot, behind the wheel of the dented 1990 Hyundai she knows will stop working one day. The car belonged to Uncle Charlie's neighbor, who planned to donate it to Purple Heart. Instead, Clarissa ended up with it.

She reminisces about the 2015 Silver Toyota she paid for with her bonus from her law firm. And that her boyfriend used to move out of their shared apartment. He'd promised to return it. Instead, he'd changed the registration and title from her name to his while Clarissa was in physical therapy for her leg. Pulling a fabric rubber band from her pocket, she ties her mud brown hair into a knot.

"Did I really ask too much of Pete," she asks herself. "I needed a place to live, to save the money I'm paying in rent. I needed to have enough time to look for a full-time job with benefits, and enough money for a decent haircut and makeup for the job interview. He had the house to himself and the money from Uncle Charlie's investments."

With balled fists, Clarissa hits the steering wheel in frustration. Pocketing her car keys, she exits the car and shuts the door behind her. Looking the vehicle over from hood to trunk, she's afraid someone will have it towed, mistaking it for junk. She pulls the generic eye drops from her pocket, squirts a drop in each eye, and doesn't bother with the residue that drips down her cheeks.

The chime sounds as she opens the door to the Wawa. It feels like the arctic inside. Clarissa is probably the one employee who is grateful that the store overdoes the air conditioning. Her body jitters. The cashier waves a greeting. Clarissa mimics the wave, not remembering his name.

"Getting' Red Bull?" he asks. He's wearing a hoodie under his Wawa T-shirt. The sleeves are pulled down to cover his hands.

"Uh, yeah, I guess. Gotta stay awake, right?" Clarissa answers. She walks back towards the refrigerators containing the cold beverages.

"Man, just get a fountain soda and refill it. I ain't gonna tell on ya," the cashier calls out to her.

Clarissa opens the refrigerator door and stands in the opening, allowing even more cold air to blow across her sweaty body. She pulls a can of Red Bull from the rack.

"I appreciate it, but if we get any kind of inspection you and I are both screwed, and you know it," she says walking back to the cashier. She keeps her head down, hoping her lack of eye contact will limit conversation. As Clarissa puts the can on the counter she notices beads of condensation forming on the can's sides despite the store's frigid temperature.

The cashier punches a few buttons, and the cash register drawer clangs open. Clarissa reaches into her pocket and pulls out a pile of coins. "Shit, youse think they'd fire us for a few sodas?" the cashier asks. "Effn A, for eight bucks an hour they can give us a few sodas."

Clarissa uses every ounce of energy to control her trembling fingers as she sorts through the coins to make the correct amount of money for the Red Bull. "It's not a chance I can take. I need every penny of the twenty-seven forty-two I get after Uncle Sam takes his share," she says, pocketing two dimes.

"See, that's what I effn mean. They's prolly makin' a dolla' fitty on that Red Bull. They could give you that dolla' fitty," the cashier says, as he rolls his head on his shoulders. He pulls one sleeve of the hoodie up over his hand, scoops up the coins and sorts them into the correct slots in the register.

Clarissa flicks the tab and takes a long draw on the soda.

She closes her eyes, swallowing. "Yeah, life sucks," she says, and walks to the sandwich counter to start putting together premade sandwiches for the morning commuters.

Chapter 21

Tuesday morning at Forever Friends, and Lily and Chelsea are handing out cat breakfast in the C-wing. Lily opens Twinkle's cage to put in a paper plate with some Fancy Feast tuna delight. "I hope to have you hang out with Skittle this morning," Lily says.

"Seriously, Lil, you're too funny. I think you treat these animals better than some children get treated," Chelsea quips.

"Well, today is the first day of the outreach program I'm starting at the Haddon Township school, so I will be interacting with some children today, too." Lily closes Twinkle's cage door and moves on to the next. "So how was the meet last night?" she asks.

"Sheesh, it was scary." Chelsea takes a deep breath and shudders, red tendrils of hair shaking to the tips. "Honestly, I was actually afraid of Burrow."

Lily gives her an appraising look. "I can't believe YOU were afraid of anything, ever."

"You didn't see his reaction." Chelsea flutters her uncommonly long eyelashes. "Holy mackerel, when I tell you that every hair on his body stood up, I mean EVERY HAIR." She puffs out her chest and opens her arms as if to make herself appear more significant. "I was glad Martin sent me out of the play area."

"How was Clarissa reacting?" Lily asks.

"She was a mess. She's sobbing, yelling, "No, no, I need that dog." She saw the way Burrow was reacting to her. Yet, she was insistent she wanted to take him home." Chelsea pauses.

Lily waits for her to continue.

"Martin was coolheaded with her. I'm telling you, I wouldn't get in a car with an animal reacting to me that way." Chelsea gives an exaggerated shrug of her shoulders and flips her hands palms up.

"There're a lot of strange people in this world. We only experience a few of them in our world here," Lily says, as she continues to pass out cat food.

"I know it. You should meet the folks I come across at my bartending gig." Chelsea flicks her hair out of her eyes.

"I can only imagine." Lily tosses the empty cans of Fancy Feast into the trash. "Okay then, breakfast is served. I'm going to head to my little space." Lily opens the door again to Twinkle's cage. Curling Twinkle against her chest, she heads for her desk.

"I'm right behind you," Chelsea says, grabbing the trash bag to take out to the dumpster.

Martin is at the front desk, "Good morning, Lily, Chelsea." He thrusts his chin in the direction of the C-wing. "I bet your chins were wagging away in the cat room." He looks from one to the other.

"Well," Lily shrugs, "Chelsea said the meet didn't go well last night."

"You minx," he shouts. "You're seriously going to pretend innocent Chelsea here started the conversation?"

Twinkle squirms in Lily's arms. "You're scaring poor Twinkle," Lily blurts, and rushes past him, closing the door to the staff area behind her.

Chelsea glances after her frowning, "Was I not supposed to tell Lily the meet didn't go well last night?" she asks Martin, a bit incredulous.

"No, no," he says in a normal tone of voice. "I expected you to talk about it. I enjoy giving Lily a hard time, the way she acts superior and everything." Martin goes to the staff area and slowly opens the door. He slides in and closes the door behind him, with a quick glance at Lily.

"I'm offended by that 'superior' comment." Lily swipes a pretend tear from her cheek.

"Don't even try it. I'm not buying the innocent act." Martin laughs and sits at his desk.

"Seriously, tell me about it." Lily spins in her chair to face him.

"Honestly, I'm sure you heard it all. The dog was great with Mickey, great with Chelsea, growled and barked when it saw Clarissa and me. I asked her to step out of sight. I approached the pen, talked to him, and he settled enough that I felt safe entering the pen. He sniffed at me and seemed to calm down. Clarissa came back into view, and he started barking again, and charged the fence." He frowns.

"Chelsea finally got Clarissa to go back into the shelter. I made sure Mickey felt comfortable with Burrow before I let her take him home." He shakes his head again. "I didn't want him turning on Mickey."

"She's a good judge of character, canine and human," Lily says.

"I know, but what the hell set Burrow off? Clarissa's crying and shouting at me. 'I know the dog. I've been in Pete's house with him.' I didn't want to call her a liar, but clearly this dog has issues with her. Maybe the owner kept him under control when she was around. I don't know. I do know I wasn't putting that dog in a car with her. Who knows what would've happened?"

"I hear you," Lily says.

"Then I suggested she come back and take a look at some of our other great animals if she wanted to adopt. She became furious." He tosses his head as if swishing long hair off his face, "Mister," he says in falsetto, "I don't want some mangy mutt. I want my cousin's dog." Martin puts his hands on the desk and blows out a long breath. "Then she stormed out."

"Please tell me she didn't say 'mangy mutt,'" Lily snarls, her cheeks flushing red.

"Don't quote me. That was one upset woman." Martin

grimaces. "I made some notes and put the file back on your desk. But now what do we do? We can't list him for adoption until we know what set him off."

"Well, maybe Ingrid and Doc could have a few sessions with him," Lily suggests. "Mickey hasn't said anything about him having problems with anyone who's been at her house. You know Mickey, she'd have no concerns about telling us she was returning a foster or reporting a problem."

Martin nods. "Well, I'll talk to Ingrid and see what she thinks. She's our in-house Cesar Millan," he chuckles, referring to Ingrid's extensive certifications.

"Speaking of Doc, I'm going to go get Skittle and see if he does well with Twinkle again." Lily gets up from her chair and heads to the medical area.

Doc and Mitchell are working with Caesar. "Good morning, Doc, how's he doing?" Lily asks.

"Well, I had him on the prescription food all weekend, but he still is having some issues. I'm going to try giving him baby food and see how that sits with him. Since I'm taking Barkley for an ultrasound tomorrow, if I find the baby food doesn't make a difference, I may take Caesar as well."

Lily gives Doc a shy smile. "Trying to get the old two for the price of one, Doc?"

He shrugs, "Our Board of Directors cares about expenses. I hope I'll get enough machine time for two ultrasounds. I know I should give him more time on the baby food, but he's clearly suffering, I hate to make him wait if it's some type of obstruction." Doc frowns.

Doc's compassion knows no bounds. Some of the staff joke they wish they could see him instead of their own doctors.

"Um, Caesar has a lot of hair, Doc?" Lily leaves the rest of the question unspoken.

"Yes, I know." He shifts his gaze to Mitchell. "Mitchell here is going to shave his belly." Mitchell is the vet tech who assists Doc.

"Yep, a real treat." Mitchell smiles wryly, his left eyebrow arches. His pupils narrow behind tortoiseshell glasses as he concentrates on shaving Caesar.

"And what tremendous job experience it is." Doc's dimples flash. Doc has been mentoring Mitchell for a more challenging animal-related career. He sees Mitchell's drive and wants to help him develop a career path.

"I'll leave you to it," Lily says. She walks over to Skittle's kennel. She leashes him up and takes him for a quick walk around the grounds before going back to her desk. Ingrid is in and chatting with Martin.

"Wow, we're full to the brim in here today," she exclaims.

"Not for too long, though," Lily says as she unleashes Skittle. "I'm going to the Thomas Edison school at two."

Ingrid squats down and scratches Skittles' ears. "This little guy is cute. He also seems a bit less jittery today."

"I was thinking the same thing," Lily smiles. "Maybe you could try putting him in with another dog this afternoon. He did well with Twinkle yesterday."

"I'll review our new recruits and see what might work well," Ingrid says. She tilts her head to the left and then to the right. She bites her lower lip. Then her eyes brighten, and her eyebrows lift. "Perhaps he and Ethel would work. She's pretty easygoing."

"My friend Lucinda's Pooh would be perfect. That is if Lucinda worked at the shelter instead of for the federal government," Lily says.

Ingrid and Martin both slip out of the staff area. Ingrid has more assessments to complete. Martin has lots of administrative items to take care of. Lily turns back to her desk and hunkers down to email and website updates.

CHAPTER 22

Lily pulls her car into the lot of the Thomas Edison school in Haddon Township. As she gets out of the car, she takes a deep breath and turns her face to the sky, allowing the warming rays of the sun to energize her. Today's fluffy cumulous clouds are beautifully reflected in the school's windows. Hearing a bark, Lily breaks from her reverie.

Connie is in the parking lot walking with Annie, a sweet dog surrendered eight months ago. A boxer mix, she has the face of a boxer and the stature and coat markings of an Australian cattle dog. Unfortunately, she's arthritic and has difficulty going up and down stairs. Since Connie and her husband live in a ranch home, with stepless access to a yard, they are an excellent placement. They have an older Scottie who is deaf. While they've been willing to foster Annie, they can't handle the veterinary costs of two older dogs, so they've been unable to adopt her.

Connie waves to Lily. She is in her late fifties and has the boundless energy of Lily's dog Crockett. Lily thinks if one could bottle the energy of Connie and Crockett, it would light an entire town.

"Hi, Lily. Beautiful day." Connie's shoulder length black hair perfectly frames her apple cheeks.

"Gosh, it is," responds Lily. She walks over to them and lets Annie smell her fist before patting her gently. "I'll go inside and check in with Kathy Klapper. I know there's an entrance with no stairs. Let me find out which one it is so it won't be so hard on you and poor Annie."

"We'll be right here," Connie assures her.

As Lily approaches the school, a short, middle-aged, blonde woman bustles out of the front door. Lily stifles a giggle. If this woman were a brunette, she could pass for Connie's sister. They have the same facial structure, and they are almost the same height and body size.

"You must be Lily. I'm Kathy Klapper," the woman says extending her hand.

"I'm Lily," she says shaking the offered hand. "Connie's here with Annie. They're waiting in the lot." Lily inclines her head in the direction of the parking lot.

"That's great. Boy, this is a good day for this experiment. People are a bit tense with all of the excitement at the high school."

Lily gives her a bewildered look.

"Oh, maybe you don't know," Kathy exclaims. "One of our high school students was found dead over the weekend."

Lily blanches. "I, unfortunately, know it all too well. It was my friend and me who stumbled upon her. I'm sorry I didn't make the connection right away."

Kathy covers her mouth with both hands, and her eyes go wide. "Goodness me, that's horrible. How on earth did that happen?"

"We were walking our dogs, and they all started barking and pulling us up a certain trail." Lily stifles a nervous laugh. "Um, forgive me, I don't mean to make light of the situation. We thought they were after a squirrel or a groundhog. When my friend realized it was a person, she was quite unnerved."

"I can imagine," Kathy says. Then she frowns. "Actually, I can't. I hope that never happens to me."

"It's not an experience I want to relive," Lily says in a matter-of-fact tone.

"Yes, well since it's such a nice day, Miss Cooke thought she'd bring the children outside. Is that okay?" Kathy asks.

"Sure," says Lily. "You show me where you want us, and we'll wait there for the children."

Kathy leads Lily to the recess space for the children. There are several plastic walls simulating rock piles, connected by rope and plank bridges, and basketball hoops framed in painted lines to simulate a court. The entire area is fringed with large maple and oak trees which provide comfortable shade. Under one of the trees, closer to the school, there's a set of Teflon-coated metal benches, organized in a "U" shape. Annie can be in the middle, while the children sit around.

Lily goes back to where Connie and Annie are waiting and walks them over to the bench area. As they arrive, a tall young woman is leading four children out of the school, followed by Kathy Klapper. Each child is carrying a book. Two of the children see Annie and stop in their tracks. "Justin, Melissa, let's keep moving forward," the young teacher says.

Connie has Annie lie down and sits beside her, at the open end of the "U". Lily hangs back. The teacher approaches and says, "Good afternoon, I'm Miss Cooke."

"I'm Connie Distefano, and this is Annie," Connie says.

"Students say hello to Mrs. Distefano."

"Good afternoon, Mrs. Distefano," murmur all four children, none of them making eye contact.

"Everyone take a seat. As I explained, we're going to practice our reading today. Annie has come to be our audience," Miss Cooke says.

Lily sidles over to Kathy. "So, how have the students been reacting to the news about Eva?" she asks.

"Well, here in grade school it isn't too bad. I was at the high school this morning, and things were more stressful." Kathy frowns. "Eva, she was a bit of a loner. Her few good friends are fairly traumatized." She pauses. "The police have spoken to each of them."

"Have the police told you anything? Was this some type of freak accident?" Lily asks.

"As you can imagine, they aren't elaborating in detail. The officers did say it appeared the death may have been accidental." She hesitates and looks from side to side to ensure there aren't any students within hearing distance. "Eva didn't come to school that day. No one knows what she was doing at Cooper River." She pauses again. "One of her friends believes she may have been getting pressured to sell drugs." Kathy lowers her voice even more. "Eva's mother is in a rehab program."

"So, the mother was selling drugs?" Lily asks.

Kathy frowns and nods. "It appears she was. Of course, I don't know if all I've heard is fact or rumor, but one of Eva's friends told us Eva found out her mother was selling drugs, and Eva was conflicted about it."

"That's horrible," Lily says. "How'd she find out?"

"I'm not a hundred percent certain. Apparently someone, or a group of people, told Eva her mother owed them money and Eva was going to have to pay it back."

"How much money?" Lily asks.

"A substantial amount, more than one would expect a teenage girl and a single parent to have laying around," Kathy says.

"You two look very conspiratorial," Connie interrupts. Lily and Kathy both jump. Neither heard her approach. "Sheesh, I didn't mean to scare you."

Kathy looks over at where Miss Cooke and the children are.

"Miss Cooke saw how placid Annie is and told me she'd be fine holding the leash." Connie pauses. "I actually think the child who's reading now wasn't comfortable with me being there."

"Please don't take it personally," Kathy begins an apology.

"Not at all, not at all," Connie brushes one hand at Kathy. "As long as Miss Cooke is okay with Annie, I'm fine standing on the sidelines. Believe me, Annie isn't going to suddenly jump up and start running." She smiles at Lily.

"You can take that to the bank," Lily says. "We're talking about the poor girl who was found dead."

"I heard the news story on KYW. How'd she die?" Connie looks at Kathy.

"It's a bit of speculation at this point," Kathy says, then looks down at her watch. "Oh, dear, I'm due to be in the principal's office for a meeting in five minutes. Lily, can I give you a call after Miss Cooke and I discuss how today went?"

"Sure thing, now hurry along, I don't want you getting detention for being tardy," Lily says as Kathy leaves.

Connie says, "So...?"

"There are rumors the girl who was found dead was being pressured to sell drugs. And some students say they think her mother is selling drugs," Lily says.

"You know, I am grateful almost every day my children are grown and out of school," Connie says. "Look at what happened last month in Wisconsin. Teenaged kids, dressed and excited about their prom, get shot instead of enjoying a night of fun and dancing."

"I can't imagine." Lily shakes her head. "I worry about my nieces and nephews. How does one even try to prepare a child for such an experience? Are they going to be placing armed guards at the entrance for every school event?"

"I know. Geez, when I was a high school student, our biggest concern was not getting caught with alcohol in the car," Connie giggles. "Those were the days of long prom dresses. We girls had bottles tucked under our skirts so the chaperones wouldn't see them when they looked in our cars."

Lily feigns horror. "Connie DiStefano, I am shocked, shocked to hear this story."

"Oh, sure you are." Connie's eyes brighten. "I suppose you have no tales of high school shenanigans?"

"I may have known a few people who tucked joints in their pantyhose," Lily demurs.

Connie puts a hand to each side of her face as if in complete shock. "Didn't they get sweat on them?" she asks.

"They didn't spend much time there." Lily laughs and looks over to the seating area where Miss Cooke is beckoning to them. "I think we're being summoned."

Lily and Connie walk over to the children.

"Would anyone like to give Annie a treat?" Connie asks. She pulls a Ziploc bag from her pocket. Annie lumbers to her feet at the sight of the package.

Two of the children are nodding eagerly. Connie instructs them to hold their palm out flat. She places a treat on each child's palm. Annie leans her head in and licks up one, then the other. The children giggle. The boy wipes his hand on his pants.

"Thank you for bringing Annie today, Mrs. Distefano," Miss Cooke says. The children mumble their thank yous.

"You're very welcome. It's clear Annie greatly enjoyed hearing the stories," Connie says with unbridled enthusiasm. She replaces the Ziploc bag in her pocket and accepts the leash from Miss Cooke.

Miss Cooke leads the children back into the school. Lily rejoins Connie, and they walk back to their parked cars.

"Would you like some help getting Annie in the car?" Lily asks.

"You can hold the leash while I set up the ramp," Connie responds. When they reach Connie's car, she kicks the bumper releasing the hatch. She withdraws a ramp and places it against the fender.

Annie hesitantly puts one foot on the ramp, and gathering her reserves haltingly climbs into the back of the car. She lies down on a dog bed .

"I'm sure my husband will be entertained by everything I learned today." Connie winks at Lily.

Lily blushes. "On that note, I need to head home. I'll give you a call later in the week."

"Sounds great, Lily. Have a good night." Connie waves as Lily heads to her car.

Chapter 23

Lily ponders her conversation with Kathy on her drive home. She realizes, not for the first time, how lucky she and her siblings were to have had a more traditional childhood. Her mom continued to work part-time after Lily and Ivy were born. She was ready to go back to full-time work when Ivy started kindergarten. Then Iris burst into the world. Lily laughs to herself. She and Ivy have joked since high school that Tyler must have been a miracle pregnancy. Any woman would have used triple birth control after having a child like Iris.

She feels heartsick for the girl, Eva. She can't imagine a teenager having to deal with her mother selling drugs. Although in her former career, Lily saw plenty of things previously inconceivable to her. Wrinkling her nose, Lily realizes her car reeks of overheated cumin. She sniffs at herself, realizing the odor is coming from her T-shirt. She's glad they were outdoors for the reading exercise, and hopes Kathy assumed the smell was from the playground or the cafeteria.

Lily arrives home, steering into her driveway. She looks into the large bay window in the living room and spies Boone in his usual napping place on the couch. Hearing the car, Boone lifts his head up, his face alight. Lily turns off the car and heads for the front door and Boone's hearty barked greeting.

"What, Boone?" Lily asks him. "Tyler went out today? Well, I sure hope Crockett didn't disturb your nap." As the words are leaving her mouth, Crockett comes running from the back of the house. Boone rolls his eyes. "Boone, don't roll your eyes." Lily squats down and scratches Crockett's ears.

She takes both leashes from the wooden rack. "Boone, there's a treat for you. Wait till you see who's joining us on our walk." Lily received a text from Eileen saying she'd join them on their evening walk.

Lily pats her pockets and realizes she needs some plastic bags. She goes into the kitchen to get a few. When she returns to the living room, she sees Eileen pulling into the driveway. Lily takes a firm hold of each leash and heads outside.

"Hello, Eileen, beautiful night for a walk," Lily says, handing Eileen Boone's leash. He may have his stubborn side, but he doesn't leap at every person they pass. "I'm glad you asked to join us. What's going on with the investigation of the girl found at Cooper River?"

"Geez, Lily, get right to the point, why don't you?" Eileen smirks sarcastically. Today she looks like a model for REI. She has on the stereotypical lightweight khaki trekking shorts, layered lightweight tank tops, a solid one underneath a printed one, and some big league walking shoes.

"I greeted you and commented on the weather when we came through the door. Now I want information," Lily sneers.

"Here's a bit of information. I think you'd better put some water on those sad-looking flowers." Eileen juts her chin in the direction of the impatiens.

"I told Kelly not to trust me with those," Lily sighs. "I definitely did not inherit my mother's gardening talents."

"Lily, pouring a cup of water a day on a wilted plant isn't talent. It's common sense."

"Good grief, remind me when we get back." Lily waves a hand towards the flowers.

They start walking but stop after about ten yards when Boone smells something under a pine tree that requires an extensive sniffing investigation. He then gives the spot a proper marking to show he was there. Lily turns to Eileen to resume their conversation and almost has her arm ripped from the socket when Crockett spots a rabbit.

Lily digs in her heels, gripping the leash with both hands. Crockett is about to leap into a beautiful bed of newly planted geraniums and snapdragons. After close to a minute of relentless barking, he sullenly concedes this particular rabbit got away, and the group resumes walking.

"It's been so stressful." Eileen sighs. "We've been talking to some of the students about grief over losing a fellow student. And the police have been interviewing students. Of course, teachers are perturbed when students are being pulled out of classes, though we all know it needs to happen. Parents are unsettled, and some of the parents are missing work because the police can't talk one-on-one with a student without a parent present. And all the parents insist their child couldn't possibly know anything." She gives a disconcerted sigh.

They stop again to allow Boone to sniff an oak tree and mark more territory. "I know most of the kids are good kids and aren't involved. I also understand the police have a job to do. Unless someone steps forward with information voluntarily, how are they going to solve this brainteaser?" Her shoulders are pulled as tight as the rope holding the main sail of a tall ship.

"It has to be nerve-racking." Lily tries to give compassionate encouragement while bending down to clean up after Crockett.

"It doesn't stop there," Eileen continues. She gets cut off as a squirrel scampers up a tree in front of them. Crockett begins leaping at the trunk of the tree, running around it on his hind legs, steadying himself against the trunk with his front legs. He believes, if he exerts enough effort, he will climb.

"Yeah, I feel a little like him," Eileen continues. "He knows he wants the squirrel, but he can't reach it."

"I hear you. I feel the same myself," Lily laughs. "So what else is going on?"

"During the interviews, someone told the police the girl was selling illegal drugs to staff." She rolls her head to the left and then to the right, trying to loosen her rigid neck muscles.

Lily halts jerking Crockett's leash. "Unbelievable. Do you

think the person was trying to divert attention?" Crockett gives a bark, straining to move forward.

"You know," Eileen continues. "That's what I thought at first. We're all under contract, and substance abuse of any kind would result in termination, especially on-site of the school. It seems ridiculous. The police have been judicious. They're trying to get more information and narrow the search a bit. We're all on edge, concerned we're going to be subjected to drug tests." Eileen's shoulders rise higher, and Lily notices the muscles in her back are as taut as guitar strings.

"Oh, my God, do you think the drug testing staff could happen?" Lily asks as they halt.

Boone has planted his feet, wanting to turn left. He will remain immobile until left is their trajectory. Eileen and Lily glance at each other, stifling giggles. They indulge him. The desire to continue their conversation outweighs choosing a different direction.

"Maybe, with a union rep to witness every test," Eileen continues, her neck muscles loosening a bit. "I think they're going to start by interviewing non-classroom staff. You know the cafeteria, custodial, teachers aids. Unfortunately, we all know the girl's mother was having a substance issue and there's this rumor that the mother's dealer got the girl involved in selling drugs. It's too horrible to think about. But predators prey on the vulnerable."

"Phew, this is unbelievable. I can see why you're so stressed, as if work isn't daunting enough. How long will the investigation take?" Lily asks.

"Hopefully I'll know more tomorrow. Let's change the subject. What happened with the guy you went on a few dates with?" Eileen beams with a hopeful smile.

"Oh, um," Lily stammers. "Can we say it didn't work out?"

"C'mon, Lily. What was wrong with this one? You have to give people a chance." Eileen takes a lecturing tone.

"I gave him every chance," Lily chokes out.

Eileen opens her mouth to continue, and Lily cuts her off.

"He died. That makes it a hard relationship to maintain," she snaps, flustered..

Crockett chooses this moment to break into a run. He and Lily dash forward a half block.

When Eileen and Boone catch up, Eileen is apologetic. "Oh my God, I'm sorry. Why haven't you said anything?"

"Honestly, it's too painful." Lily pauses, turning to face her friend. Her eyes are brimming with tears. "We seemed completely compatible. The other night I told Mickey I thought he was my soul mate."

Eileen gives Lily a measured look.

"Thank you for not scoffing. Mickey did," Lily says.

"I like to consider myself more tactful than Mickey," Eileen responds. "What evidence do you have for this assessment?" Each word is enunciated carefully, allowing Eileen to remove judgment from the question.

"This is going to sound outlandish. Promise me you won't laugh," Lily says.

Eileen nods.

"He made me feel complete."

"I'll bet that made you feel fabulous."

"It did." Lily gives a rueful shake of her head.

"I don't understand why you wouldn't have shared such amazing news with me?" Eileen tilts her head with a querying glance.

"I was savoring the feeling. Also, I was on the edge of an inappropriate job conflict. It was Pete, the guy who was volunteering at the shelter. The guy whose dog Mickey is currently fostering." Lily's voice falters, and she reaches into her pocket for a Kleenex, wiping at her eyes and blowing her nose.

"Oh, Lily," Eileen exclaims. She throws one arm around Lily in a half hug. "You do seem to outdo all of us in the relationship drama department."

"Well," Lily smiles at her, "I guess we all have to excel somewhere."

"How did he die?" Eileen asks.

"I don't know. The state police were called in for a wellness check because Burrow had been barking for an extended time. They found Pete dead." Lily sniffles.

Lily and Eileen continue their stroll in companionable silence. When Boone and Crockett start pulling in the direction of home, Lily and Eileen accept the route.

"The police didn't tell you anything?" Eileen asks.

"No," Lily answers. "This woman came to the shelter. She claimed to be a relative of Pete's and wanted to adopt his dog." Lily gives an involuntary shiver. "I called the state troopers to see if she was legit. All they told me was the case resided in Burlington County."

"Did she adopt him?" Eileen asks.

"Oh boy, there's a story for another walk." Lily glances sideways at Eileen. "I'll give you the Readers Digest version. The dog had a violently aggressive reaction when this woman approached him. Martin told her we absolutely couldn't release him to her. She made a real scene at the shelter."

"Goodness, can she sue the shelter? Do people sue for dog custody?" Eileen involuntarily giggles.

"I'm not too sure what will happen next."

The dogs have now successfully steered them back to the house. Eileen hands over Boone's leash. "Don't forget to water those flowers," she says as she embraces Lily in a hug.

Chapter 24

With mixed emotions, Lily is back on the job at Forever Friends on Wednesday morning. The experiment yesterday at the Thomas Edison school left her elated, and sharing the news of Pete's death with Eileen is helping her cope with the grief. Eileen's comment that Lily was always looking for flaws in men, not giving any of them a chance, distressed her. Lily likes to consider herself selective, not judgmental.

Opening the door to the D-wing, Lily finds Ethel's kennel empty. She pumps both fists in the air then quickly drops her arms to her sides. She's grateful there was no one there to witness her show of celebration. Being mocked for rejoicing about an adoption would only increase her feelings of social awkwardness.

She stops in front of Dylan's kennel. "Okay, Dylan, you are now our veteran guest. Let's give it the extra tail wag today and see what happens." Dylan dutifully wags his tail at her. "Rufus, Hooch, same to you, let's see some enthusiasm." They answer her with hearty barks.

Lily moves on to the C-wing and finds Anna handing out breakfast, "Good morning, Anna. Where's Chelsea?" she asks.

"Good morning, Lily. Our schedules have changed." Anna pulls an empty paper plate from a cage. "Chelsea wants to take a summer class that conflicted with her schedule. She Martin and I worked out some swaps."

"Good for her. I'll be back to help you in a minute," Lily says, and closes the door. She proceeds to the front desk. Ethel's adoption paperwork is on the counter. Lily picks it up to check out Ethel's new family, a couple who came in over the weekend to get acquainted. They came back for her, and they're going to call her Elsa. It seems more of a cat name to Lily, but it will do for a dog, too.

Doc emerges from the medical area. "I'm back from the ultrasounds," he says.

"Ultrasounds, plural?" Lily raises an eyebrow.

"Yes, indeed. I got one for both Caesar and Barkley. Caesar has a thickening of the wall of his colon. It could be a few different things, but given diarrhea, I think he might have IBS." He pauses. "I'm going to try some low dose steroids and see how he responds."

"That's great. Hopefully, the steroids will clear things up, and if we can find a digestible food, we'll know exactly what to tell a potential family. What about Barkley?"

Doc rolls his lips together until they disappear from his face. He blows out his breath. "Barkley's results aren't as optimistic. The reason his leg is bothering him is a rather large mass that's unfortunately both in his leg and his hip. I did a biopsy, and I'm not optimistic. I'm fairly certain it's cancer."

"Oh, Doc," Lily's eyes begin to well. "Can you remove the mass?"

Doc pauses, "Anything is possible, but I'm not certain surgery is a good option. If it's cancer we'll have to assess how far it's spread and develop a prognosis. Two of the other doctors there looked at the ultrasound, and we discussed things. We'll wait for the biopsy results, but you need to prepare yourself. Making Barkley comfortable may be the best we can do."

The front door is thrown wide and Martin bounds in. He looks from Doc to Lily and notices the emotion clouding Lily's face. "Doc, are you making our Lily wilt like a flower without enough water?" he asks.

"I'm guilty as charged." Doc ducks his head like a child who is caught trying to steal a cookie after being told not to touch them. "We've got a fairly sad prognosis for poor Barkley," Doc says.

Martin walks over and gives Lily a sympathetic pat on the shoulder. "I admire your emotional investment, but sometimes things aren't in our control."

"Oh, geez, Martin, the philosopher role doesn't suit you," she chides him. "By the way, when were you planning to tell me about Chelsea's schedule changed?" Feigning anger, Lily puts both hands on her hips.

"There's my cue to retreat to my domain. I'll let you know when I have the biopsy results." Doc heads back to Medical.

"Well," Martin breezily moves to the new subject. "Chelsea wanted to take a summer science class that has a lab on Wednesday afternoons. She was going to try to work here in the morning, go to the lab and then come back, but I thought that would be too hard on her. Besides, Anna is starting to get tired of working all weekend. So Chelsea is now working Sundays and Anna Wednesdays."

"You're a softie under that gruff exterior, Martin. Will Wednesdays work with Anna's school schedule?" Lily knows Anna is in the vet tech program at Camden County.

"Anna is about to finish her last class. She only has a co-op left before she graduates. Anyone with a brain will try to keep her after her co-op is done. Unfortunately." He frowns.

"Let's hope whoever she does her co-op with doesn't have one of those," Lily jokes. "It's so hard to watch them grow up, isn't it? Man, it's too bad that we can't get a co-op. I'm sure Doc would be a great mentor."

"Yes, he would be, and he actually is. He told me Mitchell is thinking about going back for an undergraduate degree."

"Fabulous news," Lily beams. "I guess Doc gives me the bad news and you give me the good news. It's all a balance." Lily raises one hand palm up. Then she raises the other hand palm up. She moves them up and down imitating scales.

"I guess that's it," Martin says. "How'd things go at the school yesterday?"

"Well, I think. Vice Principal Klapper said she'd discuss

things with the teacher and call me." Lily nods but her smile fades. "Right now things at the school are in a bit of upheaval."

"Oh, right. Did you find out anything about the dead girl you and Mickey found?" Martin asks.

"Um, a lot of rumors are floating about. The police haven't said whether the death was accidental or not." Lily gives an involuntary shiver. "It's creepy."

"Creepy is one word to use," Martin agrees. "What's in your hot little hands there?" He nods at the papers that Lily is holding.

"Ethel got adopted."

"All right," Martin says, and holds up his hand for a high five.

Lily hits the high five. "There you go. You're reminding me of the good news that started my day." She smiles. "Now I'd better go back and help Anna." They both enter the staff area, and Lily puts the adoption paperwork for Ethel on her desk. She heads back to the C–wing and finds Anna has finished with the cats. She walks over to the D–wing for some morning dog walking.

Her walking starts with Dylan, a big dog with a lot of energy, listed as part Doberman, part Rottweiler. Their walk turns into a jog through the grounds. After they've run a bit, Dylan does his morning duty and Lily brings him into one of the large play areas for some catch. She understands being kenneled is hard on the dogs. The more exercise they get the less anxious they will be.

Lily waves to a few volunteers who have come in to walk dogs. Lily picks up the ball and wipes the sweat from her forehead, then leashes Dylan back up. "Sorry big guy, I would love to play catch all day, but alas there's other work to get done." Dylan's ears slide back on his head, and he makes his eyes as big and round as possible. "Don't you give me a guilt trip," she admonishes him.

With Dylan returned to his kennel, Lily goes back to the staff area. As she opens the door, Martin and Ingrid instantly fall silent.

"Good morning, Ingrid." Lily pretends not to notice the abrupt end of their conversation. She knows Martin will probably last about…3, 2, 1.

"Lil, Ingrid saw an interesting news story this morning," he starts.

"Really?" Lily nonchalantly sits down in her chair, giving a small shrug of her shoulders.

"She's clearly not interested, Martin." Ingrid mischievously grins, calling Lily's bluff. Tension mounts as each tries to wait the other out. Ten seconds later:

"Tell her anyway. I hate it when she gets all sanctimonious on us," Martin says, shaking his head and pointing his forefinger at Lily.

Ingrid and Lily shift their gazes to each other and try not to laugh. While people, especially men, always complain women are the gossips, Martin beats both Lily and Ingrid in craving gossip.

"There was a story on the news today about a suspicious death," Ingrid starts.

Lily flinches. "Ingrid, I've already had bad news from Doc this morning. I worked it off jogging with Dylan. Are you going to make me have to jog with another dog?" She makes an exaggerated unhappy face.

"Well, you know I had to listen to it." Ingrid is trying to decide whether to continue. She decides to go on. "The Readers Digest version is--it's about Pete and Burrow. The reporter didn't name them. They did a story about a suspicious death, blah blah blah."

"Were there any theories?" Lily leans in towards Ingrid. Despite not wanting lousy news, she pines for explanations.

"They didn't elaborate." Ingrid shrugs.

"Well, why was it even newsworthy?" Lily asks with a hint of disappointment in her voice.

"Apparently, Pete was involved in some business to benefit disabled soldiers. For the media, this is another 'America doesn't take care of veterans' stories, I guess." Ingrid shrugs again. "That's actually what Martin and I were discussing. We want to know why the media is now interested in the story."

"I do hope we find out what happened to him. He was a good guy," Lily says, and then turns to her computer. She inwardly chastises herself for showing interest. She doesn't want to go down this road with them.

"Me, too," Ingrid says. She stands up from her chair. "Now I've got some dogs to get to know better." She leaves the staff area. Lily silently thanks her for realizing it was time to move on to something else.

CHAPTER **25**

Quinn stands in front of his locker, staring at the books on the shelves. All around him teenagers are talking about dates and movies. Locker doors clang shut as people leave for the day. Girls twirl their hair around their fingers absentmindedly, while whispering the latest post-prom gossip. The seniors are all discussing their summer jobs and plans for college. A hand slaps Quinn on the back.

"Q, did ya fall asleep standing up, or what?" A boy with frizzy blonde hair leans his shoulder on the adjacent locker.

"Funny, Coop." Quinn shifts his gaze to his friend. "Dreadin' the trig I know I need to do tonight." Quinn pulls a large book off the top shelf of his locker and drops it into the book bag at his feet. He zips the bag and tosses it over his left shoulder.

"All work, no play, Q, it'll make you dull, you know? Come watch the Hawks take on Haddonfield with me." Cooper stands up straight and mimics swinging a baseball bat. He pulls the ponytail of a girl walking by in a mini skirt. "Hey, Alice, looking good," he says with a wink.

Alice turns her head and giggles, "Uh, thanks, Cooper." Her friends scowl at Cooper, before they all pivot and continue down the hallway in a flurry of whispers.

"Think I made her day?" Cooper asks, with a tone of nonchalance. "C'mon, ball game?"

"I don't know, Coop. I've got a test Friday. If I don't get a B in trig my dad's sending me back to tutoring." Quinn's expression is neither frown nor smile.

"Q, you've been like a zombie the last two days. A little cheering for the school team will give ya energy. C'mon." Cooper pulls a baseball hat from his back pocket and jams it on his head. Reaching over Quinn's head, Cooper gives Quinn's locker door a quick push, slamming it shut.

Quinn looks at the closed door, then back at his friend. "You're a jerk, Coop. I wasn't finished in there."

"You're finished, my friend," Cooper says, swaggering down the hallway and flipping his phone out of his back pocket to send text messages while he's walking. Cooper glances over his shoulder and finds Quinn shuffling behind him. He reads and responds to a few more messages.

When Cooper reaches the exit, he backs against the door, holding it open for Quinn. Quinn squints into the sunlight, putting his hand over his eyes. "You pushed my locker door shut before I could get my hat," he complains.

"We can sit in the shade, instead of on the bleachers. Keep moving," Cooper says, releasing the door. As they saunter towards the baseball field, Cooper says, "Look at this." He hands his phone to Quinn.

Quinn laughs, "I think she's jealous." He hands the phone back. The sound of running feet gets gradually louder behind the boys. A sweaty teen draws up next to Quinn.

"Coop, I heard you pulled Alice's hair? What's that, a second-grade stunt?" Declan's got a baseball in his right hand that he's tossing in the air and catching as he walks.

Cooper laughs. "Just teasin' her. Alice is cool. That group she hangs with though…"

"Guys goin' to the game?" Declan asks.

"Yeah, come along." Cooper gives Declan a thumbs up behind Quinn's back.

Quinn sighs.

"Q forgot his hat though, so we're not sitting in the bleachers."

"Shade's good." Declan shrugs. They continue in silence as classmates zip by on bicycles, and a group of cross country runners jogs past. Tossing the ball, Declan asks, "Did you guys watch "Stranger Things"?"

"Oh, yeah, it was freaky," Cooper says. "Q?"

"Nope."

"Seriously, Q? I'm lucky. My Dad loves that stuff, so we watched it in the family room on the big TV," Declan exclaims.

"Haven't been interested in TV," Quinn mumbles.

They reach the baseball field and find a spot in the shade with a good view of the diamond. The game is already in progress, but no score yet. They watch Haddon Township's pitcher strike out two batters and clap for him. The next batter flies out to right field. The teams change sides. The first Haddon Township batter gets a single. The second hits a shot right to the center fielder. The third batter enters the box. The pitcher throws ball one, then a hard fastball right over the plate.

"Shit, that sucker had to be 90 miles an hour," Declan says. He's lying on his back in the grass, propped up on his elbows.

"He hits that, it'll go to Westmont," Cooper chuckles. He's got his legs stretched out in front of him and faux swings a bat with his arms. Quinn sits cross-legged between the two. He picks at the frayed hem of his jeans, then looks into the distance as the jangle of the Mister Softie truck is heard warbling down the street.

The pitcher throws another ball, then a slider. The batter swings hard, misses, earning a strike. Fans in the stands are calling to the batter, giving him encouragement.

The batter hits two balls hard, both foul. Declan shifts from side to side with anticipation. The pitcher winds up, throws, and the batter hits the ball straight to the shortstop. The shortstop flips the ball to the second baseman, who tags the base and flips the ball to the first baseman a second before the batter's foot touches down.

"Oh, damn, a six-four-three double play," Declan groans. He lets his elbows out so that he falls to his back in the grass, his arms forming an extended "T". "Say it ain't so."

"It's only the fourth inning. Give it time," Cooper advises, throwing a handful of grass at his friend.

Returning to a reclined position and sharing a nod with Cooper, Declan continues, "So, uh, speaking of time…"

Quinn stares vacantly at the field. The sides have changed over, and Haddon Township is back in the field. The pitcher throws a strike. The crowd claps. The pitcher throws the next pitch, and the batter only taps the ball. It rolls halfway to the pitcher's mound as the batter races towards first. The catcher jumps up, grabs the ball and hurls it to the first baseman. The ball is thrown so hard it pushes the first baseman off the base. He jumps on the base as the batter is about to tag. The crowd cheers the first baseman. Cooper and Quinn clap and cheer along. The Mister Softie truck arrives. Fans leave the bleachers to line up.

Declan grunts, "I could go for a cone." He looks at Cooper who makes no move to stand. "How long d'ya think it'll take the cops to figure out what happened to Eva?" Declan asks.

Quinn shrugs, not making eye contact with either boy.

"It's gotta have something to do with her mom, right?" Cooper asks.

"Gotta." Quinn shrugs his shoulders. "So, this's why you wanted to come out here, huh?" Quinn asks with a sigh. The next batter has stepped into the box. He shifts his weight onto his back leg and flexes his hands on the bat's pine-tarred handle.

"You can't keep it all bottled up, dude," Cooper says. The pitcher releases a fastball in the middle of the strike zone. The batter connects, drilling a shot into center field. The Haddon Township fielder shades his eyes with his non-gloved hand then steps right under the ball and catches it. The next batter strikes out on three pitches. The teams change sides again.

Quinn sighs, "All right, but keep your mouths shut." He looks pointedly from Cooper to Declan. Both nod their heads. "I'm serious. I see it on social media, and I'm never talkin' to either of you again."

Chapter 26

"We get it, Q," Cooper says, putting his hand onto Quinn's shoulder.

Shouts erupt from the stands, and the boys turn back to the game. Haddon Township has hit a home run. There was a runner on first, so Haddon Township is up two to nothing. Declan and Cooper slap hands in a high five, then keep their hands up until Quinn hits each of them.

"Coop, I see Alice in the Mister Softie line," Declan says with a wink.

"Shut up and let Q talk." Cooper pierces Declan with a glare. "Go on, Q."

Quinn looks down into his lap. Then looks in the direction of the baseball game, "About a month ago, Eva was riding her bike home from visiting her mom. This car cut her off, made her fall off the bike." He pauses, lets out a laugh. "You know Eva? She jumped up, ready to curse the guy out. There were two guys in the car. They were out of it faster than it took Eva to get up." Quinn digs his hands into the grass.

"The one guy says, 'Shut up. We're here to talk about your mother.' They crowded into Eva. They told her that her Mom had been sellin' to support her habit. Apparently, her mom was using more than she sold." Quinn clenches his jaws.

"Like what, more than she was getting paid for bagging groceries at Shop Rite?" Declan scoffs.

"Exactly, only no one gets addicted to broccoli," Quinn says. "Eva's mom was in a losing situation. She dug herself into a hole." He clenches his fists, pulling out two tufts of grass. He opens his hands letting the grass fall to the ground. He rubs the remaining grass off his hands onto his jeans.

There's a collective groan from the stands. The boys shift their attention to the field to see the teams changing sides again. Haddonfield is up to bat. The first batter drills the ball right between first and second base. He's a good runner and makes it to first while the throw from the right fielder to the cutoff man is still in the air. The second batter comes to the plate. He hits a looper into left field. The ball seems suspended in the air. The fielder misjudges the trajectory and the ball drops to the grass. Both runners are safe, and runners are now on first and second base. The catcher walks out to the mound to have a chat with his pitcher.

"So, okay, but they expected Eva to take over and sell what her mom wasn't sellin'?" Cooper asks, squinting with disbelief.

"These weren't men to negotiate with. They basically told Eva, sell pills and pay back your mother's debt, or else."

"Or else…?" Cooper asks.

"Yeah, or else what?" Declan echoes.

"You two stupid, or what?" Quinn says incredulously. "They threatened her, said they'd make sure the house burned down, kill her grandma, all sorts of shit." He shakes his head in frustration, clenching his fists and banging the left fist on top of the right.

Cheers erupt from the bleachers; the pitcher struck out the batter. The next batter steps into the box, hits two foul balls, then strikes out on a fastball. Cheers for the pitcher get louder. The catcher flips the pitcher a thumbs up, and the next batter steps to the plate. The pitcher throws a fastball that goes outside for a ball. The catcher takes his time throwing the ball back. The pitcher looks at the ball as if studying the stitching. His mouth moves in silent admonition. He takes his stance, winds up and guns a shot in middle of the strike zone. The bat connects with a loud crack. The ball is hit right to the center fielder, and the inning is over. The Haddon Township fans erupt in applause. As the teams change sides, the catcher gives the pitcher a slap on the back.

Quinn continues, "For a week she ran outta school, and didn't wait for me to ride home with. She wouldn't talk to me. A week later I rode to her house after school and sat there until she came home."

"I bet that went well," Cooper smirks sarcastically.

"Like waiting for a cobra in its nest?" Declan asks.

Quinn blows out a breath, "A cobra might've been safer." He laughs, then sniffs as he remembers he'll never see Eva again. "I tried to get 'er to talk to someone, but she wouldn't. She was scared."

"Damn, man, Eva stopped talkin' to me, too. I figured she was pissed at the world and gave her space." Cooper looks down, hunches his shoulders up around his ears, dropping them with a loud expulsion of breath. "Shit, why didn't I try harder?"

Haddon Township's pitcher goes down swinging. The first baseman steps into the box, and hits the first pitch into the outfield. The left fielder makes a running catch for the out. Haddonfield's third baseman comes to the plate and hits the first pitch directly to Haddon Township's right fielder. The teams change sides again.

"She wouldn't have told you. She only told me because I threatened to stay on the porch until her grandma came home." Quinn laughs again. "Thought I might be there with two black eyes when her grandma came home." Quinn ducks his head and raises his right shoulder to rub his nose on his T-shirt.

"Damn, you kept this to yourself. How long?" Cooper asks.

"I haven't known for too long. After a few days, I talked to my brother about it. I thought he might, I don't know, know somethin' that would help her." Quinn shrugs.

"Shit, like what, buy her green supply for the band?" Declan asks. He sits up in a cross-legged position and starts tossing the baseball in the air again.

On the field, the Haddon Township pitcher has struck out two batters. The current batter takes a ferocious swing at a baseball, and it flies over the outfielders, home run. A few fans call encouragement to the pitcher. As the next batter approaches, the pitcher studies the ball again and silently mouths something. He eyes the batter, and at a nod from the catcher, throws another fastball. He follows with two sliders, striking out the batter.

"I didn't know what he could do. I figured he'd know more than I would." Quinn scowls at his friend.

Declan continues throwing the baseball into the air and catching it.

"And, what—" Cooper starts.

"I know he asked around a bit, but other than tellin' me he 'scoped out her turf' he didn't tell me much," Quinn says.

The current Haddon Township batter slams the ball into the right field gap. It's a ground rule double, as the ball clears the fence on one bounce. The Haddon Township center fielder comes to the plate to the cheers of the crowd. He hit the first home run, and they call for him to repeat. He takes two pitches for balls. He studies the pitcher with a steely gaze. The pitcher throws a third called ball, causing hushed anticipation from the crowd. They know the next pitch will have to be a strike. Haddonfield won't want two runners on base. The pitcher must throw a strike. The pitcher winds up and throws a wild pitch that blows feet away from the catcher. The runner on second advances to third on the ball four wild pitch. The batter casually jogs to first base, uninterested in trying for an extra base. On his way, he waves to the girls who are leaning against the fence salaciously licking ice cream cones.

The Haddon Township catcher moves into the batters' box. After the pitcher throws another ball, the Haddonfield catcher holds up his glove to call time out, then strolls to the mound.

"D'ya tell the cops this when you met with them?" Cooper asks.

"Yeah, "Quinn sighs.

"Now, I get their questions," Cooper says.

Quinn squints his eyes, shaking his head.

"Cops were asking me things about Eva that didn't make sense to me. 'Was she doing drugs? Was she involved in selling drugs?' They went on and on. I thought they were trying to make Eva out as some bad girl. Now I get it," Cooper repeats.

The Haddonfield catcher returns to his position. The pitcher winds up, throws a screaming fastball. The Haddon Township batter connects. The ball blows past the shortstop into left field. The runner on third base easily scores. The Haddon Township pitcher comes to the plate amidst calls of support from the fans. They know that a hit here could seal the game. He connects with the first pitch, but the ball isn't hit hard. It dribbles to the pitcher who throws the runner out at first.

There are a few cheers from the stands for advancing the runners. The pitcher walks the next batter to load the bases and create a force out at every base.

"Me, too, I got the same questions. I made a crack about how she'd make a mint selling steroids to the jocks," Declan snorts.

"How'd that work out for ya?" Cooper asks.

"Backfired big time, I got a shit load of questions about who's using drugs in this school, in other schools, yadda, yadda," Declan says.

"Serves you right, butthead, back-talking the police," Quinn says.

"Seriously D, you can be a butthead," Cooper agrees.

"It was a joke," Declan says, getting defensive.

"Yeah, well, when a girl's dead, police aren't interested in jokin'," Quinn snarls.

There are screams from the bleachers, and the boys look up to see a grand slam sail over the heads of the fielders. Cooper and Declan jump up to join the cheering. They sit back down, cross-legged, on either side of Quinn.

So?" Declan leans in towards Quinn, "Whadda ya think happened? Did she stand up to those two, or what?"

"I don't know. I doubt it. Eva was rattled. It was probably a dealer tryin' to shake her down. I don't know. I tried to convince her to let me at least be around, ya know, in case someone started something with her." Quinn sighs.

"Uh, dude, what was your plan? Ride your bike for help?" Cooper teases.

Quinn holds up his middle finger. He lets his hand drop into his lap. "That's exactly what Eva said."

Declan snorts out a laugh. Quinn gives him a scowl. "I'm sorry, man. Eva was one tough chick. I never messed with her. These guys must've been something to scare her."

"I know," Quinn says.

"And…?" Cooper says.

"I told the police on Monday what little I knew about the men, which wasn't helpful to them at all. They acted like I'd given them the key to open the mystery box, but I know I didn't help at all."

Haddonfield is coming up to for their last at bat. The grand slam has given the Haddon Township pitcher new confidence. He swaggers to the mound. He quickly strikes out the first two batters, but the third and fourth batters get singles, removing a bit of the pitcher's swagger. After a signal from the catcher, the pitcher pauses. He winds up and throws strike one. He winds up and throws strike two. On the third pitch, the batter connects for a double. There's collective disappointment from the bleachers.

"What did Eva tell you?" Cooper asks.

"What the car looked like and a general description of the men that fits half the men in South Jersey. Damn it." Quinn pounds his fists together, then bounces the left one on the right one several times.

The crowd claps in unison. Haddon Township has won. Forming two lines, the teams walk by each other slapping hands. People are climbing down from the bleachers. Alice waves her friends away and casually leans back against the first base line fence, watching the three boys in the shade.

Declan leans back on to his elbows, "I wonder if we'll ever know the truth."

"Won't matter," Quinn says. "It won't bring her back."

Chapter 27

Lily leaves the shelter for the day, pondering the news story that Ingrid heard. Pete had told her he and some pals were going to form a partnership. All of them were ex-military, some retired and others discharged after suffering career-ending injuries. Pete was an only child and referred to these fellow soldiers as brothers. Having siblings of her own, it is difficult for Lily to understand Pete's bond with fellow soldiers. She would have embraced the opportunity to delve into the subject. Alas, that opportunity has passed.

"Excuse me. You're Lily, right?" Lily is shaken from her reverie. She turns to see a woman wearing navy blue scrubs. Her hair is pulled into a knot at the base of her neck and several sweaty tendrils are plastered to her face. Lily pauses, trying to recall who the woman is.

"We met Monday. I'm Clarissa… Pete's cousin." The woman stutters out. She sways a bit on her feet as if she might faint.

"Of course, thank you for reminding me. I meet a lot of people in my job. Sometimes my brain needs a hint or two to recall everyone's name," Lily explains, polite but leery.

Clarissa shifts her weight from one foot to the other. "They didn't let me adopt Burrow on Monday. I… Well, I'd like to have another try. Maybe we could meet somewhere less formal, like maybe that woman's house." Her voice quivers. She turns her gaze to the ground six inches in front of Lily's feet. "I know I was incredibly emotional Monday. I'd just found out Pete was dead. His dog… should be with family."

Lily's spine stiffens against the implied request to forgo rules. A strict adherence to regulations and guidelines is ingrained in her personality. When people suggest circumventing rules she becomes suspicious. She pauses before answering, recalling Martin's admonition to be as good with people as she is with animals. "Clarissa, we never allow potential adopters to know the addresses of foster families. It's part of the agreement we have with people who accept the responsibility of foster care. We respect their privacy and do not compromise it."

"Okay, I get it, but maybe we could meet in a park." Clarissa's voice has trailed off and her gaze hasn't left the ground in front of Lily's feet.

"No, Clarissa, we only hold dog meets on the grounds of the shelter. We follow a rigid safety protocol. Her pity for the woman is heading to annoyance. She's been in the tepid air of the shelter for ten hours, and she wants to shower and relax.

"I… I want Burrow to be with family. I don't want strangers having him. It's not fair." Clarissa kicks at the gravel of the parking lot.

"Clarissa, I'm sympathetic to the grief you're feeling for the loss of your cousin. If we don't follow regulations the shelter will be shut down. Think of the animals that will be killed if they're not able to come here until they're adopted." Lily pauses allowing her words to take effect. She casually glances at her watch. "It's too late today to try and set something up. Besides, we need to find out why Burrow reacted in the way he did."

"I think I was just too emotional, from learning about Pete being dead. I've been to Pete's house with the dog roaming free, no leash, nothing. He's fine with me." Clarissa has taken on a pleading tone.

"Give us some time to figure out Burrow's reaction. I assure you he's being treated very well at the foster family's house. I've interacted with him outside of the shelter."

Clarissa's gaze locks on to Lily's, "So, you go there to see him?"

"That's part of my job. I have to assess whether an animal in a foster situation is receiving proper care." Lily measures her words with painstaking rigor. "Give us a call next week after we've had time to work with Burrow and we can try another meet."

"Sure, okay, thanks," Clarissa stutters out. Her gaze seems calculating. She backs towards an incredibly dusty and dented car. "I'll call you."

Lily gets in her car, turns on the air conditioning, and moves the vents to blow directly on her sweaty body. She has sympathy for the woman, but she also has her protocols to follow. She makes a mental note to discuss things with Ingrid and Martin. Putting her car into gear, she pulls out of the Forever Friends lot. Clarissa remains parked.

As she pulls into her driveway, Lily spots Boone looking out the front window and forces all thoughts of work from her mind. Boone's ears lift. His eyes go bright. Lily leaves her car and walks up the front steps. She opens her door and Boone meanders to her. She kneels so he can give her a faceful of licks. Lily pulls back, ruffling his ears. "Well, Boone, my friend, it's good to see you, too. Where's your buddy?"

He gives her a perplexed look that says, "Buddy? What buddy?"

"Where's our boy, Crockett?" His ears fall around his cheeks and the brightness dims from his eyes. "Boone, you know you're my favorite. Isn't that enough?" She scratches his ears again. Mickey is always telling her not to talk baby talk to animals. Lily scoffs at her, knowing Boone and Crockett are not children. When the dogs are by themselves, she can't imagine Boone snickering to Crockett, "Mommy loves me more than you. She said so." Although, given how Boone feels about Crockett, anything is possible.

Lily walks through the house, and looks out the back window to see Tyler playing catch with Crockett. Grabbing a glass and filling it at the sink, she returns to the front stoop where she pours half the water on each of the plants Kelly gave her. She thinks, "If I can remember to do this every day, I might keep these alive after all."

She walks back through the house with Boone on her heels. She puts the glass into the sink, then continues to the back door.

"Hello," she calls, opening the back door and stepping outside. Crockett bounds over, his tail wagging as fast as a propeller blade on a helicopter about to take flight. "Hi, Crockett." Lily bends down, receiving licks while scratching his back. Sniffing the air, she asks Tyler, "Did you cut the grass?"

"Yeah, I couldn't find the tennis balls any longer," he says sarcastically.

"Awesome, it had gotten a bit high." Lily smiles at him. "Well, let's take advantage of your motivation. Would you want to light the grill while I walk the boys?"

"Sure. I've got burgers upstairs from my Saturday night BBQ if you're in the mood for those."

"To quote you, my brother, if you're cooking it, I'm eating it. It's been a tough day. Let me walk the boys. When I get back, I'll mix up some salad." Lily brightens. She can check a chore from her list of things to get done.

"Right," he says, "hopefully I didn't wear Crockett out."

Lily laughs at the thought of Crockett being tired. Crockett doesn't have an off button; he is always ready to go.

Lily goes back into the house, Crockett following her. She grabs the leashes and some plastic bags. As they walk into the living room, Boone's face becomes an exaggerated frown. Lily stifles a laugh. She wonders, "Is this the same dog who was just lit up like a lamp post?" She attaches the leashes to their collars, and they head out. About five feet from the door, Boone nearly floods the lawn.

"Gee whiz, Boone, how much water did you have today?" Lily heads towards an intramural league playing field where Boone and Crockett can get in some uninterrupted walking amidst various animal essences in the trees and brush near the homes on the far side of the area.

The field has football goalposts at each end. In front of the posts are large nets used for soccer. In these small towns, sports fields serve many purposes. Since school is still in session, the grass is neatly trimmed. Along the long sides of the area are four sets of three-row metal bleachers. There are trash cans and recycling containers at the ends of the bleachers. The trash cans are handy for dropping off dog waste.

Lily and the boys walk along the near edge of the field towards the trees. Boone spies a rabbit and starts to canter in its direction. Crockett starts barking, and the rabbit scampers off before they get anywhere close. Boone fixes Crockett with a frown. Lily stifles another giggle, thinking this is the look she and Ivy shared when Iris wanted to tag along with them.

They complete two loops around the field. Lily's eyes begin to itch, alerting her to a rising pollen count, so she steers the boys towards home. She feels a bit guilty for the shorter than usual walk, but rationalizes Crockett got his exercise with Tyler. After dinner, she and Boone can take another jaunt.

Back at the house Boone and Crockett each get a bowl of kibble. Lily rinses their water dishes, refilling them with fresh water. Sniffing, she inhales the scent of fat hitting hot charcoal. The scent lures Boone. When the kibble is finished he heads for the back door, whiskers twitching. Lily opens the door to let both boys out to keep Tyler company.

CHAPTER 28

Lily washes and chops Spring Mix and cucumbers, splitting them into two salad bowls. Placing a fork in each dish, Lily cradles them between her left arm and her torso. Grabbing some napkins with her left hand and dressing with her right, she uses her hip to open the back door. Boone and Crockett intercept Lily, attempting to cause a spill. Navigating eight paws and two wagging tails she reaches the folding card table without incident. Tyler has placed a growler on the table, along with two hamburger buns and two bags of barbecue-flavor potato chips. A frosty mug sits on the table in front of each folding chair.

"Gosh, those things have sure come in handy," Lily says, using her chin to point. She purchased the mugs in a boutique liquor store as the perfect Christmas present for Tyler. The mugs have liquid between two planes of plastic. They keep contents cold and they don't shatter in Tyler's freezer, where they seem to permanently reside.

"So, are we eating caveman style, or should I bring us a few plates?" she teases, as she sets the items she was carrying on the table.

"If you want a plate, you can get one," he teases back. "I brought the mugs." He uses a large spatula to turn the burgers over.

"And I'm grateful. Be right back." She returns to the house, grabs two plastic plates, and opens the refrigerator to collect ketchup and cheese before returning outside. Placing everything on the table, Lily pops the lid on the growler.

"What have we here?" Lily asks, not caring what brand of beer. It is cold, it is alcohol, and it will be perfect.

"That's the latest from Lunacy. I think it's Lunar Solstice Lager, or some such crazy name. It's pretty tasty and about eight percent," Tyler grins. New Jersey has seen a rise in the development of microbreweries. In a state with antiquated liquor license laws, dating back to prohibition, people have found a loophole. Microbreweries can sell beer made on the premises, as long as they don't sell food. People can either buy food at area restaurants to consume at the microbrewery or buy growlers of beer to drink at local BYOB restaurants. The rise of microbreweries has benefited many businesses and downtown shopping areas.

"Well, I'm sure I'll love it. How was your day?" Lily takes a seat, and pours beer into one of the frosty mugs, and takes a long swallow.

"Pretty good, I had a few client meetings, so I actually had to put on long pants." Tyler smirks. "I changed the website a bit for my realtor client in Haddon Township. Now you can get a virtual tour of houses right on the site. I also put in some sections where people can submit comments or ask questions, but they don't appear on the site so there's confidentiality and the site stays clean." He picks up a roll, slides in a burger, and hands it to Lily. Then he picks up the second roll, adds a burger, and sits down on the other chair. Boone and Crockett each lie down in the grass. They feign disinterest but let a piece of burger fall to the ground and they will be on it in seconds.

"You know, both clients today were talking about the dead high school girl," Tyler continues, after a bite of burger. "Did you know there's a staff person who's accused of buying drugs from her? Seriously, can you imagine selling drugs to one of your teachers?" He starts to chuckle.

"Okay, first, no I can't imagine selling drugs, period. Second, Eileen told me there were rumors that staff bought drugs from her, but as of last night nothing's been made public." Lily pauses and tilts her head a bit, knowing she sounded like an adult lecturing a child.

"Hey Lil, have more beer. You're wound too tight," Tyler snickers. He lifts the bun on his burger to squirt on more ketchup. Then he pulls a few pieces of lettuce from the salad bowl and places them on top of the ketchup. "This is a weird way to serve burger toppings, you know?" He takes a bite, follows it with a swig of beer.

"Well, my brother, that's what's called a salad," Lily mocks him. She tells him about Barkley, the news story Ingrid heard, pantomimes Martin relaying the gossip.

"You know, I feel bad for Martin. That guy needs to hire some men to work there. You women are merciless," Tyler laughs.

"Oh, believe me, he dishes it out as much as he takes it," Lily says. "He likes to act all authoritarian. He's a big teddy bear, with no filter between his brain and his mouth."

Tyler almost chokes on his bite of burger.

"You know, I have to watch for a Memorial Day sale and get us a real outdoor table," Lily muses.

"So you can make me move it every time the grass needs to be cut?" Tyler asks with a raised eyebrow.

"Mmm, no, I was thinking of making you build a deck onto the back of the house," Lily teases him.

"I know you're joking, but a deck. A deck would be awesome." Tyler has sat up straighter. "We could get some cool tiki torches. Oh, and we could put an awning up to keep the sun off in the middle of summer."

"Tyler, with your friends, it's either an awning or tiki torches, not both. I can't afford the fire insurance." Lily pours another sip of beer.

"I would act offended by that remark, except I know it's true." Tyler shakes his head. He sits back patting his stomach. "That hit the spot."

Lily leans back as well. "It sure did. That was tasty beer." She folds her hands, resting them in her lap.

They sit in silence for a while. As the sun starts to fade, Lily finally stands up. "I'd like to give Boone a bit more of a walk. Would you distract Crockett for a bit?

Tyler stands. He saunters to the tennis ball lying in the grass. This sufficiently distracts Crockett.

Grabbing up the empty plates and bowls, Lily heads to the house with Boone on her heels. Lily sees that Boone's water bowl is empty and refills it after she sets the dishes down. He greedily drinks it all.

"Watching us eat worked up a thirst, huh?" Lily asks him. "Let's take a walk, just you and me, okay?"

As he saunters to the front door, Boone's ears lift higher on his head. Grabbing another plastic bag, Lily follows him. They walk a few blocks through the neighborhood, listening to the sounds of children at play in the yards they pass. At a few houses, people sit on porches. Everyone waves to Lily as she and Boone pass by. Lily breezily returns the waves.

When they get back, Lily notices the flowers from Kelly are still wilted. "I'd better put some more water on those," she says, as if making conversation with Boone. Ignoring her, he climbs the three steps to the front door. Lily unlocks the door and holds it open for Boone.

When the inner door swings wide, there's Crockett sitting just beyond its arc. He stands and furiously wags his tail. "Hi, Crockett. Did you play catch with Tyler?" She smiles at him. Boone walks past him, heading for the kitchen. Lily closes the front door, hanging Boone's leash and her keys on the rack by the door. Crockett scampers after her, as she walks towards the kitchen.

Boone appears to have taken root, staring at the cabinet in which the dog treats are kept. While washing and drying her hands, Lily realizes that Tyler has put all the dinner dishes into the dishwasher. Removing a bag of Beggin' Strips from the cabinet, she tears it open and gives half a strip to each dog.

She fills a glass with water, retraces her path through the

house, and stands outside to pour half a glass of water on each plant. She repeats this process, thinking each plant probably needs a whole glass and reminding herself to get a watering can the next time she is in Target or Walmart. She closes and locks both doors. Boone has curled into a ball on one end of the couch, snoring loudly. Crockett is sitting on the floor following her movements.

"Okay, my friend, time for my shower." She scratches Crockett's ears. He goes over to the recliner and hops up, settling himself. Lily heads to the bathroom for a cooling shower.

CHAPTER 29

It is Thursday morning at Mickey's home, Nero keeps trying to get Burrow to open up.

Boy, I got one big drink of water in the kitchen. I checked the whole floor for any treats left as a surprise for me. There was nothing. Mom is out doing her rounds, walking other dogs, and feeding cats. It's okay. I don't get jealous. I like giving her an up and down sniffing when she comes home. My new friend Burrow has been brooding and moody since the other night.

Typically when Mom leaves with a dog, they have found their family and are off to their new homes. Instead, she brought this one back. He's unapproachable with a capital UN. I see he's looking out the window. I think I'll wander over and try to get him talking.

"Yo, Burrow, anything good passing by the window?"

I jump onto the couch and sit down next to him.

"A few scrawny squirrels running across the porch. They weren't even worth the effort to work up a growl," Burrow mumbles.

"No cats? I swear they come by to irritate me," I let my tongue hang out, giving him a wide grin.

"Nope. I could go for a good cat chase, too."

"So, are you ever going to tell me what happened the other night?" I decide to be direct. I've never met a dude who's so hard to get information from.

"Are you going to keep nagging me until I tell you?" Burrow gives me that piercing glare, that is a mark of his breed. "I'm not trying to be a jerk. I know you're trying to help." He blows out a breath. "There was this woman who used to come over to Pete's house. One of those humans you instinctively know not to trust. You know what I mean?" He glances my way.

"Oh, yeah… But honestly, I don't know. I guess I'm lucky. All of the humans I've met are good." I've heard about bad ones, but I've been lucky enough not to meet them.

"Well, there was something about her. I could tell Pete didn't particularly like her. She always seemed to want something from him. She would come in all nice, but she never gave me a hand to sniff, never scratched my ears." Burrow pauses, pretending to focus on something outside. I can tell he's thinking. The hair above his eyes keeps flipping up and down, as if the hairs on his head are powered by brain activity. "Even though Pete didn't seem to like her, I was never allowed to growl at her." He gives me a rueful glance.

"The last time I saw her, it was the same thing. She put on this fake niceness, forced smiles, but wouldn't come near me. Then she said something about money. Pete got angry. His voice got loud, and his body stiffened. You know how humans sometimes are like tree trunks? Like a cat could climb them? I'm not sure what they were discussing. She kept saying something about Pete's parents." He tilts his head to one side, looking thoughtful. "It was a rare time I saw Pete get angry. He yelled something at her like 'Burrow is the inheritance.' I didn't understand. Then she went to the bathroom. She was in there for as long as a three mile jog."

Burrow rests his muzzle on the windowsill. It seems like forever until he finally picks his head back up. "When she came out of the bathroom, she said something about 'that dumb dog isn't family.' I don't know what she meant. However, being the only dog present, I knew who she was referring to with that 'dumb dog' comment."

"So, she's one of those?" I ask. Some humans don't think us

dogs are smart. I give a little growl. We dogs love our humans, but we are loyal to our canine pack.

"Right. I knew she didn't like me," Burrow continues. "I didn't much like her."

He pauses again. His gaze is intense. I sure hope no one tries to break in while he's living with us. There's this human expression that describes it perfectly: "Pity the fool." Seriously, some dogs you know are all bark. This Burrow, ah, nope, I'd not want to be on his bad side.

Burrow turns to face me continues his tale. "When I saw her pretending to be nice, pretending to like me, I lost it." He shakes his big head as if trying to dislodge some ear mites. "I still wonder if she put something in Pete's medicine to make him sick."

"What'cha mean?" I ask.

"Pete got these headaches. He would often be in a bed a whole day with them. Sometimes I didn't get a walk on those days. He'd let me out in the yard, but no walking." He frowns. "The last time Pete had a headache, something was different. He took the medicine the way he usually did, but it made him sicker. Pete could barely stand, had to crawl to the bathroom for more tablets. I tried to keep him in bed, herd him away from the bathroom. He shouted at me, even pushed me away."

"And…?" I ask.

"And I backed away. Pete'd never been angry with me. He'd use that stern, command voice, those humans use when they want to assert themselves, but never yelled at me. I let him take more pills, and then I laid down on the bed with him." Burrow turns his head away. I stay silent, giving him space. This is the most the dude has shared since he's been here.

After a bit, Burrow turns towards me. "This other guy, Jim, he lived with us for a bit. When Pete was sick, Jim took me for walks."

"Where'd he go? Wasn't he there when Pete was sick?" I ask, this being the first time Burrow's mentioned Jim.

"I don't know. I wish Jim had been there that night. I howled and howled for a human to come. By the time one did, it was too late. Pete was dead." Burrow makes a grumbling sound from his throat, as if he accidentally ate one of those bones from a chicken. Those suckers break into bits quickly. Next thing you know they're stabbing you in the throat.

Burrow continues, "If Jim came to fetch me, I'd live with him, but no way I was leaving here to go with her."

"Oh, well, I can definitely understand you not wanting to leave this house." I grin 'cause I've got Mom wrapped around my paw. "Hey, look whose car is pulling up." I start my customary welcoming barks because I see Mom's car.

"Yeah, you definitely rule the roost here." He is smiling like he means I'm not in charge. But I run this place.

Chapter 30

On the way to Forever Friends, Lily has an odd feeling. She thinks a familiar old and dilapidated car is traveling behind her. Once on the job, the thought is forgotten as the morning tasks are completed. She and Ingrid transfer a transport of ten dogs from the St. Hubert's van into kennels.

"We are packed to the rafters in here now." Ingrid swipes at a trickle of sweat on her forehead with the towel she is holding.

Lily lets out a laugh. Reaching over, she wipes dog hair from Ingrid's face. "You need to remember to use the side of the towel that didn't touch the dog."

"Phew, that's why I have my hair in a braid," Ingrid chuckles, pointing to it. "If I did the ponytail thing like you and Chelsea, my head would be like a Swiffer cloth."

"I'm convinced Chelsea is impervious to anything resembling dirt." Lily wipes her hands on her jeans. Leaving the D-Wing, they hear Martin using his instructive tone. They come out of the hallway to find the new guy behind the front desk, sandwiched between Martin and Angelo. There is a four-foot-high counter right inside the front door where potential adoptive families can get information, pick up adoption forms, and talk to staff.

"Ah, and here's the true backbone of the organization," Martin beams. "Lily, Ingrid, this is Larry." He gestures with his hand. The three exchange handshakes. Larry is about twenty, tall and thin, sporting close-cropped blonde hair and a goatee.

"Ingrid is our Animal Behaviorist and Lily our Adoption Coordinator. Larry's going to be on ten to eight Thursday through Sunday." Larry nonchalantly shrugs.

"We call it the trial by fire start." Ingrid winks and Larry smirks. "Don't worry," Ingrid continues, "I'm coming in Saturday morning, and Chelsea works Sunday. Also, on the weekends we get a host of volunteers. You'll get relieved when there are fewer people." She gives a wide smile. "Make sure you wear your steel-tipped shoes. It gets crowded behind that desk."

"Oh, yeah, you'll truly enjoy working with Chelsea," Lily adds with a head bob. Hiking a thumb over her shoulder, she then addresses Martin. "Bossman, we've got the new arrivals kenneled."

"Great," Martin responds. "When you're ready for assessments, take the guys here and show Larry the ropes. I'll cover the front." He turns to Larry. "These two are masters at what they do. Watch and learn."

"Flattery will get you everywhere," Lily says, patting Martin on the back. "Give me a few minutes to sort through the paperwork." She gives Angelo and Larry a nod, and then heads for the staff area.

"Yes, let us know when you've finished your intro to the front of the operation, and we'll take over," Ingrid says over her shoulder, as she follows Lily. She closes the door behind them. "Oh my goodness, wait till Larry meets Chelsea," she giggles.

"I hope his eyes don't fall out." Lily stifles a laugh. "He'll get the live and in-person experience on day two." She turns to her desk, pauses, then back to Ingrid. "Wait a minute. You just worked a Saturday event. Why didn't Martin ask me to work this weekend?"

"Well," Ingrid starts, measuring her tone as Lily's eyes narrow. "He was going to ask you. I told him I'd take it." Ingrid puts up a hand in a blocking gesture. "Don't give me that look of yours. You were upset last week. I figured you needed the day off more than me."

"That's sweet of you." Lily puts a hand on Ingrid's shoulder. "It was a rough week last week. You don't have to work extra, though. I'll come in."

"Oh no, no, no, you won't," Ingrid says, wagging one finger at chin level. "I got him to give me off the Friday before Memorial Day. I'm getting a long weekend."

"You devil," Lily exclaims, dropping her hands to her lap.

Ingrid's smile is broad and beaming. "I know. I accept it. I haven't had a long weekend in…" She lifts her chin pondering. "See, I can't even remember the last time."

"Well, good for you," Lily says. "By the way, last night when I was leaving I saw the woman who wanted to adopt Burrow in the parking lot." Ingrid's jovial expression falls from her face, as she casts an inquiring look at Lily. "I was thinking maybe you could pay Mickey a visit at her house, see if you can work your magic."

"You're really invested in placing this dog," Ingrid states.

"I feel sorry for her, Clarissa. She seems, I don't know, lonely." Lily stops and ponders. "Burrow is important to her. Besides, we can't adopt him out at all if we don't know what set him off." She gives a shrug of nonchalance.

"If things are calm tonight, I'll give Mickey a call and chat with her. However, I've kind of got a lot of dogs here to assess," Ingrid says.

"I know it's like working in the post office, there're always dogs to get adopted," Lily concedes, turning to her computer.

After about forty-five minutes, Lily says, "We ready to divide and conquer?"

"Mmm" Ingrid holds up one index finger to finish what she's reading. "You know, not to contradict Mr. Bossman out there…"

Lily leans on the desk putting her head on top of one fist, and gives Ingrid an appraising stare.

"My preference would be to take Angelo with us and leave Larry with Martin." Ingrid finishes.

"I think that's a great suggestion," Lily says. "You tell him."

Ingrid snorts out a laugh, then stands and walks over to the closed door. Lily grabs the clipboards of paperwork, following her.

"Ahhh, awesome, are we assessment ready?" Martin beams, rubbing his hands together as if trying to warm them on a cold day.

"You know, Martin…" Ingrid begins.

Martin looks from Angelo to Larry. "Prepare yourselves. Ingrid has her negotiating voice on."

"Well, it's wrong for Lily and me to deprive Larry of the incredible experience of learning the operation from you," Ingrid continues, completely serious. "Angelo should come with us. Larry should stay with you. It's his first day."

Martin wipes pretend sweat from his brow. He lifts one foot shaking it as if to dislodge something from the sole of his shoe. "The BS got incredibly thick in here," he laughs.

"We're thinking of the safety side, boss," Lily adds.

"You drive a hard bargain." Martin shakes his head as if saying not really. "Angelo, you head out with the ladies. Larry, you get to hang with me some more." He snaps his fingers. "Actually, maybe you should hang out with Mitchell and Doc for a bit."

"See, a perfect idea," Ingrid smiles.

Ingrid, Lily, and Angelo head for D-wing. Martin punches the intercom on the phone and says, "Doc, you in there?"

"Martin, you know you don't need the intercom. We hear you when you use your everyday voice," Doc responds.

"So, I'm sending Larry back," Martin says, not bothering to push the intercom button.

"See, heard you loud and clear," Doc says. The smile in his voice is evident.

"I swear I'm the Rodney Dangerfield of this organization." Martin laughs and looks at Larry, "Head on back there. Learn a bit about the medical area."

"Sure." Larry lopes off.

Martin answers the ringing telephone, "Forever Friends, Martin speaking."

"Good afternoon. May I speak to Lily Dreyfus?" says a female voice.

"Lily is out and about with some dogs right now. Can I help you?" Martin asks.

"This is Kathy Klapper from the Haddon Township school system," she says.

"Hi, Kathy. How did the 'Read to a Dog' trial go on Tuesday?" Martin asks.

"The students benefited from it. We'd love to have another. We were wondering if they could come back next week? Same day and time?" Kathy says.

"Lily will be thrilled. I'll let her know you called, and have her get back to you today," Martin says.

"Thank you very much," Kathy says, disconnecting.

Martin scribbles, "Call KK from Haddon T" on a Post-it, goes into the staff area and sticks it on Lily's desk.

Chapter 31

Around 1:00 pm, Lily, Angelo, and Ingrid return to the front desk.

"Martin, I need a snack and a bathroom break," Lily says. She heads towards the tiny kitchen area walled off behind the waiting room.

"Angelo could use a break, too," Ingrid says. "He prefers cats to dogs, but he was stoic."

"Yeah." Angelo shrugs.

"Miss Dreyfuss, before you go to the kitchen…" Martin calls.

Lily does an about-face.

"Kathy from Haddon Township called. I told her you'd call back," Martin says with no facial expression.

"Whoa, what's with the glum expression?" Lily hurries over to the desk.

"Well, she told me a bit, but wanted to talk to you," Martin says, pretending to read something on the front desk computer.

"Uh, Martin…?" Angelo says. "You know you have to touch the mouse or you'll just keep staring at the screen saver, right?"

"Darn, don't give me up so fast." Martin laughs out loud. He turns his glistening eyes to Lily's scowling face. "She wants to have you come out again."

"Oh, yeah." Lily holds out a fist. Martin bumps it.

Lily and Ingrid head towards the kitchen. They find a box of Dunkin' Munchkins on the counter.

"Shoot, what are those doing in here?" Lily nods at the box as she opens the refrigerator and grabs two bottles of water. She hands one to Ingrid.

"Someone's determined to ruin our girlish figures," Ingrid says with a laugh. "Don't worry, I'm prepared." She pulls a brown paper bag from one of the cabinets, and takes out a bag of trail mix. "Help yourself." She opens the bag and sets it on the counter.

"Thanks," Lily says. "We'll leave those Munchkins for the boys. They're in their twenties and they have functioning metabolisms." She reaches into the bag to take a handful of trail mix.

"So, is it me or does Larry look like Shaggy from Scooby Doo?" Ingrid asks as she takes another handful of trail mix.

Lily barks out a laugh. "Oh my God. That didn't occur to me, but—"

"It was the first thought I had when I saw him," Ingrid says.

"We won't have to worry about who'll eat the donuts if he's anything like Shaggy," Lily laughs.

"You got that right," Ingrid says. She reseals the trail mix bag and puts it back in the cabinet.

"I'm going to get Skittle to hang out with me while I make phone calls," Lily says, as she enters the medical area. She can see Doc and Larry's shadows through the textured glass of the exam room door. She grabs a leash and gets Skittle leashed up for the short walk back to the staff area.

Seated at her desk, Lily lifts the phone and calls Kathy Klapper. After a period on hold, Kathy's voice comes on the line.

"Lily, how are you?"

"I'm doing well, Kathy. How are things at the school?"

"Still pretty tense at the high school, but the lower grades are good."

"I suppose it's too soon to have learned much more about Eva?"

"We know her death was not natural. Of course, you probably surmised that, finding her as you did."

"She was in an odd location, but admittedly I've gone off trail more than once with my dogs. I've tripped on branches more than once too. I could see someone tripping and hitting their head, falling, twisting an ankle."

"Well, yes, all of that is possible. Rumor is, Eva had some bruising on her arms and torso. As if someone held her against her will."

"Oh, no. How do you know this?"

"The police told the principal the death did not appear to be accidental. They wanted to question more students." Kathy pauses.

"Goodness, they don't think another student did this, do they?"

"I don't think so. We had very few absences that day. We had a few seniors who we know were probably playing hooky on a beautiful Friday, but their parents were contacted and 'confirmed' an ailment kept them home." Kathy lets out a grunt of disapproval.

"Wait, you mean parents lie for kids playing hooky?" Lily is aghast. "My parents would've strung me up if they found out I played hooky."

"Yours? I would have been grounded for the summer. I certainly don't allow my grandchildren to skip school."

"Do they live with you?"

There is an inhale of breath. "Yes," Kathy quickly states. "When they're not with their father. He often has to travel for his job."

"So, the parents are divorced?"

"Not exactly," Kathy says. She pauses for several breaths. "I apologize, this is one of those instances where my mouth worked faster than my brain. I don't want to give you too much information, but my daughter is in rehab, and when their father has to travel the grandchildren stay with me."

"I'm sorry to hear about your daughter. Was she in an accident?"

Kathy pauses. "No. It's not physical rehabilitation. She's in a drug rehabilitation program."

"Good for her for getting the help she needs. She must be comforted knowing you are there to help with the children."

"One day she'll realize how lucky she is." Kathy takes a regretful tone. "I apologize again. I didn't mean to go down this path with you. It's one of the reasons Eva's situation is so painful for me. It mirrors my own children's situation. I can't imagine losing one of them. Eva's grandmother must be devastated."

"I'm sure she is. Do the police still think there might be some type of drug connection?"

"Sadly, yes. Drugs are prevalent in our society. Parents don't realize giving Oxycontin to teenagers after they have their wisdom teeth pulled can have devastating, lasting effects."

"Oxycontin." Lily bursts out causing Skittle to jump to all fours from his blanket. "I was given an ice pack and told to take Tylenol."

"Me, too. I don't want to talk about the reasons we see doctors and dentists prescribing these powerful medications. Let's change the subject to something pleasant, shall we?"

"Absolutely, Martin tells me you'd like us to come out again?" Lily smiles broadly.

"Yes, yes, and you know there isn't much time left in the school year. Could we try to do every Tuesday at two until school ends?" Kathy has a hopeful tone.

"I'll talk to Connie and see what works for her. If she can't do every week, there're other good candidates." Lily thinks about Boone. Little girls love Boone.

"Okay, you let me know. Consistency is best for the students. Of course, I can understand if someone can't make a commitment for every week. Will you call me and let me know what can be done?"

"I sure will. I'm quite excited about this program," Lily says happily. They disconnect. Lily leans back in her chair. She reaches down and gives Skittle a scratch on his ears. "Little friend, first some calls for the school, then we'll work on finding you a foster home."

Chapter 32

The steam from an industrial dishwasher makes the temperature in the cafeteria kitchen unbearable. Tony's hands are moist under the rubber gloves he uses to pull the dishes out and stack them in preparation for the next day's lunch service. He grips each plate carefully so as not to drop any.

"How do you stand it?" Clarissa asks as she comes up beside him. The hair that has escaped the knot at her neck clings damply to her face. She has loaded the last of the trays into the cleaning unit.

"Prefer it to too much air conditioning," Tony answers. "That makes every joint ache. Besides, a few more weeks and then I'm off for the summer, collecting unemployment." Tony's eyes survey Clarissa from the top of her damp hair down to her worn sneakers, where one big toe is threatening to pop through the thin blue canvas. He can't tell if she is nervous or tired. She always seems on edge. He knows she comes to this job from a midnight-to-six shift at the Wawa. However, the police were asking him some very pointed questions this morning. He is starting to wonder. "Clarissa..." he trails off as their supervisor enters the kitchen.

George Mack marches over to where they stand. "Clarissa, you free for a bit?" he asks.

"Um, yeah, I guess," Clarissa stutters out.

"Good, head on up to Administration; the police are talking to staff today." George gives a perfunctory nod.

"About what?" Clarissa asks.

"You telling me you didn't hear a student died?" Sarcasm drips from George's words like the sweat that's dripping from Tony and Clarissa's faces.

"I talked to them pre-shift," Tony volunteers.

"I don't know anything about it," Clarissa blurts.

"Then it shouldn't take long," George says, and turns around to leave the kitchen.

Clarissa watches him leave, her mouth slightly hanging open as if she were about to say something else, but no sound comes out. She lifts one arm and uses the sleeve of her shirt to wipe the sweat from her face.

"Don't worry, it's nothing," Tony tries to reassure her. "They only ask questions about our interactions with the students. Did we observe anybody acting strange? Stuff like that."

Clarissa places her hands on her hips and exhales loudly. "Do they act strange? They're teenagers. Martians would probably seem more normal. Crap."

Tony laughs, "Listen, they know we don't interact with the kids. The teachers are all hiding behind their contracts, so we part-timers make easy targets."

"Great, exactly what I need. I've been up since 11:30 last night." Clarissa scratches at her hairline with one hand. Tony notices her chipped and chewed fingernails.

"Let them know you're a night shift, or is it a morning shift, person." He tries to give encouragement.

"Clarissa, I meant today," George yells, sticking his head back into the kitchen.

"Here, I'll take care of those for you." Tony catches the gloves as they fall free of Clarissa's trembling fingers. "Too bad we're not allowed to have soda anymore. You could probably use a good jolt of caffeine."

"Yeah, something," Clarissa mutters. She leaves the kitchen and decides to stop in the restroom before she goes up to the administrative office. She splashes cold water on her face from the sink, wipes her hands with a paper towel, and reties the knot in her hair. She surveys herself in the mirror, then reaches into her pocket to pull out generic eye drops, squirts two drops in each eye, and holds her eyes closed for thirty seconds. Using the paper towel that she dried her hands on, she rubs the eye drop residue from her face.

She reevaluates herself in the mirror. Not surprisingly, her eyes are still red. Leaving the bathroom with a grunt of frustration, she heads to Administration. The district's Superintendent of Schools is standing in the doorway in a neatly pressed, tailored suit. He backs away as Clarissa enters, as if afraid she might soil his clothes.

"Oh good, Clarissa, thanks for coming up," Kathy Klapper, the Assistant Principal, says. "The officers are in the conference room." She points to the left.

"Thanks," Clarissa mumbles as she shuffles towards the conference room. When she enters, the two officers are standing next to the conference table with their heads bowed together in conversation. Kathy Klapper follows behind her.

"The officers are asking staff a few questions about Eva. I can sit in with you if you'd like," Kathy offers.

Clarissa's head jolts up from its downward position. Her gaze travels from Kathy to each officer/ "Do I need representation?"

"Of course not. I didn't mean to give that impression." Kathy flutters her hands in front of her. "I meant…"

"I think we can take it from here," says one of the officers. Kathy retreats through the doorway and the officer closes it. "I'm Officer Jones, this is Officer Walters." He extends his hand.

Clarissa wipes her damp palm on her pants, extending her hand for a weak shake. "Clarissa," she mumbles.

"Have a seat. We're asking people a few questions. You may have observed something helpful and not even realize you did," Officer Jones states, as he takes the seat directly opposite Clarissa. Officer Walters sits down next to him.

"I…I only work in the cafeteria part-time," Clarissa stutters out.

"Sure, I bet that's not an easy task," Officer Jones says.

"I… I don't interact with the students. I prep food and then I clean up," Clarissa offers.

"Sure, there's no reason to be nervous," Officer Jones offers. Officer Walters has picked up a pen and he's scribbling notes into a spiral-bound notebook.

"I'm not nervous," Clarissa spits out. She quickly lifts her head, looking pointedly at each officer.

"I apologize. You, uh, seemed nervous. I was trying to reassure you," Officer Jones says.

"I work at Wawa from midnight to six before coming here. Right now is most people's eight at night. I need to head home and sleep."

"Sure, we'll try to be quick." The officers share a glance. They've both noticed the tremor in Clarissa's hands as well as the red-rimmed, sunken eyes. "Did you know the deceased, Eva Livin—"

"No," Clarissa barks before he finishes the question.

The officers don't react. They maintain eye contact with her. "That was pretty quick," Officer Jones says with a smile.

"I don't interact with the students. I prep food, then I clean up," Clarissa rushes out in one breathe. She lifts her right forefinger to her mouth to chew on a raggedy nail bed.

"They never talk to you while you're cleaning up? Maybe ask you to take their trays to the station, anything like that?" Officer Jones is breezily nonchalant.

"I don't talk to them," Clarissa says, removing her forefinger from her mouth. She holds her hands in her lap for ten seconds, then moves her right middle finger to her mouth, chewing on the skin of it.

"But do they try to talk to you?" Officer Jones asks again.

"Some of the smart asses say stuff. I ignore them," Clarissa answers. She shifts in her seat, putting her hands underneath her thighs.

"Stuff, like what exactly?" Officer Jones asks.

"The kinda shit teenagers say. I don't have children. I don't speak their lingo."

"So, you're not certain the comments are directed at you?" Officer Jones leans forward slightly. Officer Walters continues writing in the notebook.

"I told you. I don't talk to them," Clarissa says. Her voice is rising with each word. She keeps her head slightly bowed to keep the officers from looking her in the eyes.

"How do you get to work every day?" Officer Jones asks.

"I drive," Clarissa mumbles.

"What do you drive?" Officer Jones asks.

"Why is it relevant?" Clarissa clenches her jaws as she answers. She shifts in her seat bringing her right forefinger to her mouth again.

"I was asking. What type of car?" Officer Jones says with a shrug.

"Hyundai," Clarissa grudgingly offers.

"That was my first car. Bought a used one right before I started at the academy," Officer Jones eyes gleam with wistful nostalgia. "Hmm, that was a '98. Don't see many of them anymore."

There's a pause. Clarissa continues to chew on the skin on her forefinger.

"So, you park here at the school, then?" Officer Jones asks. He clasps his hands on top of the conference table

"In the neighborhood," Clarissa mumbles. She drops her hand into her lap momentarily then returns it to her mouth.

"So, at the end of the day, do you run into students? Perhaps when walking to your car," Officer Jones asks.

"I leave before they do, usually." Clarissa shifts as she places her right hand under her thigh again.

"Okay, but what about when you leave at the same time as them?" Officer Jones persists.

"Listen, I don't talk to the students. I've got nothin' in common with teenagers." Clarissa leans onto the table, raising her gaze without lifting her head.

"I understand. Sometimes they'll pass you while you're going to your car, though, right?" Officer Jones asks.

"Maybe sometimes, I don't talk to 'em," Clarissa answers dropping her gaze to the table.

CHAPTER 33

"Do you take any prescription medications?" Officer Jones asks.

Clarissa's head jolts up. She glares at Officer Jones. "I don't see what that has to do with anything." Her tone is guarded.

"I was wondering if you ever take anything which prohibited you from driving," Officer Jones continues in his nonchalant tone of voice.

"No." Clarissa returns her focus to the conference table.

"Nothing? You work a difficult schedule. Ever need a sleep aid?"

"No," she says forcefully. Clarissa's entire right arm begins to shake. She lifts her right forefinger back to her mouth, chewing the nail.

"It must be hard working different shifts. Sometimes I have to work the night shift, then I can't get to sleep when I get home…"

Silence.

"You don't have that problem?"

Silence.

"Ever any problems staying awake?"

Clarissa slams her hand flat on the conference room table. Neither Officer Jones nor Officer Walters indicate they're bothered by the noise. The edge of her finger is starting to bleed. "Not when I can actually get home and get some sleep," she growls.

Officer Walters looks up. He pulls a tissue from the box in the middle of the table, handing it to Clarissa. "Your finger is bleeding," he says without emotion.

Clarissa takes the tissue from him, wrapping it around her forefinger. She holds it in place with her left hand.

"Do you take anything that would produce dopamine? Drugs for Parkinson's, maybe?" Officer Jones continues.

"What does that have to do with anything?" Clarissa's torso starts to quiver.

"I noticed the tremors in your hands. I thought you might be using one of the Parkinson's medications," Officer Jones offers.

"Like I could afford it at eight bucks an hour." Her tone has become sarcastic. Clarissa squeezes her right forefinger harder with her left hand. The tremors temporarily cease.

"So, you aren't on the school district's medical plan?"

"Can't be, I'm part-time, non-contract." Clarissa's left hand is sweating. When she lets go of the tissue it's stuck to her left palm. She removes the wet mass and begins tearing it into tiny pieces, making a tiny mound in front of her.

"Well, you mentioned another job. Wawa, I believe. I hear they have good medical benefits."

"Maybe, if you're full time. I'm not."

"So, what type of medical insurance do you have?"

"Nothing," Clarissa mumbles.

"Not an Affordable Care Act plan?"

Clarissa cackles with the expulsion of breath. "Affordable Care Act? Don't make me laugh. What an inappropriately named law." She shakes her head as she continues laughing.

"So, you don't have an Affordable Care Act plan, then?"

"No, I can't 'AFFORD' a plan," Clarissa yells, making air quotes on the word "afford". A few pieces of wet tissue still cling to her left palm.

"What happens when you get sick?"

"I drag myself to work, no matter what." Clarissa shifts in her chair and put her hands under her thighs again. Her arms continue to tremble.

"Flu?"

"Haven't had it," Clarissa mumbles.

"You're lucky. Especially being around children. Phew, last

year, my son brought home a cold from third grade. The whole family got it, and we kept passing it back and forth to each other."

Clarissa remains silent, staring at the pile of bloody tissue pieces on the table.

"You know, some of the students we talked to told us Eva was selling illegal pain killers."

"So?" Clarissa shrugs.

"Well, without health insurance, when you've been sick, have you ever purchased something from someone to help with your symptoms?"

"No," Clarissa mumbles.

"Never?"

"No," Clarissa says more adamantly.

"So, you work a very odd schedule. Is that by choice?"

"Choice?" Clarissa lifts her eyes to meet those of Officer Jones without moving her head.

"Do you work an unusual schedule so you can be home to help with a child or parent?"

"I live alone." Clarissa drops her eyes back to the pile of wet Kleenex. She begins to lift her right hand back to her mouth, stops midway. Self-consciously, she slides her hand back under her right thigh.

"Night owl?"

"Is there a point?" Pulling her head up, eyes red, she locks her gaze with Officer Jones.

"Wondering why you don't have a more regular schedule," the officer says. He holds Clarissa's gaze until she drops her head again.

"It's none of your business what schedule I keep."

"How long have you worked at the school here?"

"This is my first school year."

"Why did you take this job?"

"Money, I needed money, there're bills to pay." Clarissa shifts in her seat again but doesn't remove her hands from under her thighs.

"What did you do before this?"

"Law firm-- I was a paralegal," Clarissa blandly responds.

"So, this was a career change for you?"

"It's none of your damn business. I want to go home and get to sleep before my midnight to six," Clarissa snaps, brazenly glaring at Officer Jones.

"I'm sorry. I didn't mean to pry. It's interesting you would leave a career, which probably had excellent medical benefits—"

"Leave?" Clarissa shrieks. "Leave, like voluntary? Jerks told me twelve weeks was all they would hold my job. Twelve weeks. I still had the damn cast on. The stupid doctor wouldn't give me the approval to go back to work, said I couldn't do the walking and standing my job required, so they 'let me go' — 'let' like I asked, and they gave me permission," Clarissa shouts.

"Ah, so you lost your job and your medical benefits due to an injury? And you didn't have any family or friends who could help with your recovery, parents?" Officer Jones asks.

"My mother died when I was in high school, cancer. My father died of a broken heart, not that that was the diagnosis, but that's what happened." Clarissa drops her head into her hands and begins to cry. "Just a month before I graduated high school. I was an orphan."

The two police officers sit quietly while Clarissa sobs. They lock eyes with each other in silent communication. After a few minutes, Clarissa reaches for the box of tissues, removes two to wipe her eyes and blow her nose. She lifts her gaze resignedly to the officers.

"We're very sorry for your loss. What a tremendous hardship for a young woman to bear, all alone. You should be incredibly proud of what you've accomplished since high school," Officer Jones says.

"Yeah, how proud they'd be if they could see me now," Clarissa scoffs, looking down at her sweat-stained top.

"So, back to your injury, how did you manage your expenses after losing your job?"

"I was on COBRA for a bit for medical, but I couldn't keep paying. I got some unemployment for a while." She pauses, shakes her head. "Uncle Charlie and Aunt Joann were helping me. I was hoping these two part-time jobs would be a temporary blip, and I'd find another paralegal job." Clarissa sniffs, rubs her nose with the tissues.

"And this Uncle and Aunt, they stopped helping you?"

"They died, crashed into by a drunk driver coming home from the shore," Clarissa sobs. She drops her face back into her hands.

"When did this happen?"

"Last August," Clarissa grabs more tissues from the box, burying her face in her hands. "I couldn't keep up with the payments for COBRA, and it got revoked. I have no insurance, so I haven't seen a doctor in months. My leg hurts after twelve hours of standing on it, and you people won't let me go home to get some sleep." She slaps both hands onto the table. Bits of torn tissue float into the air.

"So, you're managing with over-the-counter medication?"

"As best I can."

"That can't be easy."

"It isn't."

"Wow, twelve hours, standing, concrete floors, not sure I could do it," Officer Jones says, turning his gaze to officer Walters.

"My wife works at Macy's. She's shot when she gets home," Officer Walters adds. "I've got the little one in bed before she comes in the door."

"You're good. Don't tell my wife. She's a nurse at Virtua. I give a lot of foot massages," Officer Jones smirks.

"Huh, you do?" Officer Walters gets a glimmer in his eye.

"To my wife only," Officer Jones adds pointedly.

Clarissa loudly clears her throat.

"Sorry. We got distracted. Ever get offered something stronger than over the counter stuff?" Officer Jones turns his gaze back on Clarissa.

Clarissa says nothing.

"You know, like a teenager gets their wisdom teeth out and offers you their leftover oxy?"

Clarissa barks out a laugh. "These kids? Offer something? FOR FREE?" She gives a maniacal cackle.

In rapid succession, Officer Jones and Walters fire more questions at Clarissa.

"Well, then maybe someone offered you something for a price?"

"It'd be completely understandable if you'd buy it."

"You're not the first person we've met in these circumstances."

"You might not have gotten it here. Maybe someone from Wawa offered you their extra medication. Thought they were helping?"

Clarissa begins chewing on a finger of her left hand. The officers glance at each other, then sit quietly. "Big help it was," she mumbles.

"I'm sorry, did you say something?" Officer Jones shifts forward in his seat.

Clarissa breaks down into wracking sobs. Her shoulders quiver as she gulps for air. "Damn cashier, had the shift before I got to Wawa. One night she worked the midnight to eight on overtime. When I came in, she saw me hobbling and told me she could help," Clarissa splutters out, as she gulps for air.

"So, she offered you a prescription pill?"

"I didn't know she was a dealer. I thought she was friendly. Yeah, then the next time I was hobbling it was $10 a pill. What an idiot I was to trust her." Clarissa continues to sob. She sniffs loudly.

"Does she still work at Wawa?"

"No, I don't remember why she left. She'd meet me after my shift sometimes. I don't know what happened. None of this has anything to do with that girl." Clarissa stands. "I'm leaving. You have no legal right to keep me here."

"I'm sorry we kept you as long as we did—" Officer Jones starts, but he is speaking to the back of a head as Clarissa hurries out the door.

CHAPTER 34

Leaving the comfort of her air conditioned car on Friday morning, Lily's shoulders slump in the humidity as if a wet blanket had been placed on her shoulders. She takes in the threatening sky, hoping they can get the dogs walked before the downpour. She snickers as she wonders what the new guy would think if she sent him out in the rain to walk dogs.

She opens the door to the D–wing to earnest barking. "Good morning, good morning." Lily waves her right hand as if holding a conductor's baton. "You sound great. Keep it going."

Lily opens the door to the C–wing to find Chelsea handing out breakfast. Today her tangle of red tendrils is rolled into a ball secured with what looks like chopsticks. "Good morning, Chelsea."

Chelsea glances in Lily's direction, and Lily notices some very uncharacteristic circles under her eyes. "It's morning, Lily. I'm not so sure about good."

"You look a bit worse for wear today." Lily moves her gaze up and down, surveying Chelsea head to toe.

"I took a friend's shift at the bar last night. With that extra-innings baseball game, they stayed open later than usual," Chelsea half groans.

"Well, I'll take some pity on you and let you stick with the cats. I'll get dog breakfast started, which will tame a bit of the barking."

"Actually, the barking will keep me awake." Chelsea flashes Lily a smile.

"If that doesn't do it, we'll have Martin sing to you."

"Oh God no, no, anything but that."

Lily stows her bag in her desk and checks the supply of disposable ponchos she and Ingrid keep ready. There's enough for everyone today. She gets the dogs' breakfast passed out, then starts walking the dogs when they've finished eating. The clouds have transformed from the color of pebbles strewn on the beach to a menacing grey. In a movie, she thinks, here's where the villain bursts forth. Despite wanting to give all the dogs a lengthy walk, Lily decides to stop each walk at fifteen minutes so all the dogs can get one in before the deluge. On her third walk, she spots two volunteers, also walking dogs. She breathes a sigh of relief. With three people walking them, all the dogs should get their exercise before it rains.

Chelsea is working fast at scrubbing the kennels despite her lack of sleep. "Don't wear yourself out; you've got to make it through a full day," Lily teases. She returns the third dog to her kennel and leashes up the next one. She and the volunteers rotate in and out of the shelter and the grounds. When there are only two dogs left to walk, Lily leaves them for the volunteers and heads for the staff area. As she opens the door, she hears raindrops drumming a staccato beat on the window.

"Good morning, Lily. Did you get them all walked before the rain?" Ingrid tilts her head at the window.

"We did, but I think the volunteers are getting a little wet." Lily flops onto her chair. "I'm so glad they came in this morning."

"Do you think our new staff person will be back today?" Ingrid grins.

"I don't think we did enough yesterday to scare him away." Lily gives Ingrid a wink.

"So, let's think about what to teach him today," Ingrid says. Collectively, they review the work needing to be accomplished, divide the tasks and the new employee immersion. The door is flung open.

"It's Friday," Martin croons in a tenor voice as he bounds

into the staff area. He looks from Lily to Ingrid. "Oh boy, what are you two scheming away at?"

"Well, boss," Ingrid shifts in her seat. "Since we had a transport of ten dogs yesterday, we're discussing whether to give Larry some intro to dog handling and assessments."

Lily chimes in. "Ingrid and Angelo are going to assess those small beagle mixes, and we can let Larry assist. Then I'll show him the different databases and our adoption files. He can work on getting records updated. Then, in the afternoon, we thought he could interact with the volunteers who come in for the Feline Companion shifts. Those two young ladies from Cherry Hill East are on the schedule."

"Okay, now let me get this straight." Martin clasps his hands behind his back like General Patton surveying the troops. "You're going to make poor Larry spend most of the morning doing geeky computer stuff with Broom Hilda here, and then his reward is to spend the afternoon with two cute eighteen-year-old girls playing with cats?" Martin chuckles.

"You know, buddy," Lily huffs with indignation, "one day you're going to have a staff person who isn't as easygoing as me and you're going to get slapped with a harassment suit."

"Yeah, seriously," Ingrid joins the fray. "If you're going to call her a witch, at least make it be an attractive one. Who's that woman in 'Midnight Texas'? She's badass. So is Lily."

"You're so right." Lily snaps her fingers. "Olivia Charity, that's who I want to be compared to."

"Wait a doggone minute here," Martin throws his hands in the air. "Isn't that the character who has a closet full of submachine guns? You're telling me I can't refer to you as a comic strip witch, but a gun-toting assailant is okay? Who makes up these rules?" His voice has risen two octaves.

Ingrid and Lily exchange glances and try to suppress their laughter. "Martin, are you telling us you read Charlaine Harris?" Ingrid asks.

"Oh, what, I can't read books?"

"You're not exactly her target market." Lily stifles giggles.

"Well, it so happens I am a well-rounded person," Martin says, putting one hand flat against his chest.

Ingrid cannot suppress the laughter any longer. "Seriously, YOU read Charlaine Harris?"

"Okay, my wife reads her stuff. She watches that HBO show with the vampires."

"Hmm, a more reasonable explanation," Lily concedes. "Besides, Olivia isn't a witch." She takes her chin in her hand as if truly pondering something significant. "Then Alyssa Milano: refer to me as Phoebe Holliwell. Her skill was premonitions, and who wouldn't want to be as successful as she was?" Lily smiles.

"Works for me," exclaims Ingrid. "On that note, let me go get Larry and teach him a few dog tricks."

Lily decides to head to the medical area to check on Barkley and Skittle. As she approaches the set of ten large dog kennels, Skittle jumps to standing, wagging his tail.

"Getting to like me, huh?" Lily says. "Let me look in on Barkley, then you can come hang out with me for a bit."

Looking into Barkley's kennel, his eyes are open, but he doesn't attempt to stand. She opens the kennel door and kneels. Barkley sniffs her hand. She pets his head and scratches his ears.

"Is Doc taking good care of you? Keeping you free of pain?"

Barkley closes his eyes, grunting out his breath. Lily continues to pet him for a while. When it appears he is asleep, she stands silently and closes the kennel door. Wiping away a tear, she grabs a leash and opens Skittle's kennel. Attaching the leash to his collar, they walk towards the exit.

She can hear Chelsea's voice from the front desk. "Sure, um, well, I think…"

Lily frowns. She knows Chelsea didn't get enough sleep last night, but this is uncharacteristic of her. She could hold a conversation with a vulture. Lily opens the door to leave Medical.

CHAPTER 35

At the front desk stands the embodiment of a granite statue come to life. The man is about six feet five, with brown, buzz cut hair that's growing out. His broad shoulders make Lily think of Chris Hemsworth.

Chelsea acknowledges Lily with a nod of her head. "Say her name and she appears. This gentleman's asking about Burrow."

"Hi, there," Lily says, extending her hand hoping it doesn't get crushed in this guy's gigantic grip.

"I'm Jim, Jim Davidson. I was a good friend of Pete Russo's." He closes his eyes and takes a deep breath. "I was wondering if we could talk about me adopting Burrow?"

"Sure, let me take care of my friend Skittle, here." She goes to the staff area. Martin is on the phone. Detaching the leash, Lily lets Skittle into the space, and closes the baby gate so he can't run out behind her.

"Why don't we sit down over here in our reception area?" Lily indicates the chairs and tables across from the counter. Jim waits for her to walk past him, then follows.

Lily takes a seat, watching as Jim perches on one of the folding chairs. She has a vision of the Jolly Green Giant in a kindergarten classroom. "I apologize for such small furniture," she says.

Jim waves his hand in a "no bother" gesture. "I'm a marine; we adapt to our surroundings." He smiles and distinguished crinkles around his eyes and mouth become evident.

"Were you in the service with Pete?"

"Pete, yes." He shakes his head. "Pete was my best friend. It's terrible what's happened."

"You live in New Jersey?"

"I retired from the service back in February and I'd been living temporarily with Pete." He pauses. "Being in the Corps is like living a gypsy existence, staying with family or friends when not deployed."

"You weren't there when Pete died?" Lily tentatively asks, wondering why Pete hadn't mentioned anyone living with him.

"I've been visiting family the last two weeks." He pauses. "I've missed a lot of family gatherings, being in the service. They had me making up for lost time." He pauses, breathes in deeply, then continues. "This is awful. I was wondering why Pete wasn't answering my text messages. He was supposed to pick me up at the airport yesterday." He breaks off and then sighs. "Then I called a friend of ours, Matt, to ask if he'd heard from Pete, and, and…" He breaks off. "Sorry."

"Take your time," Lily says, resisting the urge to wrap her arms around him.

"Matt said Pete wasn't answering his texts either." Jim locks eyes with Lily, the intensity of his gaze causing her to flinch. He huffs out a sigh, reducing the power of his gaze. "I suggested that since Matt was here, in New Jersey, he could drive over to the house and check on Pete. Millennials," Jim scoffs. "Sorry, I didn't mean…"

"I've got a 30-year-old brother. I can relate." Lily smiles. "I sometimes have to ask the younger staff here to translate his texts for me."

"How does someone let more than a week go by with somebody not answering their texts, and not drive over to their house?" The intensity rises in Jim's eyes again. "They'd been working on a project together. They should have been talking regularly. Anyway, Matt did drive out and found out Pete was dead. He's been talking to the police to put more of a timeline around, around…"

Jim breaks off, swallowing a sob. Lily concentrates on the story, oblivious to the swirl of visitors going in and out of the shelter's front door.

"I don't understand how this could've happened," he says.

"Do the police know how Pete died?" Lily asks.

"Matt didn't say." Jim's gaze narrows with suspicion.

"Learning of his death was a shock to us," Lily says. "I dropped my phone when the state trooper called." She blushes but recovers her business demeanor. "Pete was a great supporter of ours. He would bring Burrow to adoption events and tell people what a difference Burrow made in his life."

"Yeah, that dog, that dog was important to Pete," Jim muses. "Well, that's why I'm here." He smiles.

Lily finds herself smiling. When Jim smiles, he looks like Boone: his whole face lights up.

"You see, Pete made me the executor of his estate. I'm supposed to care for Burrow." He pauses. "I sure hope you haven't adopted him to someone else." His brow furrows in concern.

Lily releases the breath she was holding. "When Burrow was surrendered to us, the police asked us not to list him as available for adoption until they could notify the next of kin." She pauses, flashing back to the meeting with Clarissa. "We set Burrow up with one of our foster families. Um, however…" She pauses.

"Don't worry. The police told me I could adopt Burrow. It's why I'm here. I just need to find out what I need to do," he says in a concise, declarative tone.

"Great," Lily assures him. "But here's a situation we've experienced: a dog is surrendered, and a family member is angry they can't come right in and take the dog out of the shelter. I sympathize with their frustration, but we're obligated to make an assessment." Lily sits up straighter, using what Tyler refers to as her 'mom tone.'

"I retired as a major in the Marine Corps. If there's one thing I completely understand, it's procedures," Jim says.

"Of course," Lily says, wondering if Jim was Pete's commanding officer. Lifting her head, she catches sight of Martin trying to watch them unobtrusively. He's being about as subtle as a fire engine with its siren blaring. Lily raises her chin to him in an 'I've got this' gesture.

Martin interprets the motion as an invitation. "Lily, everything okay here?" He walks over.

Jim stands up, dwarfing Martin. Lily laughs before she can stop herself.

"Lily's going to tell me what I need to do to adopt Burrow." Jim extends a hand towards Martin.

"Well, adoption is her business." He shakes Jim's hand. "Be careful though; she'll have you taking home two additional dogs and a cat to boot." He laughs. As he leaves them, he winks at Lily when he is out of Jim's line of vision.

Standing up as well and regaining her composure, Lily says, "Jim, have a seat. I need to get in touch with the woman who is currently fostering Burrow and see if we can arrange a meet. We have to ensure the two of you are compatible and that you can handle him. I'll have Chelsea give you the adoption application to complete. Now, when can we set up the meet? Are you available tonight?" She is standing as tall as her posture will allow, feeling the need to mirror his ramrod physique.

"As I mentioned, I was living with Pete, but I can't live there now. I'm staying with Matt until things, well, resolve let's say." Jim looks eager. Lily thinks that now he resembles Boone waiting for a Milk Bone.

"Okay, and Burrow needs to meet anyone living in the house, especially if there are children." Lily briefly considers batting her eyelashes and flirting like Chelsea, but doesn't attempt it.

"He's not married and doesn't have children. I'll give him a call. He was expecting me to come home with Burrow tonight. He's out shopping for food and bowls." Grinning, the crinkles around Jim's eyes reappear. "He lives in a duplex his parents own. They live downstairs, and he lives upstairs. Do you need to meet his parents?" he asks.

"Weeelll…" Lily draws out the word, raising her face to the ceiling in thought. She lowers her face and returns eye contact with Jim. "If technically they don't live in the same house it isn't required, but you might want them to come, especially if they'll be in the yard when he's out there too. He's a big dog." Lily clasps her hands at her waist. She finds she has a strong desire to lean in as she is talking.

"I understand." Jim tilts his head to the side as if pondering a deep thought. "They're at work and won't be home until later. I'd like to move things along, but with these requirements maybe we won't be able to do it until tomorrow." He frowns.

"Let me contact the foster parent and see what we can arrange for tonight." Lily nods and walks towards the front desk. Chelsea wiggles a forefinger at her in a "come here" gesture. When Lily gets to the counter, she sees Chelsea is holding a tissue. Eyes sparkling, she wipes at Lily's chin.

"I think you've got a little drool there," she whispers.

"Bitch," Lily mouths. Chelsea stifles a laugh and Lily returns to the staff area.

CHAPTER 36

"Lil-eeeeeeeee," Martin shrieks, as she opens the door to the staff area.

Lily puts a finger to her lips in a shushing gesture and closes the door.

"Oh, good golly, if you were a dog you'd have been licking that guy's face." Martin laughs. "You'd better not tease Chelsea for an extremely long time."

"Not you too," Lily retorts. "Chelsea pretended to wipe drool off my chin." She thrusts her chin forward to emphasize there is no drool on it.

The smile on Martin's face threatens to burst his cheekbones. "I can't wait to tell Ingrid." He continues to chuckle.

Lily feels her face flush and quickly turns from him to her desk. She mutters, "Forgive me for showing compassion on the job." She leans over and pets Skittle. "I thought I was supposed to work on my people skills."

"My constructive criticism on the job applies to all humans: the tall, dark, and handsome ones as much as the coworkers whose style is different than your own."

Lily looks back at Martin. Ignoring the jibe, she changes the subject, "I'm concerned we never determined why Burrow had an aggressive reaction to Clarissa."

"We may never know the cause," Martin says. "Let's have Mickey bring Burrow out and see what happens with this guy. One way or the other, we've got to get Burrow adopted."

"I'll text Mickey and see if we can get a meet set up tonight." As she reaches for her cell phone, Ingrid pushes open the door.

Ingrid is smiling broadly. She whispers, "Okay, who's the guy in the waiting room? Chelsea is about to melt into a puddle out there 'helping' him fill out an adoption application." She does air quotes around the word "helping".

Martin bursts out laughing. "Chelsea? You should've seen Lily, here, with him." He jerks his thumb at Lily.

"Shush, Martin, not so loud." Ingrid admonishes him. She turns to Lily, who is putting down her cell phone. "Is it me? Or does he look like David Beckham?"

"I was thinking Chris Hemsworth," Lily says, instantly slapping one hand over her mouth. She had not intended for that comment to slip out.

"You two are a riot," Martin says in the lowest decibel voice they have ever heard. "Geez, you act like you don't see a man every day." Lily and Ingrid share a silent look. In mutual agreement they do not comment. They both know this conversation is going to be pantomimed for Martin's wife tonight.

Lily puts on her most professional tone. "He was a friend of Pete Russo's and was apparently willed custody of Burrow."

"Willed?" Ingrid exclaims. "Someone 'willed' custody of their dog? I love my cats, but good golly they aren't in a 'will'." She does the air quotes again around the words "willed" and "will".

"It was put in the will how custody would be handled, I guess," Lily stammers, "I didn't ask to read the will."

"She couldn't ask anything." Martin is using his falsetto voice again. "She was having a hard time not drooling all over him." He takes a hand and wipes his chin.

"Martin, enough teasing Lily," Ingrid admonishes him.

Lily's phone rings, and she quickly answers it. "Hello, Mickey."

"Hello, yourself," Mickey answers. "I guess you forgot. I was making your house my last stop tonight to feed and walk Boone and Crockett because you were worried you might get caught up in helping the new guy during the Friday crush. I was going to let the boys all hang out together in the yard, maybe help myself to a glass of wine—"

Lily has swiveled her chair so its back is to Martin and Ingrid. She cuts in, "You're right. It's been a busy today. How about if after you feed and walk Boone and Crockett, you leave Nero at my house and bring Burrow here. Would that work?"

Martin is snickering something about using shelter resources for personal gain. Ingrid quiets him with a wave of her hand.

"Sounds like a plan," Lily agrees, and ends the call. As she rises from her chair, Martin and Ingrid mirror her movement. "Oh no," Lily puts up a stop traffic hand. "You two are going to stay put."

"You're no fun, Lil, you know?" Ingrid teases.

Lily tosses her head. "I'm a lot of fun; unfortunately, not the kind you two want." She opens the door, steps over the baby gate, and closes it behind her.

The reception area is now packed with people. Angelo is behind the desk looking a bit frazzled, "What's up?" Lily asks.

"That family would like to meet both Rufus and Jethro," he says, pointing to a group in the reception area.

Lily goes back to the staff area and cracks the door open. Martin and Ingrid are still whispering to each other. "If you could pull yourselves away from gossiping for a bit, we have a family who want to meet two dogs," she says.

"We're on it, ma'am." Ingrid gives a mock salute.

Friday nights get hectic at the shelter. Those are the families with children who "can't wait" until Saturday morning. It's a good thing, too. Saturdays at a shelter are like the night before Thanksgiving at an airport.

Lily walks back to the reception area. Chelsea is perched on the chair next to Jim. She seems to have fully recovered from a night of not enough sleep. Lily gently puts her hand on Chelsea's shoulder. "Chelsea, thank you for helping Jim with the application." Her voice drips sweetness.

"Oh, gosh." Chelsea quickly stands up. "Jim, you've had one interesting life. It was so nice to meet you, sir." She practically bounces off, the chopsticks holding her hair in place dancing as her head bobs.

Jim appears unfazed by the attention. "Can I get Burrow tonight?" he asks with a very hopeful expression on his face.

"The foster parent can bring him by at 6:30," Lily says.

"Lily, thank you very much." Jim stands. His eyes sparkle like those of the children who are at the shelter to pick out a new pet.

"We'll see you later," Lily says, and heads back to the staff area. She sits down at her desk with Burrow's file. She double-checks all the forms for completeness. If the meet works out, Burrow can go home with Jim. Lily smiles to herself. She thinks of what a warm and fuzzy story she'll have to share with Eileen.

CHAPTER 37

Later that evening, Angelo and Larry are sitting at Wendy's on a dinner break. They're talking Phillies baseball, bemoaning a season without Chase Utley and Jimmy Rollins. Larry's cell phone pings. He glances down at it.

"Sweet," he says.

Angelo raises an eyebrow in question.

"My girlfriend's baking eddies," he says. Then he chuckles, "She's baking now so we can get baked later."

Angelo laughs. "What's she making?"

"Oatmeal cookies."

"Really, oatmeal cookies? That's not the usual. She must be a good baker. I dump green in with a boxed brownie mix."

"Dude, I'm too lazy for even that. I have a bowl." Larry takes a bite of his burger. When he's finished chewing, he says, "She's all weird about the taste, says chocolate doesn't taste right. You're not eating the brownies for the taste of them."

"Women," Angelo snorts. He pops the last of his burger into his mouth, chews thoughtfully. "So, who's your plug?"

"Well, usually my girlfriend picks it up, but when I'm out, there's one around Cherry Hill East high," Larry says. "You need one?" He asks. He gives Angelo a questioning look. "They're not hard to come by."

"I know," Angelo says looking out the window to break eye contact. Blowing out a breath, he looks back at Larry.

"Dude?" Larry asks.

"Mine died," Angelo says, looking out the window again.

Larry whistles. "Dude, you mean Eva was your plug?"

"You knew Eva?" Angelo asks, turning from the window.

"I didn't 'know her' know her. I knew of her." Larry strokes his goatee. "Felt sorry for her. What happened to her sucks."

Angelo puts his head in his hands and begins massaging his temples.

"Dude?"

"Okay, it's eating at me. My friends are all like, 'you gotta let it go' but I can't let it go." He runs his hands through his hair.

Larry watches him in silence.

"I was there. I was in the park. I thought I might catch her there. You know pick up some green?" Angelo says. "The thing is, I heard arguing. I think some woman was trying to shake Eva down, get a frequent buyers discount, or something."

"Frequent buyers discount? You mean they have those? It's not like you're buying at Walmart."

"I know it sounds ridiculous. I heard this woman shout something like, 'C'mon I just bought last week.' something like that. I didn't want to get involved with some crazy woman's shit, you know?" He looks up at the ceiling; blows out his breath. "Now, I feel horrible. It was the day Eva died. I should have intervened or something; let them know I was there."

"Man, you don't know this particular woman is the one who killed her," Larry says.

"Right, but what if she was? I could've saved Eva's life; instead, I went off to Krispy Kreme and got coffee. I bought my stuff later from somebody else. I was too impatient to get involved in some junkies' argument." Angelo puts his head back into his hands.

"D'you tell the cops?"

"Tell 'em what exactly? Officer, I wanted to buy marijuana and heard some junkie arguing with my dealer. I was too much of a shithead to step in?"

"I see your point. You could've said you were taking a walk, heard two women arguing…"

"Coulda, woulda, shoulda—"

"Listen, not that it'll help, but I would've done the same thing. Mornings are tough enough without dealing with a catfight."

"Yeah," Angelo looking down at his watch. "We'd better head back. Fridays get crazy."

They dump their trash in a nearby trash can and head out to the parking lot.

Chapter 38

Lily staffs the front desk while Larry and Angelo are getting some dinner. The morning rain has completely passed through, and it's a bright, sunny evening. A small Toyota Rav 4 pulls into the lot. Jim and a younger man emerge. Jim's friend is in his twenties, well-built and tall, though dwarfed by Jim. "Hi," she greets them as they come in the door.

Jim introduces Matt as a fellow marine. Coming around from the C–wing, Ingrid announces, "Doggie and kitty dinners are served."

"Awesome, and fewer dinners too," Lily quips.

"I know it." Ingrid pumps a fist. "She juts her chin in the direction of the parking lot, "Mickey's pulling in."

Lily looks at her watch and says, "Right on time. Do we play rock-paper-scissors to see who gets the dog and who gets the men?"

"I'll take the dog," Ingrid says. "At least it isn't Nero. The way I smell, he'd mistake me for a giant cat." She heads out the front door.

Lily walks into the waiting room. "Okay, Jim, Matt, we'll give them a minute or two to get settled before I take you back to meet with Burrow." Lily goes to autopilot during the explanation, having done it many times. "Our foster parent, Mickey, will have him on the leash in the play area. We'll let him smell you through the fencing. If he responds well, we'll let you inside," she explains.

"He knows us." Matt smiles broadly. "He'll be glad to see us."

"Let Lily tell us the drill," Jim barks out like a command.

"Jim, I'm not one of your enlisted men anymore. I can make conversation with the lady," Matt pointedly responds.

"It's about respect—"

"So," Lily cuts in, "as I was saying, we have procedures we need to follow." Lily's tone is all business. They head outside towards the play area, where Ingrid, Mickey, and Burrow are waiting. Deciding on full disclosure, Lily says, "I should tell you we had another person come out to meet him." Jim and Matt lock eyes. "The meet didn't go well. Burrow had a strong adverse reaction. So we need to follow the procedure closely to keep everyone safe."

Jim lowers his head a bit then says, "It wasn't perchance a woman who came out?"

"Yes, she said she was a relative of Pete's," Lily answers.

Matt guffaws, and Jim gives him a glare that immediately silences him. The group is about ten yards from the pen. Burrow lets out a bark. He is standing on his hind legs, paws against the fence, wagging his tail so fast that if it were a propeller, he would take flight.

"Burrow," Jim says as he approaches the fencing. "Corporal, I'm glad to see you too."

"Okay, okay," Ingrid says sternly. "Burrow, sit." Burrow immediately sits, but with his tail still wagging. His eyes are as bright as a shooting star. "Jim, come into the pen and let him give you a sniff," Ingrid instructs.

Jim opens the gate. Just as he closes it, Burrow breaks free from Ingrid and leaps up to lick Jim's face as Jim kneels on the ground. "I guess this meet is going okay," laughs Ingrid.

Turning from the group, Lily swipes at a tear that's collecting in the corner of her eye.

"My friend, I'm sorry it took me so long to get here," Jim talks to Burrow. "You're going to live with me. Everything's going to be okay."

Ingrid comes out of the pen and turns to Matt, "I have to go back and staff the front desk. I'll leave the two of you in Lily's capable hands."

"Thanks so much." Matt extends his hand and Ingrid shakes it.

"Matt, we're going to let you into the pen now." Lily opens the gate and Matt walks in. Burrow gives another friendly bark, but he doesn't leave Jim's side. Matt walks over to them. He gives Burrow a scratch between the ears.

"Good to see you again, Burrow," he says.

Mickey walks over and extends her hand. "I'm Michelle. Burrow's been staying with me and my very exuberant Newfoundland, Nero."

Jim stands, giving a sly smile, and asks. "Nero? As in Nero Wolf?"

"A man of good literary taste, I see." Mickey smiles. "Being as my mom named me for Mickey Spillane, all my dogs get great detective names."

"Gosh, when we found out about Pete, we were worried sick about Burrow." Jim smiles, "We sure thank you folks, for taking good care of him. He was important to Pete. Most people don't know, but Pete's parents were killed by a drunk driver about six months after he retired from the Marine Corps. He was devastated, had a terrible time trying to get through it. Finding Burrow turned his life around."

"Wow, we didn't know," Lily says. "Pete was fairly reserved and didn't talk much about himself when he came to events. We knew Pete had retired from the Marines and he was great with Burrow." She is learning more and more about him posthumously.

Burrow is sniffing Matt. He jumps up, putting his paws on Matt's shoulders.

"Matt," Lily laughs. "You're getting what we call a doggie hug."

"It's good to see him so happy," Mickey says. "He was getting along well with Nero, but you could tell there was a sadness there. Phew, and after that other meet—"

Lily shoots her the stink eye, causing Mickey not to finish the sentence.

Lily picks up the end of Burrow's leash and hands it to Jim. "Let's finish the paperwork and let these men get home." Everyone starts walking towards the shelter.

Jim picks up the conversation. "Ladies, I'm assuming the woman you met was Pete's cousin, Clarissa. She's related to Pete, but they weren't close. Well, to put things nicely, I'm not sure how genuine her intentions were."

Lily and Mickey glance at each other but know not to ask questions.

"Yeah, that's putting it mildly," Matt says caustically. Jim scowls, but Matt ignores him. "Man, I know it's Pete's personal business, and we shouldn't be sharing it with strangers, but let's not pretend she was something important to Pete. She didn't appreciate you moving in either, cutting in on—"

"Yes, so," Jim interrupts, "what more do I need to do to adopt my friend here?"

"Come on back into the shelter. We need you to sign a few forms and, well, pay the adoption fee," Lily says.

Jim gives Burrow's leash to Mickey and he and Lily go back into the shelter. Other people are milling about looking at dogs and cats. Ingrid is processing adoption applications and chatting with people like a veteran retail clerk.

Lily finishes up with Jim's paperwork, and wishes him and Burrow well. Mickey is outside chatting away with Matt. She gives him her business card, and one to Jim as well, telling them if they ever need a dog walker or to have Burrow boarded for a time she can help out. She's a good businesswoman who offers her services without a high-pressure sales pitch.

Lily turns from the front door to find Ingrid standing behind her. Angelo and Larry are back from their break and behind the desk again. "High five me, partner, we had a good day," Lily says.

"Not so fast there, Miss. You haven't caught up on my major adoption coup today." Ingrid beams.

"What?" Lily asks.

"An older couple came in looking for a small dog." Ingrid is intentionally talking slowly, dragging the story out. "They wanted one that was housebroken, which I know we never guarantee, but we can usually tell who is and who isn't."

"Ingrid, spit it out already," Lily groans.

"I had them meet Skittle, and they LOVED him." She smiles broadly.

"Oh my God." Lily throws her arms around Ingrid. "You got Skittle adopted? I've been kicking myself for not being able to find him a foster home."

"I know it, my friend. When I met this couple, I thought, what could be more perfect? He's small, he needs a quiet environment. I've been bursting to tell you. With how crazy it was this afternoon and your fixation on Burrow's reunion, this was my first opportunity." Ingrid's satisfaction is pulsating from her body.

"Gosh that's great, and on that note I am calling it Pinot Noir time." Ingrid and Lily slap their hands in a high five. Lily gathers her things and leaves the shelter. She meets Mickey in the parking lot. "Off to my house?" she asks.

"You bet, but wait until I tell you what I found out from young Matt. "Mickey gives a wink getting into her car.

"I'm not sure how much more excitement I can take for one day. Tell me when you get to my house," Lily says, as she heads over to her car.

CHAPTER 39

An eruption of barking commences as Lily and Mickey pull their cars into the driveway at Lily's house. They enter and find Nero and Crockett standing just inside the front door. Nero's tail is wagging, with Crockett standing under him.

"Well, what a nice welcome home," Lily tells them as she closes the door. Boone is lazing on the couch. His eyes go bright as he stands to give himself a whole body shake. He joins the barking chorus.

"Okay, okay, everybody out to the backyard." Lily stops to scratch Boone's head, rubbing his ears a little. "You too, Mr. Boone."

When Mickey opens the door, the Nero Crockett duet begins anew. "I'm going to get everyone into the yard, you get the wine glasses," Lily tells her.

As the back door opens, Crockett races out after a juvenile rabbit that's sitting in the grass. Nero is hard on his heels. Boone goes to the bottom of the steps and produces a tremendous stream, before returning to the kitchen. He glances back at Lily as if to say, "What silliness, there are cookies here I don't have to run after." Lily glances at Nero and Crockett. Neither has a rabbit in his mouth. Lily assumes the rabbit made it under the fence safely, and follows Boone inside.

Mickey is at the kitchen table with two glasses of wine.

"Let me give Boone here a cookie, then I'll join you," Lily says. She gives him a Milk Bone. He makes short work of it before heading back to the couch.

Lily peers out the window to watch a bit of Crockett leading Nero on a world-class chase around the yard, then sits at the kitchen table and takes a long sip of wine. "Boy, today is one of those days when I feel completely fulfilled from what I do for a living." She smiles contentedly.

"It's great to spend time doing something that satisfies us, but don't distract me." Mickey shakes her finger as if scolding. "While you were inside with Jim, I was chatting up Matt."

"I noticed." Lily looks obliquely at her friend. "Mickey, you could sell dog sitting to the dogless." She stands and goes to the refrigerator. She removes a tub of hummus and a plastic bag of baby carrots, and sits back down at the table.

"It's odd," Mickey says, "but Matt looked familiar. I can't figure out where I might've met him. Well, heck, I did head a marketing department, you know, but that isn't the point. Matt told me Pete was an only child, and he was devastated to lose his parents right after he took retirement. He and his dad were starting a business. His dad made a lot of money buying silly startup tech stocks like Apple." Mickey has a very smug look on her face. She dunks a carrot in the hummus.

Lily gulps the carrot in her mouth. "Apple, as in the computer?" she chokes out.

"No, Lil, the ones on the trees. Yes, his dad owned Apple stock. When his dad died, Pete needed a new partner for the business."

"Did he choose Jim?" Lily asks.

"Yes, which made for an interesting dynamic," Mickey says.

"How?" Lily asks.

"In the military, Jim outranked Pete, and now they would be on even terms."

"Jim said Pete was his best friend. Wouldn't their friendship trump military rank?" Lily muses. "And how does Matt fit in?"

"Matt doesn't want to reenlist. He was discussing joining the business with Pete."

"Doing what?" Lily asks.

"Therein lies the problem, Matt doesn't have a lot of experience, but he has energy and a creative side."

"Hmm, energy and creativity… Now who does that remind me of," Lily teases.

"I know. I jumped right onto the subject." Mickey's mouth turns down.

"What's with the frown?"

Mickey takes a sip of her wine. "Matt said he wished he'd met me two weeks ago."

"He hadn't thought about how important marketing is to any business?"

"He had no idea." Mickey pauses, pensively turning her eyes to the ceiling.

"Spit it out already."

"He and Pete argued. Never mind." Mickey flips her hand to dismiss the subject.

"I don't think so. You started the story, now finish it."

"I think Pete was giving Matt some tough love. He wanted Matt to make a life plan, and as part of it to propose what his role would be in the business." She pauses.

"That sounds reasonable," Lily shrugs.

"Matt was uncertain of the how to go about making himself a 'going concern.' I'm giving you the condensed version."

"What's the not-so-nice version?" Lily smirks.

"Pete said something along the lines of, you can't hitchhike your way through life, sometimes you have to pay for a ticket. And it went on from there." Mickey shudders remembering the story. "Matt made a nasty remark about Pete having an inheritance. Now Matt's upset because it was the last conversation they had."

"You say that like you don't believe him," Lily says. "Pete was distracted the last time I saw him. I thought it was because he was ambivalent about our relationship. Geez, he was probably thinking about his argument with Matt."

"Matt's upset. I don't know enough about him to know whether it's about the argument with Pete or about not having a defined path in life. I do think he was looking at Pete's business as an easy way to try something different." Mickey pauses, rolling her shoulders forward and then back as if the movement will aid her in choosing her next words. "Jim found out about the argument, so there was tension between Matt and Jim as well."

"I noticed. Matt made some comment about not being one of Jim's enlisted men anymore, and it rankled Jim," Lily says.

Mickey laughs. "Matt said Jim's having trouble adjusting to not being in charge. He speculates Pete had to reinforce the 'partners' part of the business relationship."

"Well, Burrow sure liked him, so their relationship couldn't have been too heated," Lily muses.

"I can't believe Jim's been living with Pete, and Pete never mentioned him to you." Mickey's eyebrows draw together.

"Believe it. I wonder if it's one of those military compartmentalizing things. If Pete didn't want to discuss a subject, it was as if it didn't exist." Lily turns thoughtful. "Ingrid told me about a news story she saw about the business Pete was trying to get started. It had to do with assisting military families."

"That's what Matt told me—refurbishing and reselling second-hand furniture. Matt said military families are always relocating while living on a tight budget. It would be beneficial to have inexpensive but good furniture. He was thinking of hiring veterans. Lots of ex-military are great at woodworking. Others are good at painting. Some are even good at upholstery." Mickey rolls her glass between her hands, flashing her flamingo-pink nails.

"Ah, and Matt lacked a niche talent?"

There's scratching at the back door. Lily gets up to let Crockett and Nero in. They take hearty drinks from their water bowls. Nero drops his dripping chin onto Mickey's lap.

"It's a good thing I love you, Woofy," she teases him. "I never have a dry pair of pants on."

Lily gives them each a biscuit and sits back down. "I still don't understand the conflict with Clarissa. Did she want to be part of the business?" She takes a bite of a carrot.

"That's the best part of this," Mickey says, setting her glass down. Waving her hands in front of her face like a fortune teller finally seeing through the mist of the crystal ball, she says, "Apparently, she felt entitled to part of the inheritance."

"Why," Lily inquires as she sips her wine.

"Matt didn't elaborate. He just said that Pete was so devastated by the loss of his parents, he couldn't cope with Clarissa nagging him about money. He took their death hard." Mickey reaches for a carrot.

"Jim did mention that." Lily gives a rueful smile. "Jim said he was ecstatic when Pete adopted Burrow, because Burrow was helping Pete turn his life around."

"Yeah, and does Jim know about you and Pete?" Mickey asks, pointing the carrot at Lily to emphasize her question. "You might have been part of that."

"I don't think so." Lily tilts her head pondering. "If he does, he gave no indication of it when we spoke today. Stop changing the subject. Why didn't Pete and Clarissa get along?"

"I don't really know. My guess is Pete was consumed with grief and Clarissa was consumed with how much Pete's parents were worth. Apparently after his parents died, Pete drafted a new will making Burrow his beneficiary and Jim the executor."

"Be for real, Mickey. People don't leave money to their dogs." Lily tosses the carrot in her hand into the hummus, which spatters on to the table. She gets up and rips a paper towel off the roll.

"Maybe taking care of Burrow was going to be a directive? And the inheritance would go into a trust for the business? So if anything happened to him, the business would still have capital? He hadn't gotten everything established and well—young guy, healthy—he didn't think he was going to die. The only update he got done was changing the executor from his dad to Jim."

Lily tosses the paper towel she used to clean up the spattered hummus into the trash. "Mickey, maybe that's the conflict between Jim and Matt. Jim's now the executor and doesn't want Matt in the business." Lily shifts in her seat.

"Well…" Mickey seems skeptical. "It could be, I guess. Or maybe we still have the facts a bit wonky. If Jim accepts my offer to have our dogs get together, maybe I can find out." Her face brightens as she taps the fingers of her right hand against her cheek.

"Maybe you will, but I think only if Matt comes along. Jim strikes me as a guy who keeps his cards close to his chest."

"True. And you don't think I could charm the information from him?" Mickey bats her eyelashes.

"I'm not touching that," Lily laughs. "You don't know how Ingrid and Martin teased me this afternoon. I was 'too charming' when I talked to Jim. Given how Martin criticized my people skills earlier this week, you'd think he'd be supportive of my efforts." Lily rolls her head to the left and then to the right. "I don't want to kick you out, but I need a shower bad, and I'm a little beat."

"Oh, sure. You've had a long day." Mickey finishes the wine in her glass. "Let me gather up Nero, and we'll be on our way." She stands up and puts the empty glass in the sink.

"Thanks, Mickey." Lily stands and puts the hummus and carrots back in the refrigerator. Filling a large glass of water from the tap, she follows Mickey into the living room to find Nero curled on the floor with Crockett nestled against him.

"Up and at 'em, Nero." Mickey pulls Nero's leash from the wooden rack by the front door. Nero opens one eye to look at her. Seeing the leash, he jumps up and gives himself a full-body shake. Crockett gives a subsequent shake and turns his eyes to Lily.

"You're not going anywhere, little boy. I'm walking Mickey to her car, then heading to the shower."

CHAPTER 40

Mickey attaches Nero's leash to his collar as Lily opens the front door. Lily exits then pauses on the landing at the top of the steps to pour half a glass of water on each of the plants at the side of the steps.

"I was wondering what the water was for," Mickey says as she and Nero pass Lily and descend the steps.

"I promised Kelly I would do my best to keep them alive."

"You promised to give me another chance to adopt Burrow. You lied." The shriek emanates from the space behind Mickey's car. Mickey halts halfway between Lily's front steps and her car. Lily draws up beside her.

Clarissa steps around the bumper of Mickey's car, her face red with fury.

Nero tenses, splaying his feet wide, pointing his tail straight out behind him. Mickey wraps a loop of the leash around each hand to maintain full control of her dog. She looks over at Lily, who can't hide her shock at seeing Clarissa on her property.

"Clarissa, what are you doing at my home?" Lily has planted her feet mirroring Nero's stance.

"You said I'd have another chance at adopting Burrow. You gave him to someone else. Someone who isn't even family to Pete. Why'd you do that? Why'd you lie to me?" Clarissa's fists are balled in front of her bouncing in the air as if to add extra emphasis to each word she utters.

"I most definitely did not lie to you." Anger rises in Lily's voice as a low growl begins deep in Nero's chest. "I told you we needed time to figure out Burrow's reaction. Another person with a rightful claim to Burrow came to the shelter. We conducted an official meet. Burrow did not react to this person the way he responded to you. We had no legitimate reason not to allow the adoption."

Mickey shushes Nero, and leans forward to place a hand on his back. "Sit," she whispers to him. Nero pauses, then sits in front of Lily and Mickey. The hairs of his coat stiffen. He's tense, as he faces a potential threat to his master.

Clarissa digs the heel of her palms into her eyes, rubbing at them. "You said we could try again. Why'd you say that if you didn't mean it?" Dropping her hands, she lunges at Lily, but Nero jumps from his seated position. Mickey is holding the leash so tight that Nero stands on his hind legs. He looks like a giant bear about to attack. From the house, Crockett is furiously barking in the bay window. The porch lights of the neighboring home turn on, and two heads peek through the glass of their front door to see what's going on.

Clarissa screams and stumbles back, falling to the ground. Mickey sternly tells Nero to sit. He resumes his seated position. His eyes are fixed on Clarissa. Lily's limbs tremble as she tries to decide what action to take. Regaining her composure, she brushes her hands on her jeans and takes a step towards Clarissa.

"Do you need a hand getting up," she asks in as soothing a voice as she can muster.

Clarissa rolls to her side and uses her hands to push to a seated position on the grass. Drawing her knees up to her chin, she hangs her head between her knees, wrapping her arms around herself. "Nothing can help now. I needed the dog. All I wanted was a second chance. No one ever gives me a second chance," she mutters into her bent legs.

Mickey reaches one hand forward, grasping Lily's elbow. She gives a gentle tug, pulling Lily back a step behind the seated Nero. Leaning into Lily, she whispers, "Should I call the police?"

Lily shakes her head. While she is still concerned about

Clarissa showing up at her home, she doesn't believe the police are necessary to convince Clarissa to see reason and understand she needs to leave. Another neighbor's porch light has come on. Lily hopes one of her neighbors hasn't called the police. She steels herself. "Clarissa, I think you need to go home. Perhaps after a night's sleep…" Lily pauses, unsure how a night's sleep will help this distraught woman. She cuts her eyes to Mickey seeking assistance. Mickey shrugs and tilts her head towards the house, indicating what she thinks they should do.

In silent agreement, both women slowly walk backwards towards the house Mickey is tugging on Nero's leash, urging him to comply with the maneuver. As they reach the steps, Clarissa drops her hands to the grass. She pushes herself to a standing position, turns on her heel and walks to a car parked across the street from Lily's home. One neighbor's porch light turns off, but the other remains bright.

Lily, Mickey, and Nero remain rooted until Clarissa's motor starts and she turns her headlights on.

"What was that?" Mickey whispers.

"I'm not sure," Lily whispers back, both of them still stunned by the scene that unfolded on her front lawn.

"How did she know where you lived?" Mickey whispers, perplexed.

"She must have followed me home," Lily stammers.

"Why?"

"I have no idea. Maybe she thought she could follow me to your house, and you would give her Burrow." Lily scrunches her face in concentration. A large furrow is forming above her eyebrows.

Clarissa's car pulls away. The remaining porch light is turned off.

"Thanks for not coming over," Mickey wryly grins, easing some of the tension.

Lily turns her head, so they are peering into each other's eyes. "This is not normal. I'm not sure how I should handle this."

"Should you call Martin?"

"Not at this time of night." Lily giggles to release her remaining tension. "If I wake his son, I'll have his wife to contend with." Lily rolls her shoulders up and down a few times. "I'd rather contend with Clarissa." They begin walking towards Mickey's car, each gazing in the direction Clarissa drove off in. "I think the excitement's over. You go ahead and head home."

"Are you sure? Make sure you lock all your doors." Mickey appears skeptical. "I have Woofy here for protection."

"I have dogs, too," Lily counters indignantly. Unable to maintain it, she laughs. "Nobody better try to take Boone's spot on the couch—he's fierce. Do you think she was high?"

Mickey hits the button on her car remote to open the back of her GMC, and Nero hops in. She pauses and faces Lily, "It's possible. Her behavior was extremely odd."

"It was. Did you notice how her hands were shaking? And what was that comment she made about no one ever giving her a second chance?"

"You got me," Mickey shrugs.

"Maybe Pete didn't offer her a chance to be involved in the business because of a drug habit…"

Nero has settled in the back of the car, and Mickey closes the door. She approaches Lily wearing a stern expression. "That's even more of a reason for you to file a police report. If she has a drug problem, her actions will be erratic and unpredictable."

Lily sighs deeply. "I hear you and understand your concern. Let me sleep on it. Our emotions are all a bit over the top. I should let things settle and evaluate them in the light of day with a clear head."

Mickey reaches up and hugs Lily. "Ever the pragmatic one, you are. Get a good night's sleep, and make sure all of your doors are locked."

"I will, Mick. And thanks for everything." Lily turns from her friend and walks into her home.

Chapter 41

It's Saturday, and Boone woke Lily at 6 a.m. for the morning walk. It was too early for her, but he needed to go out. After a short stroll and breakfast for the boys, Lily sits at the kitchen table with a glass of orange juice, pondering the events of the previous night. The phone pings, and she opens the text messages.

"How about breakfast at the Collingswood farmers market?" It's from Eileen.

Lily's mouth starts to water at the thought of a MacMillan's jelly donut. Or one of their croissants. She knows neither option is healthy and begins to rationalize: I don't indulge in sweet breakfast treats very often and there's a great stand there that sells dog treats. She decides a stop at La Pooch Patisserie is essential to this outing.

"Sounds yummy, meet you at 9:30," she texts back, thinking Eileen's the perfect person to discuss the Clarissa situation with.

"Meet you at MacMillan's stand," Eileen replies.

Lily tosses a load of jeans and Forever Friends T-shirts in the washer. She picks up a tennis ball, bouncing and catching it twice. Crockett runs in from the living room. Lily and Crockett go out to the backyard and play fetch until the washer stops. Lily moves the laundry from the washer to the dryer. She rummages through the refrigerator, making a list of things to pick up from the farmers.

She gets two Dentastix from the cabinet and heads into the living room. Boone's head rises from the couch's armrest. Crockett jumps off the recliner wagging his tail.

"I'm going to the farmers market. I expect good behavior from both of you while I'm gone." With glistening eyes, the dogs stare at the Dentastix, disregarding the subject of good behavior. She gives each dog his treat before heading to her car.

As Lily makes the short drive to Collingswood, she thinks about the reunion of Burrow and Jim, and wonders again about Burrow's strong reaction to Clarissa. Had the dog sensed conflict between Clarissa and Pete? If Clarissa does have a drug problem, was her behavior erratic enough to set Burrow's guard dog instincts on high alert? Dogs are intuitive. But Pete was a strong, formidable man. Burrow couldn't have thought Clarissa was a physical threat. Had she abused Burrow when Pete wasn't present? "I suppose this will remain a mystery," she says, as she spots a car leaving a parking space and quickly pulls into it.

The market is a beehive of activity. The farm stand on the end has a long line of people vying for its fresh strawberries and local honey. There are many young married couples pushing a stroller or with a child strapped to a parent's chest. Some of the couples have both. The atmosphere hums with conversation.

Lily mingles with the crowd. The aromas from the different stands begin to overwhelm her. She snickers as she sees people selling tuna steaks right next to a woman selling homemade soap. The scents of those two stands do not belong together. She smells the yeasty aroma of bread and knows she is nearing MacMillan's.

She finds Eileen surveying the pastries. "What looks good today?" Lily asks.

"What doesn't look good?" Eileen is wearing a teal skort and a white T-shirt. "It's a good thing I did a five-mile run last night."

"I don't run, but the boys and I had an extended walk this morning. Then Crockett and I played a game of fetch. That must've burned off some calories, right?" Lily gives an impish grin.

They each buy something to eat and drink. Eileen spots an empty table and makes a beeline for it. She sits down on one of the chairs seconds before a couple pushing a stroller can reach the table. The man and woman frown but move on into the market.

"Good move, Eileen," Lily says as she puts down her purchase.

"I know I should feel guilty, but it's every person for themselves when it comes to getting a table at the farmers market," Eileen says.

"And this table has shade. I've got two good adoption stories for you," Lily says as she takes a seat. "I also need your opinion on a weird human interaction."

"Can we start with the adoption stories? I need to hear about some warm and fuzzy moments. You're not going to believe what's been discovered at school." Eileen bites into a crumbly scone. "Mmm good, but I should have gotten some jelly for this."

"That's why I buy something with jelly already inside of it," Lily says. "I tell myself it's a fruit serving."

"A serving that's a teaspoon of fruit to a cup of sugar," Eileen mocks her.

Lily recounts Jim's meeting with Burrow and taking him home. She acts incredibly annoyed that her coworkers teased her. Eileen laughs out loud when she hears about Chelsea wiping fake drool. "You have to give it as well as take it," she says.

"I know." Lily's lips form a tight line. She continues by telling about Ingrid finding Skittle a home. "These are the reasons I love what I do."

"Those are heartwarming moments," Eileen agrees.

Sensing Eileen's need to talk, Lily holds off on the story of Clarissa. "Enough about me, what's happening at the school?" Lily asks nonchalantly.

Eileen heaves a sigh. "I told you the police were conducting interviews?"

Lily nods, encouraging her to continue. Eileen glances at the people occupying nearby tables, "It turns out some students were purchasing drugs from the student who was killed."

"Oh my God," Lily halts mid-bite. "So she was selling stuff?"

Eileen frowns, "Yeah, unfortunately. It's part of the whole opioid crisis. I want to think those drugs were developed with good intentions. However, now people are out to make money preying on the vulnerable." Eileen takes a deep breath, then continues. "But worse, there were adults purchasing drugs from her."

"No way," Lily shouts, recalling her suspicion that Clarissa was high last night. She catches glances in their direction, and lowers her voice, "Teachers?"

"Thank goodness, no." Eileen pauses. "Maybe I should say, nothing has been discovered and I hope the answer is no. There was at least one woman who works in the cafeteria."

"Oh, no, not one of the lunch ladies?" Lily raises one hand to her face feigning horror.

"I know you're mocking, Lily, but seriously, yes." Eileen shakes her head. "This woman, she works part-time preparing food and cleaning up. Apparently she bought narcotics from the girl." She stops to sip her water. "The woman didn't want to admit it, but the police put pressure on her."

"This is like something you see in a TV drama," Lily says. "I mean, this doesn't happen in suburban America, does it?"

"Lily," Eileen gives a sideways glance, "you're too naïve. Yes, this happens in suburban America every day. Clarissa claimed she couldn't get prescription pain medication because she doesn't have health insurance because she's only a part-time employee. She isn't covered by our insurance, but isn't she the type of person the Affordable Care Act was created to help?"

"Um…" Lily hesitates. She knows to be careful when talking politics, even with Eileen, though she has similar inclinations. "Yes, she's who the Act was created to help, but the insurance companies have made their plans so expensive, a lot of people took the cheapest plan they could. Then the bastards went and raised the cost of plans for small companies, like us. However, before I get on my soap box, did you say Clarissa?"

Eileen flushes, "I hope I didn't." She fumbles around the table.

"You did," Lily states. "I don't mean to harp on it, but the woman who came to the shelter, the one who had a horrendous meet with Burrow, her name was Clarissa."

Eileen holds up her free hand to pause Lily's stream of thought.

"Wait, Ei, before you cut me off. That Clarissa showed up at my house last night."

Eileen's mouth falls slightly open and her eyes widen in a querying gaze.

"She made a scene. She called me a liar, said I'd promised Burrow to her but gave him to someone else. Then she lunged at me, like she was going to grab me." Lily has placed her pastry on a napkin and is using both hands to mime Clarissa's behavior.

"Holy…" Eileen begins.

"Mickey and Nero were there. Nero let out a growl and tried to rush Clarissa. Mickey was holding the leash so tight Nero was pulled up on his back legs." Lily allows her hands to rest in her lap.

"What happened then?" Eileen asks.

"Clarissa jerked back and fell to the ground, she was so startled by Nero. Then she sat in the grass, murmuring something about never getting a second chance. Porch lights were turning on all around us. I'm sure the neighbors were enjoying the live-action drama." Lily shakes her head derisively.

"Did you call the police," Eileen asks.

"Mickey thought we should. Clarissa ended up leaving on her own, and…" Lily pauses. "Okay, I was tired. I wanted a shower and to go to sleep. I was thinking about calling them this morning when I got your text. I thought I should ask your opinion on the matter." Lily leans into the table.

"Um, well," Eileen stammers, "it does concern me that this woman knows where you live. You don't know that the cafeteria worker at the school and this woman are the same person, but, yes, I think you should make a police report."

Lily slaps her hand on the table, looking up as if a cartoon light bulb has appeared over her head. "Mickey had this weird experience with Burrow. She went to take some Tylenol, and Burrow leaped up at her and spilled the Tylenol all over the floor."

"Lily," Eileen's voice takes on a pleading tone.

"What if something about the Tylenol set the dog off? Maybe Clarissa bought the drugs and put them in Pete's Tylenol bottle?" Lily is gesturing with her hands excitedly.

"Lily, I said STOP. You're acting like a crazy conspiracy theorist," Eileen huffs in indignation.

"I'm not. Dogs have an incredible sense of smell. Boone can smell a pizza crust lying on a parking strip on trash day from a block away. Perhaps Clarissa smelled like the drugs when she came to the house?" Lily puts her hands back on the tabletop. "She appeared to be high last night."

"A woman named Clarissa taking narcotics and a woman named Clarissa killing Pete are two very different scenarios," Eileen whispers in a hushed tone. "You have no proof they're the same person. Not to mention no proof of a murder."

"If Burrow smelled narcotics in Pete's Tylenol, he would associate that smell with Clarissa." Lily points a finger at Eileen to emphasize her theory.

Eileen starts to stand. "Lil, we've finished eating. We need to vacate the table."

"But..." Lily begins in protest.

"But nothing," Eileen states. "I don't want to continue this conversation. I think you should tell the police about the incident at your home, but you need to leave out the conspiracy theory."

"Pardon me, are you leaving this table?" inquires a woman holding two cups of coffee.

"Yes, we are," Eileen says to her.

"I suppose I am now," Lily grumbles. She wants to continue the conversation, but realizes Eileen won't, and lets it rest. She can think everything over more thoroughly at home.

"Do you want to walk around a bit? I could use some fresh veggies," Eileen attempts to change the subject.

"Sure," Lily grudgingly states. "I need to get some veggies for the week. I have to ensure Tyler doesn't exist on pizza."

Eileen glances sideways, with a sardonic grin.

"Oh, okay, to ensure I don't exist on takeout, too. At least I vary the takeout. When I get Thai or Chinese food, I always get something with vegetables." Lily shrugs.

Eileen laughs. "There's something we can agree on. Your Thai food has carrots, peppers, and beans."

"And tofu, don't forget the tofu for protein." Lily holds up her index finger as if giving an instruction.

They wander amongst the vendors. Before she can stop herself, Lily says. "You know, I'll have to call Jim to see how things are going with Burrow. He was Pete's friend. Maybe he'll know why Burrow jumped at Mickey." She pauses as Eileen's shoulders tense. "I'm sorry, but I'm too curious about animal behavior. Sorry, I guess it's an occupational hazard. Oh, look fresh spinach and strawberries. I have a great salad recipe for spinach and strawberries. We need to stop."

"Lead the way, culinary goddess," Eileen mocks. They walk amongst the vendors, choosing fruits and vegetables. Lily stops at La Pooch Patisserie and purchases some pretzels for Boone and Crockett. Eileen and Lily say goodbye, and return to their respective cars.

CHAPTER 42

On the drive home Lily reflects more on what Eileen had to say. She adds it to the information Mickey gathered from Matt as well as her own interactions with Clarissa. She wonders if the tensions between Pete and Clarissa stemmed from Clarissa's drug use. Did her drug habit fuel her desire for the family fortune? Maybe Pete offered to pay for rehabilitation, and Clarissa denied her problem? There had to be a reason Burrow had such an adverse reaction to her.

Noticing two cars parked in the driveway, the last partially in the street, Lily shakes her head as she parks her car. The driveway is a double. Tyler's friend could have parked in her spot. As she exits her car and gathers up the purchases, Lily hears Crockett barking in the yard. When she opens the front door, Boone is standing there, his tail wagging.

"Hi, who's a good boy? How can you nap with that racket going on?" Lily dares not put down the bags to pet him. She can tell by the twitching of his nose that he's caught the scent of the La Pooch pretzels. Closing the door, she heads to the kitchen and puts the bags on the counter. Boone sits, giving her his most significant brown-eyed stare, the one that says it's been a millennium since he has had any tidbit of food.

"Boone, my friend, first, it's only been a few hours since breakfast. Second, if only you were obedient, I could make a mint from having you do dog commercials." She rubs his ears playfully.

She goes to the back door. Tyler and two of his friends are

outside playing catch with a tennis ball. They are using Crockett's tennis ball. The poor little guy is running himself ragged trying to get it.

"Now what type of animal abuse is going on out here?" she shouts as she opens the door. They all turn to look at her and the ball falls to the ground.

Crockett makes a beeline for it, grabs it in his mouth, and runs to Lily, dropping the saliva-covered ball at her feet.

"Gee, thanks, buddy," she says, giving him a good ear scratch.

"Yo, Lil, we were helping the little guy get some exercise," Tyler calls out. His two friends start laughing.

"Oh, complete altruism, was it?" Lily gives a mock scowl. "Well, he looks none the worse for wear. If the neighbors haven't made a noise complaint, I guess we're all fine." She gives Crockett a few extra ear scratches. He pants to cool himself off. "Which one of you is parked halfway in the street?"

"That's me." One of the men waves his arm in the air. He's got a chin full of stubble, making Lily wonder if he hasn't shaved or if he's trying for the stubble look. If it's the look, he has a few more days to go to achieve it. "I didn't want to take your spot."

"How very polite of you," Lily says. "I'm in for the day. You'd better pull in behind me."

"It's all good, Lil," Tyler says. "Max has some ideas for different graphics for a website I'm working on and then we're going to Dollar Dog Night at Citizens Bank Park. But you know before we got working, we thought we'd play some catch with Crockett."

"Uh huh, you do understand the point of 'catch' is the dog is supposed to actually get the ball at some point, right?" Lily crosses her arms in front of her chest.

"Oh, man, is that the rule we forgot?" The other friend slaps his forehead with an open palm.

"Well, he probably has a bit of an appetite and I picked up some stuff at the farmers market. Since poor Boone appears to be starving in there, I guess both boys will have a snack. You guys have fun." Lily goes back into the house with Crockett hot on her heels. She gives each dog his La Pooch treat and refills their water bowls. She puts the other purchases away.

She goes to the dryer to remove the jeans and T-shirts. She uses her hands to press out wrinkles while folding. "I wonder if Chelsea hangs up her clothes? It would explain why she doesn't look as wrinkled as I do." She laughs thinking about it.

Lily does other Saturday chores while Boone and Crockett nap in the living room. When the house is tidy and the rest of the laundry complete, she grabs a tall glass of water and heads to the living room. She flops next to Boone on the couch. The conversations with Kathy Klapper and Eileen are still swirling in her mind. She decides to call Mickey.

"Lil, do you think there would be a market for afghans made from dog hair?" Mickey says, by way of answering her phone. She's seen Lily's number come up on her Caller ID.

"Somehow, I don't think so," Lily responds. "Besides, how would you spin the hair into yarn?"

"Darn, you ruin my entrepreneurial plans," Mickey teases. "Whatcha been up to today?"

"I went to the Collingswood Market with Eileen this morning—" Lily starts.

"What did you buy at La Pooch?"

"I guess you know I can't go there without stopping at La Pooch. I got each of the boys those cool pretzels she makes." Lily begins stroking Boone's back. "Eileen provided some interesting information that could relate to our confrontation with Clarissa last night. The police found out one of the cafeteria workers at the school was buying drugs from the dead girl we stumbled across at Cooper River. Eva."

"Are you kidding me? She was what, sixteen, and she was selling drugs?" Mickey shrieks.

"It's disturbing, all right. The school vice principal I met last week told me Eva's friends reported to police that her mother had debts with dealers." She pauses. "Eva began selling narcotics to work off her mother's debt."

"Lily, that's horrible," Mickey says.

"Wait until you hear this. The name of the woman who was buying drugs is Clarissa." Lily pauses for dramatic effect.

"So what?" Mickey asks.

"Mickey, Clarissa, like the woman on my lawn last night. The woman I thought was high," Lily's voice bubbles with excitement.

"Lil…" she begins.

"There's a connection." Lily hesitates to tell Mickey the remainder of her theory. "There has to be."

"You know, they say anything is possible, but you need to have the police handle things." Mickey sounds dubious.

"Now, who's ruining someone's creative spirit?" Lily teases. "I'm determined to discover Pete's cause of death, and his cousin's behavior is unnervingly suspicious."

"I appreciate your need for closure," Mickey's tone is patronizing, "I think you're trying to force a connection."

"So, you don't think I should call the police about my theory?" Lily has trouble hiding her disappointment.

"I think you should call the police about last night. However, if you add your other theory, they won't give your report much weight. Someone impatient will start talking down to you, and treat you like some crazy conspiracy theorist."

"That's exactly what Eileen said," Lily concedes. "Two of my friends think I'm a crazy conspiracy theorist."

"You're putting words into my mouth," Mickey says, caution rising in her voice.

"I did hear the words 'crazy conspiracy theorist' from you, correct?" Lily asks.

"As it relates to what the police might think," Mickey adds, drawing out each word. "What if that good-looking state trooper who's always coming by hears your theory. He might start taking the pooches he finds to another shelter." Mickey attempts to add levity to the conversation.

"If Chelsea's relentless flirting hasn't turned him off, I doubt any crazy idea I come up with will," Lily says.

"Best not to chance it. Now I have more dog hair to vacuum up." She rings off.

CHAPTER 43

Driving to work with the windows down to catch the refreshing morning breeze, Lily is grateful for low humidity. This is a good day to be outside with the dogs. Musing over the information she's learned over the weekend, Lily weighs her strong desire to call the police against the admonitions of her friends. She wrestles with the correct course of action.

Lily arrives at the shelter and takes her usual parking space. As she leaves her car, she gives herself a morning pep talk, stands tall, and pushes back her shoulders. With her head held high she opens the door to D–wing.

"Morning Stevie, morning Mick, morning Lindsay." She does a double take at Lindsay's kennel. Lindsay is a female. Given that she's in with Mick and Stevie, Lily theorizes whoever named this group was going for a Fleetwood Mac theme. Lindsay's coat is the silky texture of an Irish setter. It is a medium brown color. "Lindsay Buckingham should be proud you're named for him. Your coat is much nicer than his hair," Lily jokes.

Lily continues down the line of kennels. "Morning Dylan, morning Hopper, morning Barney, morning Gigi, what a great little wag you have on you." Moving along the corridor, she opens the door to the C–wing. "Good morning, my band of furry friends."

Lily turns on the front desk computer and then goes to her desk. She stores her bag. Staring at the telephone, Lily wrestles with which police department to call. The incident at her home happened in Camden County. Burlington County is handling the investigation into Pete's death. She decides discussing the entire situation with a known officer is probably her best option.

"Road Station D, Officer Honeycutt."

"Hi, it's Lily from Forever Friends."

"Good morning, Lily. What a pleasant surprise."

"I thought you'd like to know we reunited Burrow with a friend of Pete Russo's."

"That's great. How'd you find him or her?"

"Him, former marine buddy, and he found us. He came in Friday. You should've seen how excited Burrow was to see him." Lily smiles at the memory. "It was a relief to us after the other meet went so badly."

"The other meet?"

"Yes." Lily gives herself a mental pat on the back for her smooth segue. "A woman came in, said she was Pete's cousin Clarissa. Unfortunately, Burrow had an aggressive reaction to her."

"How so?"

"He started barking and growling, mean growling. Chelsea was scared."

"He was aggressive with Chelsea?" Officer Honeycutt asks with some concern.

"No, he was great with Chelsea. The woman, the cousin, she couldn't get near him. Honestly, it threw all of us. We'd never seen him act out aggressively. He's a shepherd. They're guard dogs, but none of us had ever seen him be aggressive, ever." Lily slaps a palm against her forehead. She realizes she is babbling like a teenager. "We were relieved when Pete's marine buddy came to meet Burrow and everything went so well." Lily breaks off. "Until…" she pauses.

"Until what?"

"Clarissa came to the shelter Wednesday night to ask for another meeting. I told her that we needed to do some assessment with Burrow to figure out why he reacted to her the way he did. Then, when Pete's friend came to the shelter and there were no issues, we allowed him to adopt Burrow. Then Clarissa showed up at my house. She was distressed, and, well, I think she was high. She was screaming at me that I promised her a second chance, that I didn't give her one." Lily pauses.

"What made you think she was high?"

"I can't say for sure she was, but her actions were erratic. Her movements were jerky, and the things she was saying were addled. I reminded her that we needed a further assessment but we never promised to hold the dog for her. Officer Honeycutt, you know if we find a good match, we allow the adoption. At one point, she sat on the ground, muttering 'No one ever gives me a second chance' over and over." Lily places her head on the palm of her free hand, and rotates her head to give herself a brief forehead massage.

"Did you file a police report in your town?"

"I didn't. Once she left, I wanted to go to bed. My friends have told me I should've filed a report."

"I agree with your friends, Lily. If you believe she was in a drug-induced state, you should report it to the police. I'm not trying to scare you, but in our business, this kind of information is always helpful," Honeycutt says in a businesslike tone.

"All right, I'll do it today." Lily pauses. She wants to tell him her theory about Pete's death, but her resolve has ebbed during their exchange. "Thank you for listening to me."

"That's why we're here, to protect and serve." He pauses, "So, Lily…"

"Yes," she says, furrowing her brow.

"You, um, haven't stumbled over anything at Cooper River, have you?" He stifles a laugh, working hard to stay professional.

"Oh, no," Lily's face flushes. "How'd you know?"

"You and your friend are a bit of the talk of law enforcement." He pauses. "We saw the local crime report. Two women and four dogs tend to stand out in a write-up."

"Well…" Lily pauses. She decides to strike while the iron is hot. He broached the subject. "Since you know about the case, are there any suspects?"

"I haven't seen anything reported. This is most likely a drug gang-related incident. There were a few prints retrieved from the clothes and the backpack, but nothing that matches any of the databases. Sadly, not the first such occurrence." His deep, baritone voice displays his frustration with the situation.

"I can imagine." Lily tries to hide her disappointment and decides to try another tack. "Is there any chance that death is related to Pete's?"

"Why would you expect them to be related, Lily?"

Lily takes a deep breath. "I told you that Clarissa acted high at my house. A friend of mine who works in the Haddon Township school system told me a woman named Clarissa was buying oxy from Eva. Mickey, who was fostering Burrow, had a problem one night. She was trying to take Tylenol, and Burrow ran into the room and knocked the bottle out of her hands." She pauses to take a breath. "I was wondering if perhaps Clarissa, the cousin, could have bought oxy from Eva and tried to poison Pete with it by putting it into his bottle of Tylenol."

"That's an interesting theory."

"Thank you for not laughing at it."

"They train us to not laugh at the academy," Officer Honeycutt says, deadpan. There is a five-second pause, and he laughs. "That was a joke."

"I'm sorry. I didn't want to laugh inappropriately," Lily says. "So, do you think it's a viable theory?"

"Anything is possible. If it makes you feel better, I've heard crazier theories." The smile in Officer Honeycutt's voice is evident. "In all seriousness, do you want me to call my colleagues at Burlington Township or Haddon Township?"

"I would appreciate that. Like you said earlier, the more information law enforcement has, the better, right?"

"Exactly, consider it done. I'll see you the next time we have a lost dog to get reunited with their family," Officer Honeycutt says and disconnects.

Belting out a Top 40 hit, Martin dances into their space.

Lily gives an involuntary jump. "Whoa, ho, Lily, who were you talking to that you hung up so fast?" He wiggles his eyebrows.

"I was finished with my call, Martin. You certainly are chipper today." She musters a nonchalant tone.

"Flower petal, of course, I'm in a happy mood. I'm here with such good people to help find homes for a bunch of orphans. What could make me happier?" He says with a shrug.

"Did you seriously call me 'flower petal'?" Lily turns to him. Her face is a bit red.

Martin puts both hands in front of him in a stop gesture. "I'm sorry. Let's not start Monday on a bad foot." He drops his hands. "Good morning, Lily. How was your weekend?"

"No, I'm sorry. I didn't mean to snap." Lily shrugs. "Flower petal? Where'd that come from?"

"My wife dragged Christian and me to garden centers all weekend. She wants to make the place look nicer." He sits down. "I wouldn't know a pansy from a potato, and she's asking me this one or this one?" He holds up one hand then the other. "Then, is it pink or is it raspberry? Like I know the difference?"

"So, you've got flowers on the brain, huh?" Lily laughs at him.

"I sure do." Martin laughs.

Lily stands. "Well, I won't leave poor Chelsea to morning duty alone. I'm off to walk dogs." Lily strides off to the D–wing.

Chelsea has handed out breakfast. Chewing and lip-smacking sounds are coming from all the kennels. "Did I hear Martin arrive?" She's smirking.

"Crazy man came in here and called me 'flower petal,'" Lily exclaims.

Chelsea doesn't even try to stifle a laugh. "He called you what?"

"Flower petal, the crazy man called me flower petal." Lily can't help herself. She is laughing too. She grabs a leash from the rack. "How'd the new guy do this weekend?"

"Larry's a pretty cool cucumber," Chelsea says. "I stuck close to him, to make sure he had backup." Chelsea bats her lashes and grins.

"Oh, yeah, I bet you stuck close to him," Lily says sarcastically. "Let's see how these new dogs are with walking." Lily goes to Stevie's pen and leashes him up.

"Be careful out there, flower petal," Chelsea calls after her.

Lily ignores the jibe and starts the dog walking, Chelsea following soon after.

The two of them rotate between the D–wing and the grounds, getting each of the dogs a morning walk. Lily walks Dylan last and spends time in the play area with him.

CHAPTER 44

It's Tuesday morning and Anna pokes her head into the staff area. "Lily, call for you a Jim something."

"Oooohhhh, David Beckham Jim?" Ingrid says.

Lily gives her an eye roll and lifts the phone handset. "This is Lily," she says brightly.

"Hello, this is Jim. Jim Davidson."

Lily sits taller. "Hi, Jim, is everything okay with Burrow?"

Ingrid lets out a little squeal of delight and Lily turns her back to her.

"Yes, he's doing fine," he says. "I wanted to let you know the police have released Pete to us."

"Oh," Lily exclaims. "Have they figured out what happened to him?"

"Well, they're not completely forthcoming in the information area." He gives a nervous laugh. "However, they have completely ruled me out as a suspect. I also think the county probably wants the morgue space."

Lily winces. She refuses to make eye contact with Ingrid again. She is so glad they are not having this conversation in person.

He continues, "The reason I called is, I'm working on a memorial service for Pete. I know how much Burrow meant to Pete. I was wondering if I could list the shelter as a place where people could give donations?"

"The shelter is always happy to accept donations. I'll ask our person in charge of fundraising to get in touch with you," Lily wears a smile so broad she looks like a training video for a customer service helpline.

"Oh, gee," he hesitates. "I wasn't planning on anything too formal."

"Jim, I understand. We love Maria, but fundraisers are fundraisers. You don't want donation cans on the altar?" Lily lets out a laugh.

Jim laughs as well. "Correct, no cans on the altar. There's something else…" He trails off.

"Sure, Jim." Lily fills the gap in the conversation.

"Well, I believe I told you Pete's parents are deceased, and he had no siblings." He pauses. "I was wondering if anyone from the shelter would like to say a few words at the service about his volunteer work?"

Lily pauses, which Jim interprets as a negative response.

"I apologize if this is an odd request. We have a lot of folks who can talk about his leadership and his tactical skills. I thought, well, it might be nice to have someone talk about Pete from a non-military perspective. I'll understand if this is something the staff doesn't do." He pauses again.

"I'm honored you'd ask us," Lily replies. "I'm sure someone would come out to speak. If you give me the details about the service, we'll see who's available. We'll probably end up playing rock-paper-scissors to see who gets top billing." Lily cringes slightly. She is not a fan of public speaking and hopes one of the other staff will agree to give a few words.

"Choose rock, Lily. I always choose rock," Jim says. "I appreciate it. I'll call back when the details are final. I'm trying for Saturday afternoon."

"Okay, I'll tell Maria about you listing the shelter as a place for donations, and that you want things low-key. She's going to insist on calling you to say thank you. Don't worry. She's very nice and won't try to sign you up for lifetime donations," Lily says.

"Thank you, Lily. I'll be back in touch with the details as soon as I have everything together." He disconnects.

"Lil," Martin shouts. Lily whips her head in his direction.

"Lil, there's a little drool on your chin." Martin fake wipes his chin as if clearing some liquid. Ingrid bursts out laughing.

Lily gives him an obscene gesture.

"Yow, Lily that's not like you," Ingrid fake gasps. She turns to Martin and points a finger, "Would you cut her some slack?" She turns back to Lily. "Give us the skinny."

"Pete's body is being released, and Jim Davidson is in charge of making the funeral arrangements. He wants to list our shelter for donations, and he also asked if someone would say a few words at the service. You know, talk about Pete's volunteer work. How about it, Martin? Can you pull together a few words?" Lily smiles. "You know nice words. Can you speak at an appropriate decibel level?"

"You two are like two cats today." Ingrid pretends to push away from Lily.

"Don't you act all innocent," Lily points a finger at Ingrid. "David Beckham Jim." She snorts derisively.

"In all seriousness, you'd better give Kim or Maria first crack. Kim is the volunteer coordinator and Maria's in charge of fundraising. Understanding Kim's methods, remember?" Martin's tone has dropped an octave.

"I know, boss. I don't want to step on any toes or bruise any egos. I'm ready to stand up for a while. I'll go over to the offices and see if either of them can chat with me now." Lily stands up and stretches her arms over her head. She briefly goes up on her tiptoes. Then returning her heels to the floor, she drops her arms by her sides.

"Be your most charming, Lily," Ingrid encourages. "Watch those hand gestures, too," she snickers.

Lily leaves the staff area.

Ingrid turns to Martin, "A Marine Memorial Service? If Kim and Maria can't go, can I volunteer?"

"You stop," he says. "Besides, what if the service interferes with your long-awaited long weekend?"

"Oh boy, I rescind my offer immediately," Ingrid smiles. "I've got dogs to work with." She stands and heads for D–wing.

<h1 style="text-align:center">Chapter 45</h1>

At quarter to two Lily is on her way to the Thomas Edison school. Since this Saturday is Memorial Day weekend, Kim and Maria were happy to let Lily represent the shelter at the funeral. As expected, Maria insisted on calling Jim to thank him for listing the shelter for donations in Pete's memory.

I hope I can say a few words without breaking down into tears, Lily thinks to herself.

Pulling into the school parking lot, Lily spots Connie near her car. She parks as close as possible. Connie has the back open and is attaching a ramp to the bumper.

"Need a hand?" Lily asks.

"I've gotten quite good at this," Connie says. "Here, you can hold a treat at the bottom of the ramp."

Lily takes a treat from Connie. Annie approaches the ramp. She backs up a few steps, then inches forward.

"C'mon girl," Connie encourages.

Lily holds the treat in her open palm. "Look what I have for you."

Annie tentatively descends the ramp. Lily gives her the treat.

Connie tucks the ramp back into the car. "She seems a little stiffer today," Connie says, as she offers Annie a pat and attaches her leash to her collar.

"Poor girl," Lily says. As they walk towards the school, they see Kathy Klapper coming out.

"Hello," Kathy calls to them. "We're going to be in the same spot as last time." She scurries to the outdoor seating area.

As Connie, Lily, and Annie reach the space, Miss Cooke emerges with the same four children as the previous week. After everyone takes their place, Lily sidles over to Kathy, who is a bit red in the face.

"How are you?"

"It's been quite a day."

"Are the natives getting restless as the school year winds down?"

"Oh, these younger children are fine. We had an incident at the high school."

"Goodness, what now?"

"One of our part-time workers in the cafeteria was arrested."

Lily puts one hand over her heart. "Oh, my goodness, was it something to do with Eva?"

Kathy rubs her temples with her forefingers. "No," she murmurs turning to face Lily. "Apparently, the worker was involved in the death of a family member."

Lily's face registers shock. Her eyes go wide. "What happened?"

"I was in a meeting with the principal, and we were interrupted by detectives from Burlington County." Kathy looks around to see who may be able to hear her. "This woman is being charged with the death of her cousin. They say she caused a drug overdose."

Lily feels faint and grabs onto the school building wall for support. She opens her mouth, but no sound emerges.

"I think I had the same look on my face," Kathy says.

Lily struggles to gain her composure. She thinks, was I right, did Clarissa kill Pete? She turns her head left and then right. She opens her mouth again. She finally manages, "What did the police tell you?"

"Well, you remember Eva. The Camden County police determined her mother was selling drugs and using them, too. She owed money to dealers, and they pressured Eva into selling. The police have been investigating a gang operation. However, they haven't been able to make any arrests other than street level dealers," Kathy begins. "After a lot of questioning, several of the part-time staff admitted they'd purchased oxycontin from the mother and from Eva."

This is what Eileen told me Saturday, Lily thinks to herself. She nods her head, encouraging Kathy to continue.

"Well, this man who died is a completely different case. The case isn't even in Camden County. It's a Burlington County case," Kathy continues.

"Did they tell you the man's name?"

"Not directly. When Miss Gibbons was arrested, the officer told her it was for the murder of Pete Russo." Kathy's face is a mask of confusion. "No one in the Principal's office knows a Pete Russo. We have no idea who he is. I suppose I should say, was."

Gasping, Lily covers her mouth. From the strained silence, Lily realizes all eyes have turned to her.

"Oh, Miss Cooke, I apologize for the distraction. We'll move further away," Kathy chirps, and guides Lily to a place out of earshot. "One of the counselors lives in Burlington County. She called someone, but was only told that a tip called into the Burlington County police led them to look at our cafeteria worker," Kathy concludes.

Lily feels herself sway and works hard to remain upright. "Kathy, I apologize if I'm overly dramatic. Last week the state troopers brought Pete Russo's dog to our shelter," she sputters. She turns her head and sniffs back tears. "Pete's cousin Clarissa came into the shelter trying to adopt the dog, but the dog had a violent reaction to her. We couldn't let her take him. Oh, my goodness." Lily puts her face in her hands.

"But…but why would she kill her cousin and then want his dog?" Kathy asks. "Please don't tell me she killed him for the dog?"

"Um, no she didn't want the dog per se. It was clear she was NOT a dog person." Lily pauses. "And also pretty clear the dog wasn't a Clarissa canine."

"Okay, but seriously, why would she want the dog?"

Lily spits out a laugh. She shakes her head, no. "You're not going to believe what I'm about to say."

"I've been in the K through 12 system close to thirty years. Believe me, I've heard everything."

"Apparently, the dog's owner, Pete, made caring for the dog a provision of his estate. He was apparently worth a good deal of money."

"This is straight out of 'The Aristocats.'"

"The what?"

"It's a Disney movie I loved as a kid," Kathy says. "Old, rich lady leaves her estate to her cats."

"This is unbelievable," Lily says. "I heard this morning Pete's body was released, and a memorial service is in the works. I, I guess she managed to poison him with oxycontin?"

"I suppose." Kathy shrugs.

"Then I suppose the police found oxycontin in the house," Lily muses then her eyes go wide with shock. "Holy cow," she exclaims, then covers her mouth and looks towards the children. "Sorry, I didn't mean to be so loud." She turns to Kathy.

"What is it?" asks Kathy, leaning in towards Lily.

"Well, since we couldn't list Burrow for adoption until the police notified Pete's next of kin, we put him with one of our foster families." Lily pauses again. "The woman told me one night she tried to take Tylenol and Burrow jumped her, knocking Tylenol all over the floor."

"Odd."

"Very odd. He didn't hurt the woman. In fact, he backed away after she spilled the pills." Lily places her hands on her hips. "I bet Clarissa switched oxycontin into an over-the-counter pill container at Pete's house."

"He would have to have taken quite a few of them."

"Sure, but if he thought he was taking Tylenol, he might have taken more than the recommended dose. I sometimes do." Lily gives her head a brief shake.

"Well, I will be glad to put this school year behind me."

"I bet you will be. But Eva's death remains unsolved?"

"Sadly, yes." Kathy nods. "We may not find out the reason before the school year finishes," Kathy adds.

"How very distressing. It'll be hard on everyone not to get closure," Lily says. "Speaking of the school year finishing, you'd like us to come for three more weeks?"

"Yes, yes. Boy, you got me off on a tangent today. Three more weeks and then you and I can talk about fall." Kathy regains her professional demeanor.

"That's awesome. Do you need me here every week?"

"I'll leave it to you and Mrs. DiStefano," Kathy says. "Now, I'd best get back inside."

"Great chatting with you." Lily smiles at her. Lily looks over to the children and sees Connie rise with Annie's leash. The children stand and all pet Annie. This week, every child gives Annie a treat. Miss Cooke leads them back into the school. Lily walks over to Connie.

"What were you chatting about so intently?" Connie asks, as they move towards her car.

"Kathy helped me understand a great mystery," Lily says. "Do you need help getting Annie back into the car?"

"You can hold the leash while I set up the ramp." Connie hands Lily the leash, then opens the back of the car. Annie's steps are tentative, but she goes up and lies down in the back.

"So, Kathy says you can come without me next week if you'd like. I'll come if you want me here, though."

"Let me think about it. It probably would be good to have someone from the shelter here."

"Okay. I'll call you on Tuesday morning."

"Thanks," Connie says and gets into her car.

Lily gets into her car and checks her phone to see if there are any messages.

"I'M WALKING WITH YOU AND THE BOYS TONIGHT.'

It's from Eileen. "Gee, I wonder what you might want," Lily says smiling to herself.

CHAPTER 46

Lily muses on the ride home how to handle Eileen. Should she feign ignorance? Or be smug in the satisfaction she was correct to mistrust Clarissa Gibbons? "Lily, you know that feigning ignorance is not something you are very good at. Smug, you're good at." A satisfied smile settles on her face.

As she turns onto her street, she sees Eileen's car parked in front of the house. Lily pulls into her driveway. Eileen emerges from her car wearing a somber expression.

"Hi." Lily smiles brightly.

"Lily, Clarissa was arrested," Eileen blurts out. Lily opens her mouth, but Eileen cuts her off. "We'd better go inside."

They walk up the steps to the entrance of the house. When they open Lily's door, Boone and Crockett are waiting with wagging tails. "Hi, boys. How about a quick romp in the yard before we walk?" Lily asks them. She leads the way to the back door. It looks like a scene from the Pied Piper: Lily in the lead, Boone, Crockett, and Eileen following. Lily opens the back door and lets the boys out into the yard. Turning to Eileen and casually leaning against the counter, she says, "Spill it."

"Well, about one o'clock two officers came into the principal's office and asked for Clarissa Gibbons. One of the admin staff went to get her from the cafeteria. When Clarissa got to the office, they put her in handcuffs and read her her rights."

"Okay," Lily says crossing her arms in front of her chest.

"It was a real scene; when Clarissa was arrested, classes were changing. Students came from everywhere, pretending they had to be in the Principal's office. We were moving the kids along, so I didn't actually hear the rights being read." Eileen pauses.

"And…" Lily is having a hard time not letting on she knows the conclusion of this story.

"I was told the policeman said she was being arrested for the murder of Pete Russo." Eileen puts both hands on her hips. "Did you have something to do with this, Lily?" She accusingly points a forefinger at Lily.

Lily puts up her hands in surrender. "Okay, can you explain to me how you think I did this?"

"You said you were going to call the police because she had the same name as the cousin you didn't like."

"And you said there couldn't possibly be a connection. Do I remember correctly?" Lily hears Boone scratching at the back door. Pushing away from the countertop, Lily goes to the back door and lets Boone and Crockett in. Dishing up their kibble, she places both bowls on the floor, standing up straight as slowly as possible. "Eileen…?" She lets the question hang.

"I believe I said you were judging her because the dog didn't like her. I didn't think you had any kind of evidence," Eileen replies in a defensive tone.

"I see." Lily pauses. She looks Eileen straight in the eye. "I did call the police. I told them about the two names being the same. They were skeptical. However, it appears that perhaps someone did take me seriously." Lily crosses her arms in front of her chest again. "Maybe there was evidence, and the police needed a push in the right direction…?"

Eileen lets her chest deflate, and her eyes soften. "Well, I didn't actually get to talk to the officers." She shifts from foot to foot. "The rest of the staff were abuzz because no one except me had ever heard the name Pete Russo. Everyone is asking, who's this guy? I kept my lips zipped." She looks Lily in the face. "I must say you don't seem too surprised by this news." Eileen raises one eyebrow.

Lily can contain herself no longer. "Today we did 'Read to a

Dog' at the Thomas Edison school. Assistant Principal Klapper may have told me a few things." She gives her head a nod of satisfaction. "And you thought I was a crazy conspiracy theorist. Hah. It appears I may be smarter than everyone was giving me credit for."

"You knew? And you've been holding it in this entire time?" Eileen yells.

"I wanted to see if you would admit I was right." Lily cannot keep the smug tone from her voice. "Now, these dogs need a walk. Are you coming with us?"

"I think I'll wait here while you walk them."

"Good idea. I need some time alone to let my smugness subside." Lily grins at her. She gets plastic bags and then the leashes. She takes the boys for an enjoyable long romp. When they come home, they find Eileen setting the kitchen table.

The air is filled with the mouthwatering scent of peanuts and sesame. Lily spots a plastic bag on the counter.

"What have we here?" she asks Eileen. Boone and Crockett have their noses in the air and are circling each other in front of the cabinet.

"I thought Pad Thai might hit the spot," Eileen sits on one of the kitchen chairs.

Lily opens the plastic bag. "I see two containers in here?"

"Yes, I also got Singapore Noodles."

"You know, one of us doesn't run 100 miles a week. You shouldn't tempt me with two different noodle dishes." Lily smiles at her.

"Hey, I'm not forcing you to eat anything. I mean, if you want me to take the bag home with me..." Eileen stands up.

"Oh, sit." Lily waves a hand at Eileen. "Let me see if I can pull together two small salads." Lily opens the refrigerator. In the vegetable bin, she finds Spring Mix, one carrot, and a wilting rib of celery. There are also some strawberries. She puts everything on the counter, and turns to Eileen with the rib of celery in her hand.

"Thumbs up or thumbs down?"

"It's not bending in half. I say it's good enough."

Lily washes the produce and peels the carrot, before chopping everything with a sharp kitchen knife and splitting it between two bowls.

She hands the bowls to Eileen.

"Got dressing?"

Lily opens the refrigerator again. "Italian or Raspberry Vinaigrette?"

"Raspberry Vinaigrette. I don't want to mix cultures," Eileen smirks.

Lily hands Eileen the dressing.

Reaching for the plastic bag of Thai food, Lily almost steps on Boone. "Thai food is for humans. You boys have to settle for Beggin' Strips." She opens the dog treat cabinet and gives each of the dogs one strip. They chew enthusiastically.

Lily takes two plates from the cabinet, opens the container of Pad Thai, puts a portion on each plate, and hands the plates to Eileen.

"So, now that we've established you know even more than I do, I want to hear everything," Eileen says, placing the plates on the table.

Lily fills two glasses with water and sits at the table. As they eat, she relates her entire day. She tells Eileen about the call from Jim as well as the conversation with Kathy Klapper.

"This is incredible," Eileen says, taking another bite of Singapore noodles.

"This food is scrumptious," Lily says.

"You know I'm talking about Pete and Clarissa." Eileen narrows her gaze.

Lily finishes chewing a piece of fragrant tofu. "I know you are." She giggles.

"You think Clarissa actually killed her cousin to get the money?" Eileen asks. "You think she wasn't in the will?"

"I think it's why she was so intent on adopting Burrow." Lily takes another drink of water. "Pete's friend Matt told Mickey that Pete had made a new will with Burrow as the beneficiary."

Eileen almost spits out the mouthful of food.

"I think what Matt meant is probably right, but his words are confusing. I think it was that taking care of Burrow was a condition within the will," Lily continues.

Eileen looks at her watch. "It's almost six. Let's turn on the news."

They get up and push their chairs under the table. Boone and Crockett jump to their feet.

"Come on boys, we're turning on the news," Lily says. The dogs look longingly at the table, then to Lily. "I know neither of you would dare try to get on the table," Lily says in as stern a voice as she can muster.

Eileen laughs as she moves towards the living room, Crockett scampers after her. Boone continues to stare at Lily.

"Turn it around, mister." Boone turns and reluctantly follows Crockett.

Eileen has the remote control in her hand. "Who's your favorite newscaster?"

"Let's go with Jim Gardner."

Eileen hits '6' on the remote.

The sharp trumpet of intro music sounds. Jim Gardner appears on the screen.

"In shocking news, Burlington County police today made an arrest in a suspicious death." The scene flashes to the Burlington County Prosecutors Office. "Clarissa Gibbons, a cafeteria worker at Haddon Township High School, was arrested for allegedly poisoning her cousin, Pete Russo, in an attempt to gain access to a family fortune. Chad Pradelli is at the scene."

Eileen and Lily glance at each other. The scene changes to a small brick ranch home. The house has olive green shutters on the windows, and on the small, concrete porch are three wicker chairs. A man is sitting in one of the chairs and a police officer sits in another. They are in conversation.

Lily gasps.

Eileen turns to her with a querying gaze.

"Jim, I'm here at the home of Pete Russo, a decorated marine veteran," Chad begins. "Sergeant Russo was found dead in his home a week ago by the New Jersey State Police. The death was ruled suspicious by the Burlington County coroner, and police have been investigating." Police officers can be seen walking in the background. Barking is emanating from the house.

That's Jim on the porch," Lily whispers. "He adopted Burrow."

Jim and the officer stand up and go inside the house.

"The coroner has determined that Sergeant Russo was poisoned. Investigators determined that caplets found in a bottle of Tylenol in the Sergeant's home were actually oxycontin. Sergeant Russo apparently took the pills assuming they were Tylenol, and died of a drug overdose. Clarissa Gibbons' fingerprints were found on the medicine cabinet containing the bottle of Tylenol, as well as on the bottle itself." Chad turns to look at the house. "Sergeant Russo inherited a substantial amount of money from his parents, who were tragically killed in an automobile accident last year. He was planning to start a business employing former military personnel. Back to you, Jim."

The scene returns to Jim Gardner in the Action News studio. "What a terrible tragedy for a man who survived overseas combat only to be murdered at home. In other news…"

Eileen clicks the TV off. "Well I'll be dammed, Lily."

Lily looks at her friend. "A terrible thing to happen to a fabulous guy." She sobs as tears roll down her cheeks.

Eileen embraces Lily in a tight hug.

CHAPTER 47

On her drive to work Wednesday morning, Lily replays the events from yesterday in her mind, feeling dejected about the insight she's gained into Pete's life. Recovering from the tragic loss of his parents and getting his life back together, he had plans to start a business that would help other retired and injured veterans. His life cut short by an addict's need for drugs. Lily lets out a long sigh. She can take some comfort that Burrow has been adopted by one of Pete's friends. A wistful expression crosses her face. Burrow was quite comfortable with Jim and Matt.

Lily pulls into the shelter lot, parking in her usual space in the back of the lot where there's shade from oak trees that line the road. She starts her pre-work ritual, standing tall and pushing her shoulders back. She walks towards the building and enters D–Wing.

"Good morning, Dylan." She greets the dog who is now longest in residence. She receives a hearty Woof in return. She squats down to be on eye level with him. "Hey, Dylan, some of the other guests have not been named yet. I know I told the staff we needed a break from TV character names. But don't you think that chubby, very short-haired guy over there looks like Homer Simpson?"

Dylan gives a hearty Woof. Lily laughs at him. She knows reality is that his bark means he's happy to be receiving attention. Dylan doesn't really think the new shelter occupant looks like Homer Simpson. Lily stands and lets Dylan lick her hands through the bars of the kennel. Today, she decides, she'll talk to Ingrid about making a video of him playing with another dog for the website. If people see how much fun he can be, they will be more likely to want to meet him.

She'll also ask Ingrid for tips to train down Dylan's excessive barking. Unless someone wants a good watchdog, people will probably get scared when they hear him bark. She looks at the clipboard on the kennel, reading again the description Ingrid has done for him: "Hey, do you like football? Or Soccer? Guess what, so do I. I love to run. I am also good at catching a Frisbee. I do like to chew, though, so I don't play with tennis balls. Apparently, they are not strong enough for me. After a good game in the yard, I love a nice nap. Hopefully, next to you. Don't worry. I won't hog the couch. If you are an active family, I am perfect for you."

It is a good write-up. The mention of chewing is probably turning the moms off to him. If they can offer suggestions to keep him from chewing the couch, there will be a better chance of finding him a forever home.

Lily walks on to the C–wing. She calls out "Good morning" to the cats. Then she continues out to the front desk area where she finds Anna already logged on to the computer.

"Good morning, Anna," she says.

"Good morning, Lily. We've already had a call from Officer Honeycutt. He came across a dog with a collar but no tags. He wants to bring the dog down here to see if it has a chip."

"What did you tell him?"

"I told him to swing by after nine, in case we need Doc to do an exam."

"Good thinking, Anna. You're going to be running a shelter one day." Lily beams at her.

"I'll settle for a good job at a veterinary hospital when I finish my coursework, Lily."

Lily has a brief melancholy thought of being twenty and having your whole life ahead of you, then lets it pass.

"Well let me check the agenda for the day, and then we can start the morning routine," Lily says, moving to her desk.

Lily turns on her computer, making a mental note to check

with Kim on volunteer sign-ups for the off-site event in a few weeks. She muses that with it being late spring there will be lots of feral kittens arriving at the shelter. Kittens always draw people over to an adoption table. Lily checks email to see if anyone has sent out a note about a family looking for a lost dog. She finds no inquiries yet, but is hopeful the dog is chipped and can be quickly reunited with its family.

Lily stands from her desk and makes her way back to the D–wing. Anna has left the front and is assembling breakfast. As Lily enters the D–wing, she runs into two volunteers.

"Good morning, we haven't met. I'm Lily," she says extending her hand.

"I'm Carlos." The man shakes Lily's hand. "This is my wife, Izzy."

"Isabella," she says, and shakes Lily's hand. "We had our canine walking training last night and figured we would come in right away to use what we learned."

"Well, that's awesome," Lily says, assuming they are newly retired. They look to be sixtyish, but very fit and clearly early risers. "We'll have you help Anna serve up breakfast first. You'll find no one wants to walk when the chow train is coming through."

They eagerly nod. Lily turns them over to Anna. She goes into the C–wing to start the kitty morning routine. Too many folks in with the dogs, she thinks, and we'll be tripping over each other.

About halfway through the cat routine, Lily peeks into the D–wing. Carlos is in front of the kennel of the dog she thinks looks like Homer Simpson. She calls out to him.

"Carlos, don't forget the blue sheets are dogs that haven't had an assessment yet. For your first day, please stick to the dogs with the white sheets. None of us want a surprise this early in the morning." She smiles.

"Oh, right, thank you." He smiles shyly. "But he looks so calm."

Isabella says something in Spanish. Turning quickly, before

either can see, Lily laughs. Apparently, Isabella already told Carlos he shouldn't be walking that dog.

Glancing out the window to the parking lot, Lily spies a state police cruiser. After a quick stop in the bathroom to wash her hands, she grabs a leash and walks outside.

CHAPTER 48

Officer Honeycutt opens the back door of the cruiser and a giant, shaggy, labradoodle bounds out, making a beeline for Lily.

"Sit," Lily commands.

It immediately sits. Lily quickly attaches the leash to its collar.

"Phew, he was quick out of the car, good thing you move fast, Lily" Officer Honeycutt meanders over. Officer Honeycutt is wearing his New Jersey State Trooper uniform. His black, steel-tipped boots look spit-shined. The trousers have a perfect crease straight down the front of his leg. His belt buckle and badge glint in the morning sun, so shiny, one might think they were polished this morning. His uniform embodies the expression "fits like a glove."

"You can't let them fool you, Officer Honeycutt. Sometimes they wait for a chance to run." She gives the dog a scratch. "Is that how he came to find you in the first place?" She asks the dog, looking down. "Did you see an open gate and go for an adventure?"

The dog lets out another Woof, and gets up and puts his front paws on Lily's shoulders. His tail is wagging.

"So Lily…" Office Honeycutt starts. He removes his mirrored sunglasses, and the hazel flecks in his deep brown eyes twinkle in the sunlight.

"Yes?" she says, petting the dog at her feet.

"I don't know if you've heard, but an arrest was made yesterday in Pete Russo's death." His face is set, as if he were a statue, not a living, breathing human.

"I did hear. His cousin poisoned him." Lily's voice catches. She shakes her head as if clearing away a thought. "It was a waste of a good life."

"I agree. Something interesting was discovered after the arrest." He pauses.

Lily looks up, waiting patiently.

"When Miss Gibbons was fingerprinted, her prints matched those of another crime."

Lily's eyes go wide.

"Your theory wasn't as crazy as everyone thought. One of the prints we found on Eva Livingston's clothes and backpack matched Miss Gibbons."

"Seriously?" Lily steps forward in excitement. The dog jumps up and begins barking. "Sit," Lily commands.

"Yes, the prints were a match. When she was questioned about it, Clarissa admitted she'd had an altercation with Eva."

"Oh, my God. She killed Eva, too?" Lily is unable to hide the distress in her voice.

"Clarissa claims it was an accident. She says Eva tried to run from her, and she stumbled and hit her head." He appears dubious. "It could've happened that way, but she didn't report it to police. Who knows, Eva could've been alive when Clarissa left her. Clarissa's being charged with involuntary manslaughter in that case."

"Wow, how horrible. Poor Eva. She could've been laying there unconscious for who knows how long." Lily tilts her head to the other side. She shifts from foot to foot.

"You put the pieces together. That's the type of thinking that makes a good investigator, Lily." Officer Honeycutt smiles at her. "Have you considered a career in law enforcement?"

Lily blushes deeply. "Goodness, no. I haven't. This is already my second career." The dog jumps on Lily and paws at her jeans.

"Don't discount it, Lily. Nowadays changing careers can happen at any stage of life." Officer Honeycutt slips his sunglasses back on.

"I'll keep it in the back of my mind. Of course, hundreds of thousands of dollars in student debt to gain a criminal justice degree isn't very appealing." Lily frowns. She gives the dog a gentle shove so it puts all four paws back on the ground. "Well, let me get this guy inside and see if he has a chip." She turns towards the entrance of the shelter.

"All right if I come inside and wish Chelsea a good morning?" Honeycutt asks.

Lily stops in her tracks. She tries not to show her surprise. "No Chelsea today, Officer Honeycutt, she swapped Wednesdays with Anna. I'm sure Anna would love to have you come in and say hello. She may hand you a mop. She's cleaning cages." Lily smiles, giving her head a toss.

Martin's car pulls into the lot. Officer Honeycutt looks over at the car and waves to Martin. "Well, then I guess I'll be on my way. You call me if you need any more help with our friend here." Officer Honeycutt gives the dog a final pat. He quickly gets back in his vehicle.

Martin approaches Lily. "Well, what's up this morning, Lily?"

"Officer Honeycutt found a stray with a collar but no tag. Hopefully, he or she", Lily hazards a peek underneath the dog, "is chipped."

"I don't know, that sure looked like a cozy moment." Martin raises his eyebrows.

"Um, cozy isn't what I would call it." Lily giggles. "He wanted to come inside and say good morning to Chelsea and he was rather disappointed to find she wasn't in." Lily breaks into a full laugh.

"Oh, ho, you are kidding me?" Martin smiles. "All this time you've been giving her a hard time for being so flirtatious?" He hooks a thumb in the direction of the parking lot. "Perhaps tall, strong, and handsome there, enjoys the flirtation?" Martin laughs out loud, too.

"I think you're right. I thought he'd be embarrassed by all the eye fluttering and sashaying." Lily swirls her hips as she walks into the shelter, attempting to imitate Chelsea's walk.

"Which one of us gets to tell her?" Martin asks as he follows.

"Oh, I don't think we should," Lily says. Martin frowns. "Wouldn't it be more fun to let her discover the results on her own?"

"Only if I'm there to watch, spoilsport."

Lily walks the dog into Medical and takes him over to the scanning device. She runs the scanner between the shoulder blades. He is chipped. "Well, my friend, we can reunite you with a worried family." She says to the dog. She jots the name and phone number down onto a Post-it note.

"What have we here?" Mitchell has walked over. There's a smudge of sweat on his glasses.

"He seems to have wandered off from his owners. Can you kennel him while I try to reach them?" Lily asks.

"Leave it to me," Mitchell assures her, taking the leash and leading the dog to a kennel.

Returning to her desk, Lily finds Martin still simpering. Letting out a laugh in agreement that the irony of the situation is funny, she shares the amusement of the moment.

"Lily, when they get married you'd better give them one hell of a wedding present."

"Listen, don't put the cart before the horse. Our Chelsea has quite an active social life. He may have to shoot his way in." Lily cocks her hand into the shape of a pistol and lowers her thumb to signal firing.

Martin raises his eyebrows and smiles wider.

"Let me call this family and get them reunited with their lost friend," Lily says trying to redirect them both to their work obligations. She lifts the phone receiver and dials the number from the chip. There are two rings and then a harried voice answers.

"Hello?" The steady sound of a car engine is heard over the connection.

"Good morning, am I speaking to the owner of a labradoodle who answers to Albie?"

"Oh, thank goodness. Do you have him?" a woman asks. The sound of the car engine ceases.

"We do. This is Lily Dreyfus at Forever Friends Animal Shelter…"

"Oh, no. He's at a shelter? How did he get to a shelter so fast?" There's a large intake of breath.

"Don't worry. When local law enforcement finds a dog without tags, they often bring them our way."

"I don't know how he got out. I swear the gate was closed tight," the woman says in a frenzied voice.

"Yes, would you like to come in and pick him up?" Lily tries to keep the judgment from her voice, knowing dogs take the opportunities that are given to them.

"I certainly will. Like I said, I thought the gate was closed. He was on the back deck, which is screened in. I figured he'd be fine while I took the kids to school. Then I came home, and he wasn't there." A gulp of air is followed by a notable exhale, and another large inhale. "Pardon me. I must sound like a crazy person. I've been driving all around town calling his name out the window."

"It's fine. Let me give you our address so that you can come over and get him. I would suggest that you get him a tag. If he'd been wearing a tag, the officer who spotted him would have probably brought him right to your house. It might have saved you a lot of anxiety."

"Yes, I know. You're on Seminole Drive, Bassettville, correct?" the voice asks.

"Um—" Lily starts.

"My husband put this GPS gizmo app on my phone. You can get the address of incoming calls. I'll be there in about ten minutes." She disconnects.

Lily stares at the receiver and shakes her head. "You're welcome," she says. Hearing Martin scoff, she turns to face him.

"No good deed goes unpunished, Lily."

"And yet you wonder why I prefer the company of dogs to humans. Dogs always show their gratitude."

CHAPTER 49

Later that night, Lily is relaxing on the couch reading "Dayshift." Boone is on one side of her. Crockett is on the other. She relishes the escape from real life that reading a good mystery provides.

When her cell phone rings, she reaches across Boone to pick it up. He glares at her, stands up, jumps off the couch and heads for the recliner.

"Hello, Mickey," she answers with a giggle.

"It's good to hear you laugh, Lily."

"I had to reach across Boone to pick up the phone. Let's say it displeased him," Lily says. Boone has curled into a ball, his face to the back of the chair.

"If they ever make 'Grumpy Old Dogs' into a movie, you should sign him up for a screen test."

"So true. I saw Officer Honeycutt today."

"Lily, I swear that man steals dogs from people's yards to make an excuse to come to the shelter."

Lily laughs again. "You know, when I called the owner, she swore the gate to the house was closed tight. I didn't believe her. Well, I've heard it all, but now that you put that thought in my mind…"

"I was teasing. I can't see a state trooper stealing someone's dog to come and flirt with the women at a shelter."

"If he did today it had benefits for me," Lily says. She recounts what Officer Honeycutt told her about the Eva Livingston case. Then Lily tells her about Honeycutt's disappointment to find Chelsea wasn't at work.

"The woman who killed Pete also killed Eva?" Mickey is incredulous.

"Yes, it's unbelievable. I'm relieved to finally know what happened in both cases. I'm disgusted by what happened to Pete, and saddened by Eva's entire story…"

"Speaking of Pete," Mickey cuts in before Lily can become too morose. "The reason I called is Matt called me today. You know, Jim's friend?"

"Yeeeessss, what did chatty Matt have to say?"

"He told me the service for Pete is Saturday at Platt Memorial Chapels in Voorhees. They're letting Jim bring Burrow and asked if I could come. Matt said Jim will be busy with the arrangements for the service, and it'd be good to have a point person to be in charge of Burrow."

"Wait, they're allowed to take a dog to a memorial service? Are you serious?" Lily asks, dubious.

"That's what he told me. Apparently, Platt's done this before, especially for people who had a service dog. Matt said he knows Burrow is a well-behaved dog. However, since I'm skilled in dog handling, he thought it might be helpful to have me there."

"This is good news for me," Lily begins. "Jim had asked if someone at the shelter would say a few words about Pete and his volunteer work. I'll be there too. It'll be good to have a friend there for support."

"How'd you talk Maria and Kim into letting you do the speaking?"

"Surprisingly, neither of them was incredibly interested in attending a funeral on Memorial Day weekend," Lily sneers.

"Lily. I hear the sarcasm in your voice, but you know this is good for you. It'll give you closure on the relationship. Besides, the place will be full of tall, good looking marines. Who knows what connection you might make."

"Ewwwww, Mickey, that's gross. You want me to try and pick up a guy at a memorial service? That's too creepy." Lily puts her arm around Crockett. He licks her face.

"I guess asking you to flirt is asking too much. How about you chat with people. Don't pet the dog and avoid all conversation."

"Hey, I… I chat," Lily sputters.

"As long as it involves talking about an animal, you chat," Mickey says sarcastically. "If it involves emotion, you run like a rabbit chased by a dog."

"Well…"

"Don't give me the 'I'm an introvert' line again."

"But I AM an introvert. Talking to strangers doesn't come as easy to me as it does for you. I get so tongue-tied."

"Yes, yes, I've heard this excuse before. Let's move on. Since we're both going to the funeral, how about if we go together? I'll pick you up."

"That'd be good. What time will you pick me up?" Lily says relieved she'll have someone she knows to get her through the awkward mingling which invariably takes place at functions like funerals.

"One o'clock sharp," Mickey announces. "Oh, and Lily. Wear a dress."

"A dress?" Lily shrieks. Crockett jumps off the couch and runs for the back of the house.

"Surely you own something other than jeans and T-shirts. You can't go to a memorial service in jeans."

"Oh, fine, mom," Lily emphasizes the last word. "Maybe you should come by at 12:45 and inspect my outfit?"

"12:45 it is." Mickey disconnects.

Boone sits up. He jumps from the recliner and goes back to the couch. He sits next to Lily and gives her a big lick on the cheek.

Lily pats him on the head and looks into his big brown eyes. "Boone, if only I could express myself like you do. A lick on the face when you're happy and a hefty sigh when you're not."

CHAPTER 50

Jim has told me today is a big day. We are all saying goodbye to Pete. I don't understand saying goodbye to someone who is no longer here, but these humans have different routines. I'll go where I need to, and be a support for everyone. At least Jim and I are back home. It's different without Pete, but at least the house still has Pete's smell. Jim is doing his best. We've had a lot of visitors. I know it's good for Jim, but with every person who comes through the house a little more of Pete's scent is gone.

I did hear I will never have to see that awful woman Clarissa ever again. I know she did something to Pete's medicine. I don't understand all the humans are saying, but apparently she put something in Pete's Tylenol bottle. Poor Pete, he took what he thought was Tylenol. When his head still hurt, he took more. I guess his body couldn't handle whatever it was.

I tried to warn him. He wasn't acting like himself that day. I knew he got terrible headaches, but after he took Tylenol, he wasn't right. I didn't want him taking any more. I barked at him. I tried to knock the bottle out of his hands. He got angry with me. Well, I did all I could. Then I laid down on the bed with him.

Jim is coming over with the leash. He is wearing those sparkling white pants and a white cap. I know the marines wear those on the most special of occasions.

"We need to be strong for each other today," Jim ruffles my fur a bit as he attaches the leash. "I got permission to bring you. Everyone knows how important you were to Pete. I'm depending on you to be the best behaved friend."

I give Jim a Woof as we head to the car.

When we arrive at Platt Memorial Chapels, there are lots of people milling about. Boy, there is a sea of white. Jim and I get out of the car and head towards the building. It's tough navigating all of those legs. I get lots of ear scratches and pats on the back. I don't jump on anyone though. I've been told there are to be no paw prints on those white pants. Pete had this thing he would roll over those pants. He would joke with me that one dog hair would make a person fail inspection.

We go inside, and a man wearing some type of dress greets Jim. Whoa, he has a funny smell about him. I can't identify it. He smells like something that was on fire. Not the pleasant warm, campfire smell. This is more pungent. We walk with him into this auditorium of a place, and I can smell Pete. There's a table with Pete's picture. I jump up and find Pete's hat is here. Jim tells me to get down, so I do. Well, at least Pete's scent is with us.

People from outside are coming in. They are

shaking Jim's hand, and I hear Pete's name a lot. I smell something familiar yet not familiar. I'm trying to figure out what this is when I see two women in front of me. Oh, it's the nice lady from the shelter I know Pete liked and Mickey, who I lived with for a bit. I give her a sniff. Oh yeah, there is some flowery smell on her, but I can smell Nero under it. What a goof that guy is. I am grateful to them for letting me visit until Jim could take me home.

The lady from the shelter keeps tilting her head and touching her hair. She sure seems nervous. Maybe she can smell the guy in the dress too. Jim, on the other hand, has a smile a mile wide. I swear if he had a tail, he'd be wagging it. Jim hands my leash to her, and we walk over to one of the benches. Everyone is taking seats, and I'm told to sit. Different people come to the front and talk. I hear Pete's name a lot. A few of them mention my name, and I sit a little taller when I hear it.

We sit for a long time until all of the talking is complete. Mickey suggests that I could use a stretch of the legs. She's right, I could sure put down some Eau d' Burrow. Lily, that's her name, takes my leash and we follow everyone outside. Going on a bit of a romp, smelling around this place, I lay down some scent. I don't know if I'll be back here, but I want the locals to know I was here.

We get back to the Platt building, and people are standing in small groups, talking. Lily chats with some of them. She seems anxious. She keeps twirling a piece of hair around one finger, letting it go, twirling again.

Approaching us, Jim says, "Good, you're back."

"Yes, I let Burrow have a bit of a leg stretch. He was so good in there." She fidgets some more. "Um, do you know where Mickey is?"

"Oh, yes," Jim smiles. He has that tail wagging look about him again. "She said something came up. She asked if I could give you a ride home." I think the grin might split his face.

Lily turns a strange shade of pink. Then she lets out a nervous laugh. "How presumptuous of her." She looks around the parking lot. "It's very nice of you, but I'm sure you have, um, obligations today."

"Well, in fact, Matt's parents invited everyone to their house. So, no problem at all. That's where I'm headed."

Lily looks at her watch and shuffles from foot to foot. "I could go. I do have to make sure my boys get fed later." She is looking around again. "I can't believe Mickey would be so rude as to foist me off on you like this."

"It's no problem. When it's time to feed your dogs, let me know and I'll drop you at your house." Jim smiles again.

He does have a comforting smile. I remember how Jim and Pete used to laugh a lot.

"Okay," Lily smiles back.

We get back into Jim's car. He opens the door for Lily first. Then he opens the back door for me. I lay down on the seat. I'm a bit overwhelmed with all of these people. However, this Lily sure is friendly. I hope we see more of her.

Acknowledgements

There are two people without whom this book would have never become a reality. I must thank my friend and former coworker Dan Traister for having enough faith in my chutzpah and humor to make introductions on my behalf.

Dan introduced me to Merrily Taylor, who has become my most trusted writing adviser and my friend. Merrily thank you for your patience, guidance, and constructive advice. Clues From the Canines would still be a pie-in-the-sky idea without you.

Thank you to Tom Welch for his editorial efforts and the improvements made to the pacing and grammar of the book.

In books, as in life, appearances matter. Thank you to Ron Rollet for transforming my written words into the final product. I appreciate your guidance and creativity.

I must also thank all the people who, knowingly and unknowingly, provided real-life stories and assistance with research to ensure accuracy and realistic representations. In alphabetical order: Dawn Augustino, Lee Coletti, Mathew D'Ortona Jr, Colleen Koeppel, Michael Lacavita, Kathy Mettrick, and Katie Ritter.

To the slew of beta readers who kindly suffered through draft after draft as I worked through this tale, your feedback was critical in honing the details and improving the story. In alphabetical order: Michele Connell, Sharon Cooper, Ruth Dziomba, Stan Dziomba, Sabrina Flynn, Joe Francolino, Mark Lorah, Linda Millares, Shirley Raynor, Merrily Taylor, Barbara Traister, and the members of the Palombo Park Writers Workshop. As you read the final version, I hope you share in the pride I feel for this book. It would not be as good a story without your input.

To Bess Carmen and Teresa Inge, thank you for coordinating the annual Guppy Fantasy Agent submission. To those Guppies who served as Fantasy Agents, your feedback was invaluable.

Connect with Author

If you enjoyed Clues From The Canines please consider leaving a review on any of the platforms you use. Reviews generate interest and help authors keep writing.

For the latest news and a monthly blog please check out my website: **www.ReadDarlene.com**

If you enjoyed reading Lily's adventures watch for *Up Close and Pawsonal* to be released in 2023.

Twenty-five percent of any profits made from the sale of my books will be given to the Animal Welfare Association in Voorhees, New Jersey. You can find out more about their mission at: **www.awanj.org**

www.ingramcontent.com/pod-product-compliance
Lightning Source LLC
Chambersburg PA
CBHW071459140726
47997CB00005B/1780